MW00856624

"Jennifer Deibel is an amaz weaves a tale of love and forgiveness that's as beautiful as the cloth she describes. I was touched by the main characters' journeys to forgiveness and overcoming adversity, and I encourage readers to give *Heart of the Glen* a try."

Tracie Peterson, bestselling, award winning author of over 140 books, including *The Heart of Cheyenne* and the Pictures of the Heart series

Praise for *The Irish Matchmaker*

"An irresistible tale of matchmaking mishaps and second chances."

Publishers Weekly

"*The Irish Matchmaker* is an immersive story about faith and finding love in unexpected places. Deibel skillfully weaves Donal's and Catríona's stories, creating realistic characters and a fascinating storyline."

BookPage

"In her latest heartwarming historical romance, Deibel deftly matches a period-perfect early twentieth-century Irish setting with a full complement of endearing characters. The end result is an absolute delight."

Booklist

"Jennifer Deibel once again makes Ireland come alive with her lyrical writing voice and vibrantly drawn characters. The story engaged all my senses."

Reading Is My Superpower

Praise for *The Maid of Ballymacool*

"Deibel's update on the Cinderella story features sympathetic, three-dimensional characters who are easy to root for as they find their way to one another in this page-turning plot."

Publishers Weekly

"Deibel once again inventively draws on Ireland's fascinating history as inspiration for a compassionate and compelling sweet romance with a Celtic Cinderella-like flavor."

Booklist

"Jennifer Deibel has done it again with *The Maid of Ballymacool*, a hopeful historical romance novel about unrelenting faith and new beginnings with just a pinch of mystery."

BookPage

"*The Maid of Ballymacool* by Jennifer Deibel is an emotion-driven novel that will keep you reading until the last page. The story was brilliant and moving."

Interviews & Reviews

HEART
of the GLEN

Books by Jennifer Deibel

HEART
of the GLEN

JENNIFER DEIBEL

Revell

a division of Baker Publishing Group
Grand Rapids, Michigan

© 2025 by Jennifer V. Deibel

Published by Revell
a division of Baker Publishing Group
Grand Rapids, Michigan
RevellBooks.com

Printed in the United States of America

Library of Congress Cataloging-in-Publication Data
Names: Deibel, Jennifer, 1978– author.
Title: Heart of the glen / Jennifer Deibel.
Description: Grand Rapids, Michigan : Revell, a division of Baker Publishing
    Group, 2025.
Identifiers: LCCN 2024018324 | ISBN 9780800744861 (paperback) | ISBN
    9780800746711 (casebound) | ISBN 9781493448616 (ebook)
Subjects: LCGFT: Christian fiction. | Novels.
Classification: LCC PS3604.E3478 H43 2025 | DDC 813/.6—dc23/eng/20240506
LC record available at https://lccn.loc.gov/2024018324

Scripture used in this book, whether quoted or paraphrased by the characters, is from the King James Version of the Bible.

Emojis are from the open-source library OpenMoji (https://openmoji.org/) under the Creative Commons license CC BY-SA 4.0 (https://creativecommons.org/licenses/by-sa/4.0/legalcode).

Cover image by Joanna Czogala / Arcangel

Published in association with Books & Such Literary Management, BooksAndSuch.com.

Baker Publishing Group publications use paper produced from sustainable forestry practices and postconsumer waste whenever possible.

25   26   27   28   29   30   31   7   6   5   4   3   2   1

For the honor of my heavenly Father—
may Your name be greater in the eyes
of any who read these words.

For my earthy father, Jerry Martin—
thank you for being the first one to teach me about
God's "Silly Battle Plans" and for building that foundation
for me to trust Him when all seemed lost.

Glossary of Terms

a chara—[uh KHAH-duh]—friend, direct address

a chairde—[uh HARR-juh]—my friends

Ádh mór—[AH MORE]—good luck

amach leis—[uh-MAKH LESH]—out with it

a Mhaighdean—[UH WAH-juhn]—oh, heavens!

An bhfuil tú ceart go leoir—[AHN WILL TOO KART GUH LORE]—are you alright?

an laindéir mhór—[AHN LEHN-jurr WOHR]—the big lantern

An Píobaire Mór—[AHN PEE-bruh MOHR]—the Big Piper, the nickname for world champion piper, Charles MacSweeney

ar aghaidh linn—[AIR AYE LINN]—let's go

a thaisce—[UH HASH-kee]—a term of endearment meaning "my little dear"

a thiarcais—[uh HEER-kish]—oh my

buíocihas le Dia—[BWEE-huhs leh JEE-uh]—thanks be to God

cailleach—[KAH-lyahck]—a bed built into an alcove near the fireplace; usually used for the oldest member of the family; also called an outshot or snug; oddly enough, *cailleach* is also the word used for "witch"

Carrageen—[KAYR-ih-geen]—a type of seaweed native to Ireland

céad míle fáilte—[KAYD MEE-luh FALL-chuh]—a hundred thousand welcomes

céilí—[KAY-lee]—a type of Irish dance

cinnte—[KINN-chuh]—certainly/of course

comhghairdeas—[kuh-GAR-juh-huss]—congratulations

craic—[CRACK]—fun; good times; fellowship

craiceáilte—[CRACK-ahl-chuh]—crazy

créatúr—[KRAY-turr]—creature; often used to mean "poor thing."

dáiríre—[duh-REE-ruh]—really

Damhsa bruscar—[DOW-sah BROO-skar]—Brush Dance, a specific style of Sean nÓs dancing using a broom

dochreidte—[DOE-kreh-juh]—unbelievable

dubhín—[doov-EEN]—literally "tiny black," a term of endearment/pet name

fíodóireacht—[FYOH-juh-rockt]—weaving

gabh mo leithscéal—[GO MUH LEH-shkayl]—excuse me/beg your pardon

gardaí—[garr-DEE]—police

goitse—[GUH-chuh]—come here, West Ulster dialect

go deimhin—[GUH DYEM]—indeed

go díreach—[GUH JEE-rachkt]—exactly

go raibh maith agat—[GUH ROW MAH uh-GUHT]—thank you, to one person

go raibh míle maith agat—[GUH ROW MEE-luh MAH uh-GUHT]—thanks a million

Go raibh míle maith agaibh—[GUH ROW MEE-luh MAH uh-GEE]—thanks a million, to more than one person

hurley—[HURR-lee]—the "bat" used in the Gaelic game of hurling

iontach maith—[EEN-tahk MOY]—very good

Íosa —[EE-suh]—Jesus

lough—[LOCKH]—lake

Máirt na hInide—[MARCH nuh HIN-yuh-jeh]—Pancake Tuesday/Shrove Tuesday/Fat Tuesday

mo thread caorach—[MUH HRAD KEE-rockh]—my flock of sheep

muise—[MUH-shuh]—oh my

na caoirigh—[NUH KWIH-dee]—the sheep

ná dean é sin—[NAH JANN SHINN]—don't do that

na Scrioptúir—[NUH SKRIP-tooir]—the Scriptures

Naomh Íde—[NEEV EE-deh]—Saint Ide, the woman believed in Irish lore to have written a lullaby for baby Jesus

oh muise—[OH MUH-shuh]—oh goodness/oh my

peata—[PA-tuh]—a term of endearment meaning "my little dear" or "my little pet"

pleidhcíocht—[PLY-kee-awkt]—tomfoolery

plód—[PLAWD]—crowd

Rop tú mo Baile—[ROHP TOO MUH BAH-lyuh]—be thou my vision

scioból—[SHKUH-buhll]—barn

seachtain—[SHAKH-tuhn]—week

seafóid—[SHAH-foyj]—nonsense

sin é—[SHIN AY]—that's it/that'll do

siúil ar aghaidh iad—move them forward

sláinte—[SLAWN-chuh]—cheers, literally meaning "health to you"

tá brón orm—[TAH BROHN OHR-uhm]—I'm sorry

tá fáilte romhat—[TAH FALL-chuh ROWT]—you're welcome

Tír na Nóg—[TEER NUH NOHG]—the land of eternal youth

and beauty; the place you go when you dream; also sometimes used to refer to heaven

tóraithe—[TOHR-ee-huh]—historical Irish word for bandit or sheep-stealer

1

Saoirse Fagan had blood on her hands. She turned them over in her lap and studied her palms and fingertips. The crimson stain couldn't be seen, but it was there. She knew it. Could feel it seeping into her bones, forever changing who she was.

The carriage slowed and rumbled to a stop. Saoirse's gaze lifted to the roof of the enclosed cabin she'd been riding in—an undeserved kindness from the Harris-Temples as she left their employ at Waterstown House. The walls, covered in a rich burgundy fabric, spoke of an opulence Saoirse would never know. And truth be told, she found it uncomfortable. The blast of fresh air when she opened the carriage door was a welcome reminder of her true station.

She climbed out, grateful that Burke hadn't lumbered down from the driver's seat to open the door for her. She didn't deserve it. The biting February wind whipped her cloak around unsteady legs as she headed to the back to unhitch her small carpetbag from the hold.

"Thanks, Burke," she called, shielding her eyes from the sun as she glanced up at him.

He nodded gravely. "Sorry I canna stay. Her ladyship made it verra clear I'm to make it to Letterkenny before dark."

Saoirse flapped her hand. Why should he stay? There was nothing for him to do. She was more than capable of carrying her one bag containing the few possessions that remained to her in this world. All she truly had were the clothes she'd worn that fateful day when she left for Waterstown House. But so many charitable donations had been given to her, and for that she was truly grateful. But now the items weighed down her bag like a hundred pounds of lead, as they seemed to carry with them the weight of all she'd done.

"Don' give it another thought," she answered Burke finally. "I'll be grand, so."

He tugged the brim of his flatcap and nodded again before hitching the reins and rumbling away. Saoirse watched the rig roll over the hill and out of sight, then turned her attention to the foreboding structure in front of her. Though called Drumboe Castle, it didn't much resemble what Saoirse considered a castle to be. Vines crept up its outer walls, which had been plastered and whitewashed, and stretched three stories tall. In the center, a rounded bay jutted out, matching the height of the rest of the building, with arch-topped Wyatt windows flanking either side of the bay section. This was to be her new home. Though the help likely resided in a smaller outbuilding or were hidden in the basement.

Steeling her nerves with a deep breath, she hitched her bag onto her shoulder and approached the massive, dark front door. A gust of wind kicked up, whipping around her and carrying with it the echoes of screams. Saoirse squeezed her eyes shut. The screams weren't real. She knew that. And yet they haunted her. Taking another steadying breath, she lifted the heavy brass knocker and rapped it three times. An eternity seemed to stretch long like a lazy cat.

Saoirse's brows pressed together, and she knocked again. Nothing. She stepped back and looked up at the building once more, as though whether she was in the right place would be written on the wall. After all, how many Drumboe Castles could there be in County Donegal? It was only then that she noticed no smoke curled from the chimneys and every window was dark. She glanced around. The only person to be seen was a farmer herding his sheep in the field neighboring the mansion. She stepped over to one of the windows next to the bay, cupped her hands around the sides of her face, and peered in. But her view was blocked by thick drapes.

"Ye'll have no luck doin' that."

Saoirse squealed and spun around. A hunched man with wiry white hair and leathery skin stared back. Goodness, how did he cross that distance so quickly?

"I beg yer pardon?" she said.

He waved a knobby finger in the direction of the castle. "She's locked up tight. No one's there."

Saoirse's gut sank. "That can't be right." She turned and looked back up at the menacing building. "I'm to start today as the new maid."

The man tsked, and a wheezy chuckle slipped from his lips. "No need fer a maid when no one's livin' there."

The bag slipped from her shoulder and fell to the ground with a muted thud. "No one liv—" The words stuck in her

15

throat. How could no one be living here? Surely Lady Harris-Temple wouldn't have set her up for a joke? Or, worse, a sentence of abandonment?

The man shrugged. "Lord Hayes died last week. Her ladyship's gone to live wit' her sister."

Saoirse blinked, then pulled her eyes open wide. "Died? How did he die?"

The old man removed his hat and held it over his heart. "He'd been ill closin' in on a year." He turned and called something unintelligible to the sheep growing restless in the field behind him. "Then the coma came over him. Less than a day later, he was gone."

The very air seemed to suck from Saoirse's lungs. She pressed a hand to her belly, trying to stay the churning that began to swirl there. "So . . . they've . . ."

"Left," he said, shrugging as he turned and shuffled across the road. "They won't be back, you can be sure o' dat."

As though she'd been socked in the gut, Saoirse gasped. "What am I supposed to do now?" She wasn't sure if she was asking herself, the old man, or God Himself.

The man sucked in a sharp breath. "Not sure, child. What I do know is that the lord's title died wit' him." He let out a shrill whistle and his herd startled and began moving off to the south. "I s'pose there's only one thing ya can do." He looked back at her. "Go home." With that, he turned and disappeared with his sheep over the crest of the hill.

Home. The patchwork landscape surrounding her blurred as tears filled her eyes and a burning spread in her throat. If only she could go home. She'd give anything—even her own life—to have things back the way they were before. But she couldn't. The only way out of this nightmare was through and forward. She swiped at her eyes, then bent, picked up her bag, and stepped into the middle of the road. To her right, the road stretched on to the northeast and forked off. To her left, it ambled over the hill toward the Atlantic. The bubbling of the River Finn could be heard just behind the castle. If legend could be trusted, Drumboe Castle guarded a ford in that river where she could cross and head off in a completely different direction.

Spinning in a slow circle, she struggled to rein in her thoughts as the questions flooding her mind threatened to suffocate her. With the next gust of wind, the clouds overhead broke ever so slightly, allowing a thin shaft of cold sunlight to seep through. That beam of light was like a lifeline in a turbulent sea, and Saoirse clung to it with all she had. Taking the road to the west would allow her to follow the light for as long as it remained, which wouldn't be long since the sun typically sank below the horizon near four o'clock this time of year. But the more light she could follow, the better. So, she set her shoulders and started off toward the west to meet her fate.

DUNLEWEY, COUNTY DONEGAL

A guttural cry tore from Owen McCready's throat, the pain of it almost matching that of his hand, even as he swiped at his assailant. Outside, a voice called, and the man who'd attacked Owen ran from the barn, shouting a reply that garbled in his ears. In the distance, Stout's intimidating growl and bark echoed through the chilled night air as the stampeding of feet faded into the hills. Groaning, Owen cradled his injured limb against his chest and rolled to his side then sat up.

"Stout!"

One final bark punctuated the canine's warning before he appeared in the doorway of the dimly lit barn. Whimpering, the border collie hurried to his master's side and nuzzled his cheek.

"I'm alright, boy." He tousled the dog's ear with his good hand. "Did ya get 'em?"

Stout grunted.

"Attaboy." Owen struggled to his feet. "D'ya think Aileen has some bandages somewhere in the house?" His sister prided herself on her domestic abilities, but her logic on how she carried them out left quite a bit to be desired, by Owen's estimation, anyway. How many quarrels had they had over the years regarding what belonged where in their small bungalow? Eventually, Owen had had to let go and allow Aileen to run the household the way she saw fit. Between the farming and the weaving, he simply didn't have the time or energy to control every last detail.

Stout stared at him, as though his gaze alone would heal Owen's injuries.

Despite the pain radiating through his hand, Owen chuckled at his sidekick. "C'mon, let's go." The pair ambled across the field toward the house, Owen swiveling his gaze back and forth all the while in case the bandits decided to ambush him yet again. But Stout's carefree trot toward home was reassuring. That dog could sense scoundrels a mile away.

Once inside the house, Owen scrounged for bandages or some sort of wrapping in all the drawers he thought Aileen might have stashed them. Finally, he found a rolled strip of scrap fabric and took it to the basin. Mixing water from the kettle on the stove with cool, fresh water from the jug on the counter, he washed his wounds. They were more superficial than he'd guessed, for which he was grateful. The knife had just grazed below the skin, thankfully. But the pain and limited mobility would make weaving almost impossible while he healed. Never mind the fact that he couldn't risk getting blood on the newly woven tweed fabric. He shuddered at the thought of having to scrap a full ream of seventy yards because of one drop of blood. Murphy's set the highest standards for their goods—as well they should. Donegal tweed was quickly becoming the tweed of choice for royalty, landed gentry, and the overall wealthiest members of society in Ireland and Britain. As well as the first choice for most farmers in the area, given its warmth, sturdiness, and ability to block out the damp weather.

At the thought of Murphy's, Owen's musings turned back to his sister. Aileen had driven to Donegal Town to deliver their most recent order—and to find out if they'd receive a contract for another batch. With tonight's turn of events, Owen couldn't decide if he hoped they received the order or not. He shook his head. They had no choice—they needed that contract, and he'd just have to hope he healed quickly enough to get it done.

He shuffled to the stove and absently made himself a cup of tea before crossing the room to one of the two chairs flanking the small fireplace. The warmth of the turf fire spread through the space like a warm blanket on a wintry night. Sighing, Owen lowered himself into the seat and let his head rest back. Before he could even take a sip of his tea, his eyes slid shut and he drifted off into a dreamless sleep.

2

Saoirse pulled her shawl tighter around her shoulders as the wind kicked up. Though the sky was pitch-black, she could tell a storm was on the way by the mist thrashing her cheeks. No lights flickered ahead or behind her, nor to the north or the south. She slowed her steps and let her gaze sweep the dark horizon, fighting the sense of panic rising in her chest.

"Lord, help me." The whispered prayer startled her as it escaped her lips. She'd not bothered talking to the Good Laird since that fateful day. Certainly the God who created and sanctified life had closed His ears to her after what she'd done—just one more tally mark in a long line of offenses. Though this was the worst of the lot, to be sure. No matter now though. The words were already winding their way on the wind somewhere else, anyway. She ducked her head against the elements and continued her slog. At least, she presumed she was still heading the same direction she was before she stopped. In the distance somewhere, a sheep bleated, and for a moment, Saoirse considered lumbering across the hills to find the beast and hunker down with its warmth. But common sense won out. Chances were the skittish animal would just run from her anyhow.

A deep rumbling pulled her attention to the road behind her. At the crest of the hill she'd just come down, a faint light flickered and swayed as the dull, almost thunder-like sound drew nearer. Her pulse quickened and, torn between fear of a predator and relief at possible transportation, she spun this way and that, looking for a place to hide. Squinting into the inky night, she could just make out the silhouette of a lone figure sitting atop a jaunty car. It wasn't overlarge and could have been a feminine form, but the hooded cloak made it difficult to tell.

The rig rolled to a stop next to Saoirse. "Lands alive, lass, what're ya doin' out here by yerself?"

Saoirse huffed a sigh of relief at the woman's voice. "I'm afraid that's a rather long story."

The shrouded figure shifted over and waved her aboard. "*Tsk*! Well, get on up here, wouldja? Ye'll catch yer death of a cold if ya stay out all night."

Glancing around once more, Saoirse stepped up onto the open-top carriage and relief flooded her body as she sat on the wooden bench. "Thank ya." She adjusted her cape around her. "Very much."

A gloved hand slipped in front of Saoirse. "I'm Aileen. Aileen McCready."

Saoirse shook the offered hand. "Saoirse Fagan."

Aileen snapped the reins and, with a jolt, they were off. "Where're ya headed? I can drop ya on the way."

From the side of her eye, Saoirse studied the woman who appeared to be roughly the same age as herself. She shrugged. "Not sure."

"*Wheesht*! Ya hafta know where ye're goin'." She shook her head, chuckling as if Saoirse was trying to play a joke on her.

"Nope." Saoirse pulled in a deep breath. "I was to start at Drumboe Castle today—"

Aileen tipped her head. "I thought I'd heard the lord had passed away," she said, crossing herself before adding, "God rest his soul."

Saoirse nodded. "He did. Or so I've just been told."

"Och, they didn't send word to ya?"

Saoirse shrugged. "If they did, it didn't reach me in time. But I suspect the Widow Hayes was too distraught to think of it."

"'Magine." Aileen shook her head, her gaze trained on the road ahead of them. "So, ya really don't know where ye're headed. Will ya not go back home in the morn?"

Saoirse studied Aileen's profile, trying to decide how much she wanted to tell the veritable stranger next to her. "No," she finally said, opting for the safety of ambiguity. "There's nothing for me back there."

Aileen turned fully toward Saoirse for the first time. She was quiet for a moment, studying her more closely, as though weighing what she would say next. Even in the scant light from the lantern swinging on a hook, a war shone in the woman's eyes.

"Right," Aileen said at last, startling Saoirse. "Ye'll come home wit' me."

Saoirse's jaw fell slack, and she shook her head. "Oh, no, I couldn't."

A sarcastic laugh puffed from Aileen's lips. "What, ya have somewheres else to be?" When Saoirse didn't answer, Aileen tugged on the reins until the horse slowed to a halt. "Look, it won't be forever. And I'm afraid ye'll have to settle for the barn tonight. We can deal with my brother in the morning. Goodness knows it's late enough already. But ya can't stay out here alone all night. At least in the barn ye'll be warm, dry, and safe."

Mulling the woman's argument over in her mind, Saoirse tried to find a reason to decline the offer but none came to mind.

Ya don't deserve it, that's the reason.

She shook the unwanted thought away, true though it was. The fact remained, however, that Saoirse had nowhere to go, and she wasn't going to figure things out in the middle of the night in the middle of nowhere. A biting gust of wind cut through her cloak, chilling her to the bone. If nothing else, she needed out of the elements or she'd never make it anyway. Sighing, she agreed. "Thanks a million. I owe ya."

"Grand, so!" With another snap of the reins, they were off once again.

The next hour passed pleasantly, with the two women discovering they had more in common than Saoirse would've guessed. It was as if they'd been friends their whole lives.

That's 'cause she doesn't know what ya did.

Granted, Saoirse's carefully crafted answers to Aileen's questions about her past painted a rosier picture than her current reality. Not that she was lying, so much as just not being ready to divulge her darkest truths to the woman. If she did, she'd surely be back where she started, left on the side of the road with nowhere to go and no way to get there.

At long last, just when Saoirse's eyes had grown almost too heavy to keep open, the jaunty car veered a sharp right, bringing into view her home for the evening. A small, thatched cottage, with windows glowing orange from the turf fire within, sat nestled against a small knoll. The roof of the barn peeked over the knoll as lantern light forced its way through the tiny spaces between the roof slats. Her vision blurred at the idyllic sight so much like the home she left behind. Well, not exactly like she left it. But nonetheless, the sight stirred an ache so deep in her soul, it threatened to steal her breath. That, combined with the relief of being done traveling—even if only for the night—settled on her like a sleep-spelled tune from Dagda's harp.

The carriage followed the narrow road around the knoll and over to the entrance of the barn. Aileen tugged on the reins, then turned to Saoirse.

"Alright, I'll go chat with Owen. He's a grumpy one, but he'll not leave ya stranded in the middle o' Donegal overnight." She reached out and gently squeezed Saoirse's shoulder. "Just wait here and I'll come get ya in a wee while."

Saoirse nodded, pulled her cloak tighter around her shoulders, and watched Aileen scurry down from the bench and disappear into the dark night.

Owen, head lolled to one side, didn't stir when he heard the door scrape open, certain it was his sister back from her trip to Donegal Town. Next to him, Stout's tail thwapped the floor three times, confirming his sleep-laden assumption.

"Och!"

Aileen's screech jolted him fully awake. In a flash, she was kneeling before him, horror etched on her face.

"Owen Sean McCready! What's happened to ye? Are ya alright?" Her hand hovered over his bandaged one, and she scanned the rest of him as though she could determine if he had any other injuries with just a glance.

Shifting under her intense scrutiny, his chest rumbled with a low growl. "*Tóraithe*," he mumbled.

Aileen tsked. "Someone ought to do somethin' about those bandits. Haggerty again?"

He nodded.

She winced as she met his gaze. "How many did they get?"

Owen managed a weak smile, lifted his bandaged hand, and waved it gently. "Just me."

His sister puffed out a breath and sat back on her haunches. "Thanks be to God for that." She stared off for a long moment, seemingly lost in thought, while she absently scratched Stout's head. Owen guessed that she was calculating how much money they'd have lost if the band of thieves had been successful.

Blinking suddenly, she reached for his injured hand. "Lemme take a look at this." She scowled at the bandage as she carefully turned his hand over and over, looking for the end of the cloth. "Ye've made a right mess of this dressin', I'll tell ya that." Though worry clouded her eyes, humor laced her voice.

"Oh, I dunno," he replied. "I thought I did pretty well considerin' I only had one paw to work with." He couldn't help the chuckle that rattled in his chest.

"Now, I'll be the judge o' that." She unwound the bandage and examined the wound. "Looks like ya cleaned it pretty well, and it doesn't look too deep."

"I told ya it wasn't so bad." He wiggled his fingers and winced. "Hurts though."

Aileen sighed and met his gaze. "How long till ya think ye can weave?"

A pit settled firm in Owen's gut. He'd forgotten all about Murphy's. "Did we get an order?"

She leveled a heavy gaze on him. Whether that meant there was no order and they'd be hard-pressed for cash this quarter, or they hit her with a doozy of an order, he couldn't tell. "Well?" He raised his brows high.

"Aye, we did." She crossed to the hearth and grabbed some dried flowers that hung upside-down there. *Feverfew*, he thought she'd said one time. She crumbled them into a bowl and poured some hot water from the kettle into it, then left the mixture to steep. "Owen, it's massive."

She returned to sit in the chair across from him. "They loved this batch ya just sent. They, of course, love your signature barleycorn pattern. And even more so for the colors. McKean said the bluish hue with the flecks of purple put him in mind of summer on Mackoght Mountain when the heather has just started to bloom."

Owen's mouth tipped up in a smile, but the reality quickly hit of what such an order actually meant for him—and his injury. He reached up and scratched his head with his good hand. "I was afraid o' that," he mumbled to himself, though deep down pride warmed him at the core. He'd found a new combination of local flora to use in the dyes, and it pleased him to know it had paid off. He flexed his fingers and cringed. "We'll make it work. Ya can tell me all the details in the morning. I'm too tired tonight."

Sighing, Aileen crossed to the kitchen again and dunked the bandage in the tea-like substance she'd made, wrung it out, and returned to his side. Stout roused and sat up as though studying how to wrap the injury in case he had to do it himself later. His sister tenderly wound the damp fabric around his hand, then a horse's whinny echoed outside.

Owen shot to his feet. "Och! Did ya not stable the horse?"

Aileen fell back a step, her eyes grew wide, and she clapped a hand on her forehead. "Land sakes, I completely forgot!"

"How d'ya forget to stable a horse when ya park him right next to the barn?"

"Wheesht!" The remark, intended to make him hush, was her typical response when she had no feasible reply. She made quick work of finishing the bandaging, then rushed outside, leaving the door open behind her.

Owen looked to Stout, who stared back at him. "I know, buddy. Women, eh?" The black-and-white border collie huffed, licked his nose, and circled around to settle in his spot. "Don' worry," Owen called after his sister, "I'll get the door!"

Saoirse sighed and slid down from the seat of the rig. How long had she been left sitting out here? The night was pitch-black, and other than the soft orange glow that peeked out from slats in the barn, no light could be seen. The scent of the turf from the house wafted down over her head. She breathed in deep, letting the comforting aroma ground her and steady her nerves. She shuffled her way toward the knoll, hoping to crawl on top and get a glimpse of what was going on with Aileen and her brother. But before she could get there, footsteps came racing around the barn.

"I'm so sorry," Aileen's breathless voice said in a harsh

whisper. "I didn't forget about ya." She sniffled hard and wiped her hand across her mouth. "Okay, I kinda forgot about ya, but not on purpose."

Saoirse had no right to be annoyed at the delay—after all, this woman held no obligation to help her. Yet she fought the tightening in her shoulders. "It's grand," she said, hoping her voice didn't belie her fatigue and frustration. If she was honest, it was not just being left to wait so long in the jaunty car. It was everything. Her entire situation. The circumstances that had gone downhill back in Westmeath, and had spiraled from bad to worse in a matter of days, vexed her to no end, with no way out that she could see.

Aileen closed the distance between them and tugged on Saoirse's elbow, pulling her toward the barn. "Lookit, Owen's in a bad way tonight. Was attacked by bandits while I was away, but—"

"Oh my gracious," Saoirse interrupted her. "Is he alright?"

"Aye, he will be, thanks be to God." She pulled the large wooden doors open. Soft golden light and piles of hay beckoned Saoirse as Aileen approached the horse, still attached to the cart.

"Anyway," Aileen continued, "he was in no way for me to ask about ye, so ye'll just have to lay low in here tonight." She brushed her hand down the horse's neck and crooned something indistinguishable in his ear. She presumed it was some expression of how good of a boy he was.

Saoirse glanced around them, Aileen's statement about the bandits echoing in her mind. She chose to leave it alone. If there was any real danger, Aileen wouldn't suggest putting her up for the night there. Would she? "Eh . . . can I help ya unhitch the horse?" she asked.

Aileen shook her head. "Nah. Fadó and I here have our own little routine. Don't we, boyo?" She patted the draft horse's neck once more as she slipped a slice of apple from her cloak pocket. The horse nickered.

"Fadó?" Saoirse asked.

Aileen chuckled. "Aye. My brother said this fella was an old soul, even as a foal. Said he must've come to us from a long time ago."

Saoirse nodded absently and scanned her surroundings. Though rustic, as most barns were wont to be, this one was clean and tidy. Four stalls lined the eastern wall, with a work area and one additional stall on the western side. The southern wall sported hooks that held yokes, a saddle, and other farm implements. And despite the lack of a fire in the stove, it was decidedly warmer inside than it was out in the wind and impending rain.

"C'mon back here." Aileen's voice shattered Saoirse's thoughts. "We've not used this one for a creature in some time, so it's nice an' clean." She gestured to the last stall on the left.

Saoirse stared inside the small rectangle space. Aileen was rearranging fresh hay into a bed and lay the blanket on top of it before grabbing another from a shelf under one of the tables.

"This'll keep ya out o' sight more easily back here," she was saying. "In the morning, Owen usually comes in around eight o' the clock, so ye'll want to be out by then. There's a creek that runs behind the short stone wall about twenty yards north of here. Ya can hide there, and I'll bring ya some food."

Saoirse nodded. She'd need to hide? Was Owen such a

cantankerous man as that? Should she be worried for her safety? "Are ya sure about this?" she asked Aileen. "If it would trouble your brother so much if he were to find me, wouldn't it be best for me to shelter somewhere else for the night?"

"Wheesht! And where would that place be?" Though her face held a look of scolding, her voice carried the lilt of jest. "Ye'll be just fine here for tonight. I should be able to talk to Owen tomorrow. I'll see if I can convince him to let ya stay longer if ya need. Until then, sleep well and stay hidden or he'll likely confuse you for a sheep thief."

Saoirse swallowed hard. *Let's hope that doesn't happen.* "Alright," she answered. "Thank you so very much."

"*Tá fáilte romhat,*" Aileen replied.

3

Early morning mist hung suspended in the air, dampening the usual symphony of Owen's animals waking and searching for their breakfast. Beads of dew stretched across the ground like a blanket of diamonds and decorated the rustic wooden barn like the tinsel he'd seen once in a storefront in Dublin. Immune to the cold that held permanent residence in his bones, Owen tugged on the heavy door. Behind him, Stout's strident bark ripped his attention away.

"What is it, boyo?" Owen asked as he lumbered over to the canine. The fur lining Stout's back stood up, and he peered intently at the bushes cresting the hilltop between the barn and the house. "Bandits?"

Stout stood still, tail frozen in a straight line behind him, one front paw curled in midair. Slowly, he extended his paw and crept forward. A low growl rumbled in his chest.

Glad he's on my side. The thought flitted through Owen's mind like an autumn leaf on the wind as his pulse kicked up. It would be just like those blighters to lie in wait to ambush his house while he tended his flocks and worked in the weaving shed. The racket from the loom would drown out any *pleidhcíocht* the brutes might get up to. Instinctively, Owen's hands balled into fists as he wished he had a shovel or *hurley* with which to protect himself.

Suddenly Stout lunged at the bushes and chaos erupted from the branches.

"Oi! What're ya like?" Owen yelled, fists swinging wildly. Fur and barks flying, Owen fought valiantly against his foe until the realization struck that a pair of red squirrels had leapt from the plant, sending his dog into a lathered frenzy.

Owen dragged a hand down his face and sucked in a deep breath as he willed the pounding in his chest to slow. "Confound it, dog," he muttered. "C'mon, boyo."

Owen made his way back to the barn door, eager to return to his intended task. "Squirrels." He chuckled as he headed inside.

Saoirse pressed her hand over her mouth as she peered over the low stone wall. The motion was meant to both cover the sound of her huffed breathing and also to stifle her laughter. She'd never seen such a hilarious encounter between man and nature.

Her gaze flitted to the sky, and she offered a silent prayer of thanks for the dog distracting the man. She'd overslept and was just about to head to the place Aileen had told her about when she heard footsteps approaching. The canine— who was apparently called Stout, if she'd heard correctly— had barked just in time, pulling his owner's attention in the opposite direction, allowing her to slip from the small side door unnoticed. And then she'd been treated to a wee comedy show to start her day with slightly lighter spirits than she'd anticipated.

Turning, she sank back against the wall and pulled her knees to her chest, a smile still creasing her face. But as the pounding in her chest slowed and her breathing returned to normal, a chill snaked its way up her spine and settled at the base of her head.

Muise, that was close, Saoirse.

She had no idea what the man would've done had he discovered her. He looked harmless enough from the distant view she'd had. She craned her neck and risked another peek over the wall. He was nowhere to be seen, and the barn door was closed. She wasn't in any danger, was she? Surely not. Though Aileen had mentioned bandits or thieves or something, hadn't she? Suppose her brother mistook Saoirse for one of them? She shivered as her gaze drifted across the landscape, taking in the scene before her.

She was hunkered in a small square field, bordered by a low stone wall. Just beyond the north edge, the trickling of the stream Aileen had mentioned floated on the gentle morning breeze. In the neighboring field to the west, a flock of sheep wandered and munched on their breakfast of wild grasses. Beyond that stretched an endless patchwork of fields and land in as many varied shades of green as stars in the sky. To an outsider, it would seem Aileen's and her brother's farm was plopped down a thousand miles from any sort of civilization, but Saoirse knew the next farmland would be just over one rise or another.

She wondered if this community was as tight-knit as the one she'd left behind in Westmeath. The earthy scents of a turf fire, damp earth, and livestock filled the air. Saoirse's eyes drifted closed, and she drew in a deep breath, once again allowing the aroma to settle her. She loved the smell. It was the aroma of childhood and Ireland and home. Such a soft, delicate fragrance, while also heady and deep. Not harsh like . . . her stomach sank, and a cold sweat beaded on her forehead and upper lip.

No, not now. Don't think of that now. She gripped the damp earth, grounding herself in hopes of avoiding the spiraling despair that threatened to suffocate her every time she remembered it. Remembered *them*. She squeezed her eyes tighter, trying to stop the thoughts from overtaking her, even as the image of a rolling black column invaded the fortress of her mind. Her history of drawing the short straw in situations was nothing compared to the calamity she'd caused that day. She never dreamed her unique skill for making mistakes would ever harm anyone else, let alone—

The sound of the barn door scraping open jolted her back to the present.

"Stout! *Goitse!*"

Saoirse slouched even lower and grimaced. The farmer's footsteps lumbered just beyond the wall. Stout's *trot-trot-trot* across the turf grew louder, and Saoirse slowly tipped over to curl up on the ground. The dog snuffled around the other side of the wall for a moment, stopped near where Saoirse lay, and sniffed three or four times in quick succession before huffing out a hearty exhale.

"Stout!" Saoirse's unknowing host called again.

One more round of sniffing, and the dog trotted away.

Saoirse waited several minutes after the cadence of man and beast faded over a distant hill before moving an inch. The inordinate fear that she'd sit up to discover Aileen's brother and his dog waiting to catch her kept her pinned to her spot far longer than was likely necessary. Finally, she peeked over the top of the stones. Seeing the coast was clear, she stood, brushed off her skirts, and once again surveyed her surroundings before heading north to the stream, extremely parched. She'd not had anything to eat or drink since the carriage ride up yesterday afternoon.

Once at the water's edge, Saoirse knelt and scooped up an icy handful. She relished the frigid chill that trailed her throat and quickly slurped down three more scoops.

"Oh, good, ya made it!"

Saoirse's head whipped around, and she was relieved to see Aileen stepping over the wall, a basket slung on one arm.

"I was afraid Owen'd run ya off."

Owen. Saoirse seared the name into her brain. If she was to have any hope of convincing the man to let her stay until she could make a plan, she'd need to remember his name.

"He very nearly did," Saoirse said on a laugh.

"No." Aileen hurried to Saoirse's side and lowered herself down, questions pinching her face. "What happened?"

Saoirse shrugged. "It's m' own fault. I overslept. Thank God for Stout!"

"Och! That dog." Aileen shook her head.

"No, I'm serious! He trapped a squirrel or somethin' in the bushes, which distracted Owe—your brother—just long enough for me to slip out the side door."

Aileen shifted to sit cross-legged and began unwrapping the towel covering the opening of the basket. "Well, at least the dog did somethin' right." She lifted out a plate loaded with three pieces of brown bread smeared with butter, two hardboiled eggs, and some tomato slices. "Thought ya might be hungry."

Saoirse's stomach rumbled.

"And ya are, I see." Aileen laughed and held the plate out toward her.

Heat flooded Saoirse's cheeks as she sheepishly took it. "Thanks." She sank her teeth into the dense-yet-pillowy bread, and her posture sank in delight. "Oh, that's lovely. Thanks again."

Aileen flapped a hand in her direction. "Don' mention it." She reached back into the basket and produced a rustic metal teapot and cup. Steam flooded the air around them as she poured a serving and handed it to Saoirse.

"Oh, God bless you. I could cry at the sight o' that." She pulled the cup close and inhaled the pungent aroma. The first sip was pure heaven, and Saoirse was surprised at the sense of calm that washed over her.

The pair sat in silence for a long while as Saoirse finished her much-appreciated breakfast.

Far in the distance, a dog's bark floated on the breeze. "I thought sheepdogs were usually pretty good."

Aileen looked at her, brows pressed together. "Pardon?"

"Ya said earlier that at least Stout had done somethin' right. Is he not a good work-dog?"

"Oh, no, he's the best work-dog," Aileen said, eyes wide. "He just can't be bothered with anyone except Owen."

Saoirse laughed. "*Dáiríre?*"

"Yes, really!" Aileen started packing up the basket. "Never mind that I'm the one that makes sure he has enough food and gives him scraps from the garden an' all that. He's only got eyes for yer man." She stood and Saoirse joined her.

"Thanks again. Ye're a lifesaver," Saoirse said, handing her the empty dishes. "Truly."

"Don't mention it." Aileen slid the basket over her arm. "Lay low here for the day. When the sun goes down, it'll be safe ta head back into the barn, if I haven't been able to chat with him by then."

Saoirse nodded and Aileen waved and slipped back over the wall.

Saoirse gasped and sat up straight. Ice-cold rain lashed down upon her, waking her from a deep sleep she hadn't even realized she'd fallen into. With the heavy clouds overhead, it was impossible to tell if the sun was close to setting, but she couldn't stay here. She'd catch her death. Scanning the area to ensure the coast was clear, she scrambled over the wall and scurried toward the barn. No light seeped through the slats as she approached, and all was quiet—save for the pounding rain—so she sprinted toward the side door and slipped inside. The immediate warmth was welcoming, and she could only imagine how much nicer it would be with a fire burning in the stove. Saoirse let her eyes adjust to make certain she was alone.

Seeing that she was, indeed, by herself, she headed back to the stall she'd slept in the night before and made quick work of curling up in the hay and wrapping herself tightly in the blankets Aileen had given her.

The rain continued to pour, and the wind picked up even more. As she warmed, sleep threatened to overtake her again. Just as she began to drift off, the large barn door scraped open. Saoirse's heart leapt in her chest, and she looked for any way to escape. Seeing none, she held her breath and tried to lie as still as a stone. Hopefully, whoever it was wouldn't come this far back.

The ground in front of her glowed the soft orange of distant lantern light, and she rolled her lips together to stop her breath from giving her away. A deep baritone voice hummed a quiet tune as the light grew brighter. A man came into her view.

With the lantern held aloft in his left hand, he searched the shelf on the far wall for something. Then he turned and stopped short. A pair of piercing blue eyes pinned themselves on her.

Saoirse froze, held in a trance by his gaze as her heart pounded in her chest.

His face, which had first registered shock, darkened. "Who are you?"

Saoirse's voice refused to work, and all words vanished from her mind as she stared back at the man. Finally, one word surfaced. "Owen."

4

Confusion tugged Owen's brows together. A young woman—well, younger than he was, anyway—lay hunkered down in a mound of hay and blankets. *His* blankets. She looked to be maybe late-twenties, with a pair of sea glass–colored eyes peering up at him through a mop of reddish-blond ringlets. He cleared his throat. "*Gabh mo leithscéal?*"

The woman clambered to her feet, tripping over a clump of straw and stumbling in his direction. She puffed the strands of hair from her face and jutted out her right hand. "What I mean to say is, you must be Owen."

He stared at her hand as the wheels continued to spin in his mind. The woman was soaked to the bone and didn't appear to be any sort of threat. For a split second he considered whisking her down to the cottage and sitting her in front of the fire. But before he could entertain the idea fully, his protective wall flew back up, and he crossed his arms over his chest. "I'll ask ya again—who are you? Speak quickly."

She swallowed hard as her hand sank to her side. She dipped a shallow curtsy. "Beggin' yer pardon, Owen. I'm Saoirse Fagan."

"That's thrice now ye've used m' own name before I've had a chance to know yours. How d'ye"—he stopped, and a snort of disbelief puffed from his nose. His chest burned as he glanced in the direction of the house. "Aileen," he growled between clenched teeth.

At that moment, Aileen burst through the door, "Saoirse, he's comin'!"

"Too late," Owen said. Aileen slid to a halt right before running right smack into him. Her mouth bobbed like a fish as she looked between him and the strange woman hiding in their barn. His sister twitched as though she was going to stand next to the interloper, then again as though she would take her place next to him.

She finally settled into a spot equidistant to them both. "I-I see ye've met."

Owen shifted his arms to fold tighter across himself and then leveled his gaze on Aileen, hoping the derision he felt registered loud and clear.

"Alright, alright." Aileen stepped closer to him, her hands up, palms facing outward. "I was hopin' to talk to you about it today, anyway. I met Saoirse on the road home last night, and she'd nowhere to go."

Owen's lips screwed up to the side. "So, ye . . . ye told her she could live in the barn?"

"Och!" Aileen rolled her eyes. "No, ya dolt! I was goin' to bring her in after talking to ya last night, but when I saw yer hand, I got flustered and, sort of . . ."

Owen bent slightly at the waist, willing her to continue.

She shrugged, a sheepish pink hue flooding her cheeks. "I forgot about her."

"Ha!" Owen dragged a hand down his face before looking to the stranger. "And so ya figured ye'd help yerself to my barn?"

Saoirse's eyes widened, and her mouth fell open. Suddenly, Aileen's hand was on his arm.

"'Twasn't like that. When I came back out to see to Fadó and the cart, I told her to stay the night and we'd set things to right in the morning."

Suddenly, Saoirse sneezed and wrapped the plaid tighter around her shoulders.

Aileen cleared her throat. When Owen glanced her way, her brows soared, and she flicked her head ever so slightly in Saoirse's direction and then in the direction of the house. Confound the woman and her nonverbal communication. She fancied herself able to tell the whole history of Ireland with just a look, when in reality she was harder to read than a closed book. He scowled and shook his head in silent question.

She repeated the gesture, only more animatedly, which served only to deepen Owen's annoyance and offer no clarification whatsoever. He shrugged slightly as a request for elaboration.

"Good heavens, man. *Tsk.* Ye're as thick as sheep's wool." Aileen shook her head. "Will ya not invite the woman in for a cuppa tea to warm her bones?"

Oh, that. He shifted his attention back to their guest— nae, intruder. She was beginning to shiver fairly fiercely, and her eyes silently pleaded with him to take pity on her.

Sighing, he gestured toward the sliding door. "C'mon, then. I can't have ya dying of exposure in my *scioból.*" He lumbered outside without looking back to see if the ladies were following him.

Saoirse fought the hot tears that threatened to spill down her cheeks. They weren't tears of joy, relief, or even fear. They were just tears of . . . life. Her current predicament with Aileen and Owen aside, the last month had been a blur of tragedy upon hardship upon upheaval, and everything had left her reeling. She needed to get her mind off all that had transpired.

All that you caused, you mean.

She sniffled and wiped at her eyes angrily, hoping to wipe the thought away too. She focused her gaze on the path leading her to the McCreadys' house. She took advantage of her position at the back of the trio to scan Owen once more. Even from behind, he was a commanding figure. She could almost see his bright sapphire eyes illuminating the way ahead of them. He was a daunting character, to be sure. She had no doubt he could easily throw her out without giving it another thought. And yet she felt entirely captivated by him . . . captivated and safe. She scowled at the idea. It made no sense. Nothing that went on in her head made sense anymore. Not since that day. Confound it, would it never cease to invade her every waking moment? *Waking and sleeping,* she reminded herself.

The group rounded the corner at the base of the hill, and the front of the home came into view. While by no means was it a luxury accommodation, the thatch on the roof was impeccably clean and the paint and windows in good repair. Golden light glowed and flickered within as smoke from the turf fire curled lazily overhead.

Owen's shrill whistle pierced the silence, and Saoirse flinched.

"Stout!" Owen called just before opening the door.

Aileen shook her head and snorted. "That dog. C'mon, Saoirse." She hooked her arm through Saoirse's elbow and led her inside.

The gentle yet fierce warmth of the home enveloped her like a hug, and Saoirse's muscles instantly relaxed.

"Go on over by the fire. I'll put the kettle on."

Saoirse fought the temptation to sprint to the hearth, instead forcing herself to move at a respectable speed and take in the modest home. Clean and tidy, everything clearly had a place. Dried herbs and flowers hung from hooks on the kitchen wall, as well as from the ends of the mantel, which stood opposite in the open room. Two tall-back chairs flanked the fireplace, and a *cailleach* was tucked into an alcove along the north wall. Just beyond that, to the right of the hearth, a short hallway led to another bed, or perhaps to a small bedchamber. Saoirse didn't let herself wonder who slept in the outshot bed and settled herself in front of the blazing turf fire.

Her eyes drifted closed as the blessed heat washed over her frame. She opened the heavy tweed plaid she'd wrapped around herself in the barn and allowed the warmth to seep into every nook and cranny.

Just as the kettle began to scream, a scurry of paws skittered into the house. The border collie stopped short and looked from Saoirse to Aileen and back. His body was black, save for a small white patch on his chest, but his head was completely white. He looked just like her own dog, Finn. Except Finn had been brown and white. Her heart clenched at his memory, and her vision blurred. Forcing a smile on her face, she knelt down. "Hello there."

The dog huffed once, trotted over to her, and shoved his head onto the palm of Saoirse's hand to be pet. "Well, who's a good boy? Are ya a good lad?" His tail *thwap-thwapped* on the floor.

"Well, I'll be," Aileen whispered. "Owen, look."

Owen came in and shut the door behind him. He hung his flatcap on a peg and started to take his slicker off when he froze, eyes glued on Saoirse and Stout.

"He's a lovely animal," Saoirse said as she rose. Stout sat next to her foot and pawed up at her hand. Saoirse chuckled and rewarded him with more scratches on the top of his snowy head.

"Aye." Owen grunted. "And he doesn't like anybody."

Behind him, Aileen shook her head. "He doesn't." She crossed the room with a cup of tea and handed it to Saoirse. "I've never seen him do anything like this."

Saoirse smiled down at her new friend.

"I've heard dogs can tell a good person from bad," Aileen called over her shoulder as she poured a fresh cup of tea for her brother.

At that, Saoirse's smile faltered. Poor Stout must be a terrible judge of character if he liked her.

"That beast has only ever had eyes for m' brother." Aileen returned to the kitchen once more for her own cup. "Though who knows why."

Saoirse eyed Owen, who was now sitting in the chair nearest the cailleach, sipping his tea and staring into the fire. She absently wondered what that meant about Owen's character too.

5

Once again, Owen's azure eyes leveled themselves on Saoirse, and she fought not to squirm under his gaze. She'd never seen such an intoxicating color before. Coupled with the intense emotion she couldn't name behind his expression, Saoirse found it equally unsettling and impossible to look away.

"So," Owen said around a mouthful of tea. "What's yer story?"

Saoirse's pulse quickened. Of all the questions he could've posed, he had to ask that one? Hers was such a long and sordid tale. Though it hadn't always been thus. Until a month ago, her story had been like anyone else's in Ireland. Quiet, unassuming. She worked hard to eke out a living and help support her family. Though she'd always suffered from a terrible streak of what some called bad luck. It had been a running joke in her family. If things were going to go wrong for anyone in the Fagan family, it would be Saoirse. When she was a young lass, it was little things like her milk being the one to spill. But as she grew, the seeming failures grew with her. Even still, she'd never really been the cause of any true harm. But then . . . that all came crashing down. Surely, he didn't want to know all that. *Just tell him the truth—but as little of it as possible.*

She tried to paste a look of calm on her face. "I came up from Westmeath to start as a maid at Drumboe Castle only to discover the place locked up and abandoned."

Owen nodded slightly. "I'd heard the auld codger had passed. Why'd ye come all this way if there was no post to be had?"

Saoirse tugged the plaid tighter around her shoulders. "That's just it. No one sent word. So when I arrived, I was stranded. My previous employer had kindly arranged for me to ride in her enclosed carriage, but the driver had to hurry on to Letterkenny and left before I knew what was going on."

"'S desperate." Aileen tsked, shaking her head. "Leavin' a gairl stuck like that. 'Magine."

Saoirse shrugged. "I didn't know what to do, so I just started walking." She tipped her head toward Aileen. "Night had fallen when Aileen came upon me and graciously offered me a lift."

Owen grunted and drained the rest of his cup. "So, ye'll be headin' back home, then?"

It was a logical assumption, but the weight of it hit Saoirse like a sock to the gut. She wanted nothing more than to go home. For things to go back to the way they were. Images of her mother's, father's, and siblings' faces floated across her mind's eye, and she blinked against the stinging in her eyes. The lump in her throat stopped her voice, so she simply shook her head. A heavy, awkward silence yawned until it filled the room.

"I—" Saoirse's voice cracked. "I don't have a home."

Owen's gaze faltered slightly for the first time. "Oh." He cleared his throat and shifted in his seat. "What happened?"

Aileen, who stood next to his chair, swatted his shoulder. "Have ya no tact, man? What does that matter?"

Owen shot a look at his sister. "It matters. And I'm just curious." He turned back to Saoirse and waited.

"Fire," she whispered. "Everything gone. Everyone gone."

"Oh, Saoirse," Aileen whispered and clutched her chest.

"I'm sorry." True sympathy fluttered across Owen's face, and his gaze drifted to the fire in the hearth. "So ya have no plans." It came out as a quiet statement rather than a question.

"Now ya see why I invited her to stay," Aileen said. "Even just for the night. How could I abandon her to the elements?"

Her brother merely nodded, a million miles away in thought. At length, he pressed his palms to his knees and stood. "Aileen," he said, then he strolled into the kitchen.

He angled them so their backs were to Saoirse. She let her gaze fall to the ground as she lowered herself onto the low creepie stool next to the fire. She wouldn't dare sit on their chairs in her damp clothing.

Snippets of their conversation drifted into the living room. Phrases like "supposed to do," "not enough," and "barely surviving as it is," snaked their way into her ears, the deep timbre of Owen's voice allowing a clarity of words that Aileen's softer voice filtered. Saoirse glanced up just in time to see Aileen lay a hand on her brother's arm, her pleading gaze tracing his face.

Owen sighed, and Aileen threw her arms around him. The pair returned to their places by the fire, and Owen slowly lowered himself into his chair.

"You can stay through the weekend," he said, his tone

matter-of-fact. "That gives you a few days to seek out new employment and lodging."

Tears sprang to Saoirse's eyes, and she leapt from her stool and fell before Owen. "Oh, thank you so much. Truly."

He grunted what sounded like an acknowledgment, but a peculiar look had settled on his face and his gaze bore into his knee. Saoirse followed it to discover she'd clasped his uninjured hand in hers. Heat rushed to her cheeks, and she pulled her hand away—but not before noting the way his roughened skin felt against her fingers or how strong his hand was, even without him returning her grip. She stood and brushed her hands down the front of her skirts. "I'm terribly sorry. I'm just ever so grateful for your hospitality."

"I'm afraid all I can offer ya is the barn," Owen said. Next to him, Aileen shrugged, an apologetic look on her face. "We've no place fer you to sleep in here."

Saoirse shook her head, her cheeks damp from her tears. "That will suit me just fine."

Aileen stepped forward. "We'll set ya up real nice. I'll make ya a proper bed. Or, at least, a pallet that'll be more comfortable than the hard ground."

Saoirse smiled at her new friend. "Thank you," she mouthed. She took a steadying breath, and when she found her voice again, hurried to add, "And I'll help out around here however I can. I don't expect something for nothing. I'll earn my keep."

"Fine." Owen stood. "Now if ye'll excuse me, I have a few things to see to before supper. Aileen, ya'd better make with whatever grand plan ya have for that bed before the weather gets worse, and so ya have time to get dinner going."

Aileen scurried about the small home, gathering a few bits and bobs. When her arms were sufficiently loaded, she handed a small, flat pillow to Saoirse and inclined her head toward the door. "C'mon, let's get ya sorted."

Owen flexed his left hand as he trudged to the weaving shed, forcing himself not to think about the electricity that had jolted through him at Saoirse's touch. He'd held plenty a woman's hand over the course of his thirty-eight years on this earth, so the touch of a woman wasn't new to him. Granted, most of his experience was limited to a passing brush while working on a mutual task, or during a *céilí* when he held a woman close to dance. He'd never really held designs on romance. Not that he was against the notion—not by any means. And as a younger man he would've welcomed the right woman. However, life simply hadn't worked out that way for him, and once his parents had passed, and it was down to just him and Aileen to run the farm and do the weaving, there wasn't time for anything else. But that split second near the fire when Saoirse grasped his hand was a sensation he'd never experienced. She was a lovely woman, to be sure. Easy on the eyes and more than likely a delightful person to be around. But he didn't have room in his life for anything else—namely another mouth to feed. So, confound it all, why would his rebellious hand not stop tingling at the absence of her touch?

She'll be gone in a few days' time, anyway, he reminded himself. He held on to that thought like an anchor, letting it hold his wayward thoughts under the surface to drown.

Entering the shed, he lit a lantern and began to inspect the loom. He'd done not a stitch of weaving today, so it was imperative he have everything ready to start a full day of work at the crack of dawn tomorrow.

He slowly moved around the loom, checking that all was in place. The warp was already set and meticulously strung through the eyes of the heddles that would pull different strands up at a time in order to create the various patterns Owen was known for. He heaved a sigh of relief that he'd already finished the task of stringing the warp, which ran the length of the loom frame—by far the most wearisome part of the whole weaving process. One might think it a mindless task, but it was imperative to keep focused on what he was doing or risk making a mistake that would cost him at best hours of work re-stringing, or at worst a whole bolt of destroyed fabric. With that job done, Owen was set to get straight to the actual weaving in the morning.

He tugged on the ends of one string of warp to ensure it was fully tied and winced as pain sliced through his right hand. This was going to be interesting. He could weave despite his wound, no doubt. But it would not be a pleasant experience. He eyed the bandage, grateful to see no blood had leaked through the cloth but still cursed the bandits who continued to threaten his livelihood. As he closed up the shed, ensuring the door was secure, the scent of Aileen's stew drifted on the air mingled with the aroma of the turf fire burning in his hearth. His stomach rumbled in anticipation of the feast that awaited him. Okay, perhaps *feast* was a bit of an exaggeration. The truth was, they barely had enough to keep the two of them fed. Owen swallowed the disappointment of having to go with less of his favorite dish in order to feed their new guest. *Spoken like a true selfish scut.* He shook the thought free and determined to be grateful for what he had, then headed to the house and his supper.

When Owen entered the house, Saoirse stood at the counter next to Aileen, the two in quiet conversation. Stout lay at Saoirse's feet and, upon seeing Owen, thwapped his tail on the ground a few times before lumbering to his feet and trotting over to greet his master.

"Supper's almost done," Aileen said. "Just waitin' for the bread to cool enough to slice."

"Grand, so," Owen replied, hoping to drown out the growling in his gut. Stew and brown bread, his absolute favorite. The only way to top this meal would be to finish it off with some apple tart and fresh cream, but that was not to be. Not only was it the wrong season for the fruit but the extra sugar, butter, and flour required would leave them in a lurch at the end of the month.

Owen shuffled to the washbasin and cleaned his hands and face while Aileen and Saoirse set the table and dished out the steaming ambrosia, moving in a coordinated dance as though they'd been working together the whole of their lives. He dried himself and hung the rough-nubbed towel on the hook just as Aileen summoned him to the table.

The trio sat at the small table that was crowded when it was just the two of them. He offered a short prayer of thanks, and they dug in. All was quiet for a long while as everyone enjoyed the hearty stew full of lamb, potatoes, and carrots—all harvested from their land and flock—in a thick gravy broth.

Saoirse was the first to break the silence. "What can I help with tomorrow?"

Aileen flapped her hand. "Ya really don't need to work around here. We've only offered for ya to stay."

"There's work to be done in the garden, and the stock need fed," Owen said, attention fixed on his bowl as he scooped up some of the broth with a wedge of brown bread. "The sheep need moved to the eastern quarter, and I've a full day in the shed ahead of me."

"Owen," Aileen scolded.

He shrugged. If they were going to be sacrificing from their own stores to feed this woman, the least she could do was help out a bit. It would be nice to have an extra pair of hands for a few days.

"I really don't mind," Saoirse said around a mouthful of food. "I know it's a burden to feed and house me for so long, and I want to contribute as much as I can."

Owen studied her for a moment. Her strawberry ringlets had been tied back with a ribbon, but a few stray ones fell around her face. She looked from Aileen to him and back, her expression one of earnest pleading. "Truly," she added. "I want to."

Aileen pressed her lips together. "Very well, then. You can start in the garden with me and then we can work the stock together."

Owen nodded, stood, and took his dishes to the basin. "'Tis settled, then. Now, if ye'll excuse me, we've an early start tomorrow, and I must turn in."

6

Saoirse relished the feel of the cool, damp earth as she worked it between her fingers before pulling up the next weed. There weren't too many, as it was apparent Aileen worked hard to keep their garden tidy and neat. The garden and house were her domain, Aileen had told her. Owen tended to the weaving and the livestock. Saoirse suspected that Aileen also had a hand in carding and spinning the wool, which she would've done over the long, dark winter months. February, while still cold and damp, was the official start of spring, starting on Saint Bríd's Day.

"After this, we'll head to the garden shed to chit the spuds," Aileen called over her shoulder while pruning the blackberry bushes that made up the western border of the garden plot.

Saoirse nodded as she sat back on her heels, the final weed in her hand. Over the crest of the hill, the constant *clickety-clack* of the hand loom filled the air around them. It was so rhythmic and steady, one could dance to it, and Saoirse found herself drawn to the sound.

"We'll do the spuds in here," Aileen said, beckoning Saoirse over to a small, whitewashed shed—though the word *shed* was generous. It was little bigger than an outbuilding and held spades, rakes, a shovel, and some buckets, as well as a few other gardening tools. A rustic wooden shelving unit lined one wall. Saoirse joined Aileen at the shelves, and they made quick work of arranging all the tubers on a wooden tray so that the ends with the most eyes faced upwards. They'd be left to sprout so they'd be ready to plant come mid-March.

When the last seed potato was placed, Aileen brushed her hands together and sighed. "I think it's time for a cuppa."

Saoirse smiled. "I like the way you think, Aileen McCready."

Aileen laughed and closed up the shed. "I'll go put the kettle on. Would ya go see if Owen wants to come down, or if he'd like to take his tea there? Sometimes, if he's in the groove of the loom, he doesn't want to leave and break the spell."

"Of course." Saoirse chewed her lip to hide her smile. She'd been dying to get a look at the loom in action all morning. And if she was honest with herself, getting to peek at the brilliant blue of Owen's eyes again didn't make her too terribly sad either.

Muscles burning in protest after spending so much of the morning crouching in the dirt, Saoirse climbed the hill behind the McCreadys' home and finally caught a glimpse of the weaving shed. She'd not noticed it until now. Roughly half the size of the house, it stood about thirty yards away due north from the back door, whereas the barn was about thirty yards to the east. The rhythmic clacking grew louder as she approached. The door to the shed was open, and Owen's voice mingled with the loom's percussion as he sang a jaunty tune to the beat. Smooth and deep, the baritone voice sent chills skittering up Saoirse's arms. She allowed herself to indulge in her own personal concert for a moment before darkening the entrance at the threshold.

"Hallo?" The din of the loom swallowed her voice. When her eyes adjusted to the dim interior, her jaw fell slack. The contraption nearly filled the room, and so many pieces moved at once, she wasn't sure what to watch first. She had envisioned a simple frame strung longways with threads and imagined Owen snaking other thread over and under. This, however, was a different beast entirely. At least three feet wide, and twice as long, the tallest parts reached five or six feet, causing her to feel overshadowed by the monstrosity. Hundreds of threads stretched the length of the loom and went through a curtain of strings that ran perpendicular, each one passing through a small loop in the upright strings. Her gaze drifted to Owen, and she watched his lithe movements. His left hand would pull a lever hanging from the top, then catch a spindle of thread and send it hurtling back the other direction before pulling another lever. His feet pressed long pedals near the ground like she'd seen on the organ at mass. The whole process was utterly dizzying. Suddenly, she was terrified to interrupt him. What if he lost his place? Would it ruin the whole bolt of fabric? She couldn't be responsible for that. Especially not after he'd been so generous in allowing her to stay through the weekend.

She half turned to leave, then stopped. Aileen had requested she ask Owen about his tea. She couldn't decide which instinct to follow—the self-preserving one that didn't want to risk interfering with their livelihood, or the one wishing to please her hostess and do as she wished.

All at once, silence enveloped the shed. "Do ya need somethin'?"

Saoirse's head spun to meet Owen's gaze, his eyes glowing in the dim light. "Oh, sorry, I—" She cleared her throat and stepped farther into the space. "Aileen wanted me to ask if ya'd like to come down to the house for a cuppa, or if ya want ta take it up here?"

Owen pulled his flatcap off and scratched his head, then rolled it from side to side. "I'd best take it here. I've a long way to go."

Saoirse nodded, but instead of turning to the door, she took another half step closer to the loom. "It's extraordinary. How—"

"Tea!" Aileen's call jolted Saoirse from her thoughts, ripping the question she was going to ask right from her mind.

"Right." Saoirse smiled sheepishly. "Back in a sec."

The air remained quiet, and Saoirse hurried back down the hill to the house. She supposed it wasn't worth Owen getting back into a rhythm only for her to interrupt it again in a minute.

Aileen was standing in the doorway of the house, a grin splitting her face when Saoirse approached. "Get lost, didja?" She laughed.

Saoirse shrugged. "It's a right mystery, that contraption!"

"*Psh!*" Aileen shook her head. "That's why I leave the weavin' to him. He tried to teach me once, and I nearly lost the head with it all."

"I can understand why." Saoirse followed Aileen inside. "He said he'll take his tea up there. Long way to go."

"I figured as much." Aileen handed her the same basket she'd used to bring breakfast to Saoirse yesterday. "Would ya mind running this back up there? I need to start on some things here in the kitchen."

"*Cinnte*." Saoirse took the messages and scurried back up the hill, eager to get another look at the weaving process.

Owen stood, one shoulder leaned lazily against the doorjamb, a piece of straw twirling in his lips, and his gaze a million miles away into the hills.

She slowed her pace so as not to startle him. "Here ya go," she said softly.

He blinked and his gaze refocused. It seemed to take a second for him to remember where he was. After another long look at the horizon, he took the tea and bread from her hands. "T'anks."

Saoirse turned and followed the direction Owen's gaze had been fixed. "Wishin' you were somewhere else?" she asked as she poured him a cup.

He chuckled, and it rumbled low in his chest. Saoirse couldn't help but grin at the sound. "That's a loaded question," he said, taking a long draw of tea.

She hiked her thumb toward the hills. "Seems like ye'd rather be out there."

He bobbled his head from side to side, the corners of his mouth pulled downward as he considered her statement. "Perhaps. I do enjoy bein' among creation with my flock. But I enjoy this too." He glanced briefly through the door behind him, then back toward the horizon. "I'm just a mite worried about *mo thread caorach*."

Saoirse stepped closer. "Oh?"

He nodded. "Bandits have been more active of late than they've been in a while. They always want my sheep."

"Why?" She shifted her feet. "I mean, why yours specifically?"

A sly smile tickled the corner of his mouth, and he glanced at her from the side of his eye. "'Cause they're the best."

Laughter bubbled up from Saoirse's belly. "Oh, I see."

He chuckled again, and she warmed at the sound. He drained the last of his cup, then handed it back to Saoirse. "Thanks for bringin' that up." He turned and stood half in the doorway. "I need to get back to it."

Saoirse held the basket toward him. "But ye've not had your bread."

"Just set it there." He gestured to the windowsill. "I'll have it in a bit."

Saoirse did as he bade and excused herself back down the hill.

The rest of the afternoon, Saoirse helped feed the horses in the barn, mucked out their stables, and swept the building clean—all to the music of Owen's weaving. She'd planned to help Aileen move the sheep to the eastern quarter—which, as it turned out, was the field Saoirse had hidden in yesterday morning—but Aileen had said it would just be easier if she did it. Aileen wasn't sure how Stout would take to Saoirse trying to give the commands, though the animal was clearly taken with her. But more than that, she didn't want the sheep to startle at the presence of a stranger.

"They're so used to the bandits tryin' to run off with 'em," Aileen had said. "They bolt when anyone but me or Owen gets near."

Now, Saoirse tugged the heavy barn door closed and looked to where the sun had just begun to kiss the horizon. She pressed her hands to the small of her back, arched, and absently thought, *If those bandits put half as much effort into making an honest living as they do trying to steal other people's sheep, they'd be richer than they realize.*

The light outside had gone from golden to a purplish blue to gray, and finally too low for Owen to make any more progress with the weave tonight. The lantern light simply wasn't strong enough. Owen stepped from behind the machine and stretched his tight shoulders and shook his legs. A day of weaving was like a never-ending bit of céilí dancing, and he was exhausted.

Before heading back to the house, he stopped by the barn to check on the progress of things there. When he stepped inside, his brows soared. The place fairly sparkled. It hadn't been that clean in a dog's age—and Owen prided himself on keeping the tidiest barn in the parish. But somehow, his sister had managed to take it to a whole other level.

When he entered the house, the aroma of mashed potatoes, fresh bread, and tea welcomed him. The ladies were setting the table.

"Well, look who finally decided to call it a day," Aileen said. "Hurry now and wash up before this all goes devilishly cold."

His sister sure did have a way with words. "Aye, Mammy." He smiled to himself and made quick work of cleaning up.

After blessing the food, the trio dug in.

"The barn looks great," Owen told Aileen. "Well done."

Aileen, who'd just shoved a mound of spuds in her mouth,

shook her head and pointed at Saoirse with her fork. "That was all Saoirse."

Once again, Owen's brows lifted, and he turned to their guest. Saoirse's cheeks flushed, and she dropped her gaze to her food.

"Is that right?" he asked.

Saoirse lifted one shoulder and let it fall.

Owen swallowed another bite. "Well, thank you. Well done."

She nodded and her eyes briefly met his. "Happy to help." Then, after a sip of tea, she sat back. "Tomorrow, after I finish whatever you need me to do, I was going to head into town to see about employment opportunities." She grimaced slightly. "That is, if you can direct me to which town might be best."

Owen thought for a moment, trying not to pay heed to how much he admired her drive. "Well, Glentornan likely won't have what ye're lookin' for. Ya might try Ballymann to the west, or Letterkenny to the east—that might be your best option, what with tomorrow being a Sunday. Letterkenny is certainly the biggest of all your options." He paused another moment, his eyes drifting up to the ceiling in thought. "Perhaps even Glenveagh Castle, depending on what yer skills are." He sat back as well. "What do you do?"

"She's a wiz of a seamstress," Aileen offered. Owen and Saoirse both spun their heads toward her. Aileen shrugged. "We've had a lot of time to talk." She rose and started clearing the empty dishes.

"I have done a fair bit o' sewing," Saoirse said. "I've also worked as a housemaid. And I was set to be the head maid at Drumboe."

Owen nodded. She shouldn't have too much trouble finding something. Folks were always in the market for good help.
Though resources to pay that help were often scarce. But
that wasn't his problem. Saoirse was clearly a very capable
woman. Surely she'd land on her feet.

7

Saoirse lay in the dark barn and stared up at the ceiling. Every bone in her body ached from the labors of the day, and yet—as unlikely as it seemed—she felt accomplished and satisfied. This was the first honest day of work she'd done since losing her family, and it was strangely cathartic.

Her thoughts rolled back to the conversation at dinner. Owen had seemed impressed, or at least pleased, with what she'd done and with her plan for tomorrow. She smiled to herself as she recalled the look he'd given her when he found out she'd been the one cleaning the barn. She hardly knew the man, and yet she couldn't help but wonder what she could do next to bring that light to his eyes again.

Shifting onto her side, she slid her eyelids closed. In the recesses of her mind, she could still hear the constant clacking of the loom, which turned her thoughts toward the conversation about the latest order of tweed Owen and Aileen had had as they were cleaning up from dinner. Saoirse couldn't imagine how exhausted Owen must be after such intense physical labor all day long. How many days like that would it take to fill an order of that magnitude? Were the yarns all dyed, or was that yet to be done? What happened if he had to change the pattern? She shook her head against the straw-stuffed pillow, grateful that she wasn't the one to have to re-string all those threads just in order to be able to start the actual weaving.

Ferocious barking tore through the night air, ripping Saoirse from a dead sleep. Heart pounding, she pressed a hand to her chest. *Stout.*

The dog snarled, growled, then continued barking, his volume increasing by the minute. Then the sound of shuffling. Stout's ferocity intensified, and the shuffling grew louder as a mix of voices joined in. *Bandits.*

"Oi!" Relief washed over Saoirse at the sound of Owen's shout. "Away with ye, chancers! Git!"

Men laughed. A caustic, sickening sound. The ruckus died down, save for Stout's low growling. Owen's footsteps drew nearer. "Go on wit' ye," he continued. "Ye've no place here."

"Ya should've left *na caoirigh* on the hill," a gravelly voice said. "But I thank ye kindly fer roundin' them up for us." More toxic laughter.

No, the sheep! Saoirse crept toward the side door of the barn. It was both easier to open and quieter than sliding the massive main entrance ajar. As stealthily as she could, she turned the handle and opened the door just enough for her to slip outside. She didn't know what help she could be, but she wouldn't abandon her hosts in their time of need. Not again.

Owen was holding a torch, which cast an eerie orange glow over the scene. Saoirse could just make out the silhouettes of three or four large men standing opposite Owen, all seemingly itching for a fight. In the middle, Stout stood, hackles raised, teeth bared. He reminded Saoirse of her childhood dog, God rest him, when a mob of schoolboys had been teasing her for her latest mishap.

Owen waved the torch toward the bandits. "Ye'd best get, Haggerty, before I summon the *gardaí*."

A tall man with a barrel chest—apparently Haggerty—snorted. "I could get halfway to Dublin wit' yer entire flock before the first of the law ever arrived."

Saoirse ground her teeth. How could people do things like this?

"Now," Haggerty said, taking a step closer to Owen, "we can do this the easy way or the hard way." He drew a knife from his belt and held it up.

Owen switched the torch to his bandaged hand and held the other one up, palm toward the bandits. "Look, just leave and no one has to get hurt."

As the men continued to argue, Saoirse snuck around the backside of the barn, grabbing a shovel on her way, and tried to creep behind the men, hoping she could clock one of them on the back of the head and cause a distraction. But before she could, a bloodcurdling yell rent the air, and Stout started barking and growling again in earnest.

"Owen!" Saoirse screamed and sprinted to the front of the building. Owen lay in a heap on the ground, firelight glistening in the pool of blood that slowly spread from his arm. Stout stood between him and Haggerty, teeth bared. Just then, Haggerty lunged and swiped the knife at Stout. Saoirse desperately wanted to save Owen but she refused to let another dog die on her watch, so she jumped between them and swung the shovel wildly.

A sickening thud told her she'd made contact with Haggerty's head. He stumbled back a few paces and fell to the ground, his backside rolling into the air. That's when Stout pounced, landing a healthy bite square on Haggerty's rump. The man screamed for his cronies to help him. The pair jolted out of their stupor and waved their arms wildly at Stout, shouting. Stout gave his target a good shake before letting go and taking his place at Owen's side again.

"You'll pay for this, McCready," Haggerty growled. "You and yer little tart!" He scrambled to his feet with much difficulty and hobbled into the darkness, his backside covered in a glistening stain that grew bigger with each second.

Saoirse squinted into the blackness, shovel at the ready in case their leaving was a ruse. But Owen's groan drew her attention.

She hurried to his side and knelt down. "Owen, are ya alright?" Stout lay next to him and whined. Owen was curled up on one side, blood pooling around him. His eyes rolled back in his head and fluttered closed.

"Owen! Owen, stay with me!" Saoirse patted his cheeks, ignoring the coarseness of his whiskers. She picked up the torch, which was somehow still burning, and held it aloft, but it was impossible to tell where the bleeding was coming from, or how badly wounded Owen really was.

"Owen!" she called again. His eyes batted a few times, he groaned again, and then his whole body sagged lifelessly. "No!" she screamed, shaking his shoulder. "Come back!" When he didn't respond, a sob choked Saoirse, and she clapped a bloodied hand over her mouth. *Please, God, don't let him die.*

Next to her, Stout whined again. Saoirse's eyes flew open. "Stout, go get Aileen!" The dog looked at her, whimpered, and pawed at her leg before looking back at Owen. "Go!" Saoirse pointed toward the house. "Aileen, go get her!" He barked once more and bolted down the hill.

She could hear his strident barking fade as he drew nearer to the house. Saoirse brushed some hair from Owen's face and let her tears fall freely. She offered the same prayer over and over. *Please, God, don't let him die.*

After what seemed an eternity, Aileen came rushing up the hill in her dressing gown, hair disheveled, Stout leading the way.

"Owen!" she screamed and fell at his side. "What happened?"

Saoirse's breath hitched in her chest. "Bandits."

Fire flashed in Aileen's eyes. "Haggerty?"

Saoirse nodded.

Aileen muttered an oath under her breath and cursed the thieves that could have very well killed Owen or, at the very least, destroyed the McCreadys' livelihood. Then she took off her dressing gown and draped it over her brother's still form. "Keep him warm. Keep talking to him. I'll send for Doctor McGinley."

Panic seized Saoirse's chest. "Don't leave me here alone." She reached out and grasped the sleeve of Aileen's nightdress. "Please."

Aileen scrambled to her feet. "Ye'll be fine. Stout'll look after ya. I must fetch the doctor or Owen'll die." She spun on her heel and sprinted down the hill.

Saoirse swung her gaze from one horizon to another. Still no sign of Haggerty or his men, but that did nothing to quell the churning in her gut. She shifted to sit on her hip with her legs bent to one side so she could lean closer to Owen. His breaths were shallow and quiet, but he was breathing—a welcome revelation since she couldn't tell a few moments ago. And the bleeding seemed to be slowing. At least the puddle hadn't gotten any bigger in the last minute or two. "Hang in there, Owen," she crooned into his ear. "Stout and I are here, and help is on the way. Don't leave us."

Saoirse stood in front of the washbasin in the McCreadys' kitchen and stared down at the red liquid. They'd refilled the small tub with fresh water three times already, and the blood never seemed to fully wash away, adding to the unseen stains she already carried.

Owen's right arm had been almost completely sliced open, and he had other gashes on his left arm and a few in his abdomen. Thankfully, the doctor said, the ones to his belly were fairly superficial, so he wasn't in any danger of succumbing to those wounds as long as infection didn't set in. It would be a matter of time before the full extent of the aftermath of his hand injuries was apparent.

Studying her own hands, Saoirse decided they were as clean as they were going to get and turned her attention back to the doctor, who was explaining Owen's care to Aileen. Saoirse couldn't even remember how they'd gotten Owen down the hill and into the house. Had she and Aileen done that themselves? Did the doctor have a cart? Did a neighbor help? It didn't matter now. Owen was home and safe, though not out of the woods by any means.

"Change the bandages twice a day for the next three weeks. And no heavy lifting," the doctor was saying.

Aileen was writing down his instructions, but she paused, her hand hovering over the parchment. "And weaving?"

Doctor McGinley looked at her like she'd claimed to be the queen. "Aileen."

"What?" she shouted. "Tell me, we need to know!"

He laid a tender hand on Aileen's arm. "Let's leave that for now. We'll talk about it in a few days, eh?"

Aileen sucked in a shuddery breath and nodded. "Alright. Aye."

"Let's get him through tonight, and we can chat more when I come back to check on him." He turned and Saoirse's heart lurched at the look he gave her. A look as if to say, "Don't tell her he won't be weaving for a good long while. If ever."

How he could communicate that with just a look was beyond Saoirse, but she could swear that's what he was saying. Maybe it was just her own fears talking, but either way, she knew there was no way Owen was going to be able to get the Murphy's order done on time, if at all.

Doctor McGinley began packing his bag. "He'll likely sleep on for the next couple of days. That's to be expected, as is the slight temperature he's running as his body fights to heal. But if his fever spikes or the swelling gets worse, send for me right away."

Aileen and Saoirse both nodded.

"I'll be back in a few days if I don't hear from you before then." He tugged his jacket from the peg and put it on. "Take care, lassies." He stopped just before he closed the door. "Make sure yas latch this door tight, aye?"

They shared a frightened glance. "Aye," Aileen squeaked. Saoirse could only nod. With that, the doctor left them alone to care for Owen and protect their homestead.

The next two days passed by in a blur. Aileen and Saoirse traded off taking care of Owen and tending to the meals, sheep, horses, and other chores. Stout refused to leave his master's side unless forced to help with the stock. But as soon as his duties were finished, he was right back next to the cailleach.

Tuesday morning, Aileen had taken Stout to the barn to keep watch while she fed the horses and mucked the stables. Saoirse was in the house changing the dressing on Owen's right arm when he began to stir and moan.

She scooted to the edge of her chair. "It's okay, you're safe."

He mumbled something she couldn't understand, so Saoirse leaned in closer. "What was that? You're home, Owen, okay?" She brushed the hair from his forehead, willing him to fully wake.

Just as he seemed to settle back down into sleep, his eyes flew open and filled with panic. He released a loud scream, his breaths shallow.

"Shh, shh," she crooned. "You're okay. You're safe. They're gone."

Owen looked around, wildness and confusion coloring his expression. Saoirse gently took hold of his hand with one of hers and used the other to smooth the hair away from his forehead. At her touch, he stilled and his gaze found hers. After a long moment, recognition seemed to register, and he calmed.

"What happened?" His voice was gravelly and raw.

"Haggerty," she replied, not sure what, if anything, he recalled.

"The sheep!" Owen tried to sit up, grimaced, and fell back.

"The sheep are fine. But you need to rest. You've been badly injured." She gently stroked his fingers with her thumb.

His gaze drifted down to watch the motion. His expression darkened when he saw all the bandages winding up both his arms and around his torso. "How bad is it?" He gripped her fingers lightly, though to her it felt less like holding on and more like testing their movement.

"Well, you're alive," she said on a sigh. "Let's start with that."

"That bad, huh?"

"It could've been worse. Much worse, believe me." She blinked away the unbidden memory of Owen on the ground, unconscious and bleeding, and her begging God not to let him die. Was this her doing? Did she bring her own special brand of bad luck—the deadliest sort—to the McCreadys?

"Thanks for the encouragement, doc." He chuckled, but the sound faded and was followed by a groan.

"Just take it easy and rest for now, aye? Aileen and I have things well in hand." She stood and gathered the dirty bandages. "Doc McGinley should be here today or tomorrow to check on you."

8

Owen watched Saoirse dump the soiled bandages into a pot of boiling water to disinfect. She then filled the kettle and set that on to boil as well. She moved so naturally around his home, and he couldn't understand how or why she would be so familiar with everything.

"These are already looking better than Sunday," she called over her shoulder to him.

Sunday? "How long was I out?"

She paused in thought, hand poised above the tea canister. "About two days."

"Two days?" Panic surged through him. The flock must be starving. What state was the garden in? And the weaving shed? He tried to sit up again, but shooting pain throughout his entire upper body forced him to lie back down.

"It's alright. Aileen and I have been seein' to the stock and the garden," Saoirse said, as if reading his mind. "And yer neighbors have all been keeping a weather eye out for Haggerty's return." She shuffled over with a steaming cup of tea and set it on the chair she'd been sitting in a few moments ago.

"Let's sit you up a bit, aye?" She leaned over and hooked one arm around his shoulders and under his left arm. Then she looped her right hand under his right arm. The scent of tea, bread, and lye wafted from her clothes as a tendril of her hair tickled Owen's cheek. "Nice and easy now."

Owen gritted his teeth and pushed his feet against the bed to sit up and rest his back against the wall of the cailleach, ignoring the searing heat that shot through him as he did so.

"Good." She reached for the teacup. "Now, let's get some fluids in ya."

He reached out to take the cup from her, but his bandaged hands were clumsy, and he couldn't grasp it.

"Here, let me. Just sit back." She sat on the edge of the bed and gently lifted the rim to his lips. As tenderly as if she was holding a newborn babe, she tipped the cup slightly so he could sip the hot liquid. His eyes drifted closed as the tea soothed not only his parched mouth but his battered spirit as well. When he opened them, his gaze locked with hers.

"Thank you," he said, his voice hoarse and raw from his ordeal and lack of use the last few days.

She nodded and waited a moment before lifting the cup to his lips once more. He fought the urge to slurp the whole thing down in one gulp, as the first sip had awoken a three-day hunger in his belly. When she took the cup away, some of the tea sloshed out and splashed on his chin.

"Woops!" she said. Then, as if by reflex, Saoirse wiped his chin and lower lip with her thumb. Suddenly she stilled, her thumb still resting on the corner of his mouth, her touch as soft as a flower petal. Her eyes were wide, as though she'd surprised herself with the motion. Owen shared her surprise, but he was more shocked at the strength of his wish that she not remove her hand just yet. He wondered if she could feel his heart thundering through his chest.

Her eyes met his again. "More?"

He swallowed hard and whispered, "Aye."

A sudden knock at the door startled them both. Saoirse jumped up, somehow managing not to drop the cup or spill any more of the steaming liquid on him.

The strange knocking pattern repeated.

Saoirse set the cup down on the table and scurried to the door. She knocked an odd pattern in return and then waited. When two deliberate knocks sounded a second later, she unlatched the door and opened it. Aileen came in and flung her cloak on a peg, Stout trotting in behind her.

Saoirse beamed. "He's awake."

As if he understood Saoirse's words, Stout sprinted to the bed and hopped up so his front paws rested on the side of it. His tail wagged so fiercely, Owen feared it might fall off, and the dog whimpered as Owen carefully scratched his ear.

"Hiya, boyo."

Aileen screeched and rushed to her brother's side. "*Buío-cihas le Dia!*" She bent and pressed a kiss to his cheek, then pushed Stout aside and sat where Saoirse had just been.

"How do you feel?"

He smirked. "Skewered."

"Och!" She made like she was going to swat him but stopped short.

Owen chuckled. "Ya wouldn't hit a wounded man, now wouldja?"

Aileen scoffed. "I oughta, ya scallywag!" She laughed, then grew more serious again. "But truly, how do you feel?"

He pulled in a slow, deep breath, stopping when a sharp

pinching below his ribs required he exhale carefully. "I'm not really sure how I'm supposed to feel. It's not nice, I'll tell ya that much. But I'll live." He smirked again. "As long as ye don't kill me."

"Wheesht!" Aileen stood and joined Saoirse in the kitchen. She lowered her voice, but Owen could still make out her next question. "How is he?"

Saoirse looked at him and nodded. "I think he's alright. Though he's a ways to go before he can get back to all his normal things."

Just when Owen's heartbeat had returned to a normal pace, it kicked up again. Not because of Saoirse this time, but at the thought of his duties. How was he supposed to weave in this state?

"Aw, no ya don't, mister," Aileen said, shooting him a warning look and wagging her finger. "Don't be plottin' and plannin' how to get back in that shed."

How did she know that's what he'd been thinking? Then again, how could he not think about it, with such a massive order and deadline looming. "What about Murphy's?"

Aileen flapped her hand. "All in good time. We'll be grand, so."

He pinned her with a look. How could she say that? Their whole lives hung in the balance.

He tried to ignore her glassy eyes and the hitch in her voice when she said, "We have to be."

Owen tried to think about anything but the weight sinking in his gut—but to no avail. He hated seeing his sister upset. Hated that this was their lot. That he couldn't be some highfalutin landed gentleman with nary a care in the world. He needed a distraction. They all did. When Aileen went to double-check that the door was latched, he saw his chance.

"What was all the nonsense before?" he asked, adjusting himself in the bed.

"What're ye on about?" Aileen asked.

Owen reached down and mimicked the knocking pattern on the wooden frame of the bed. Stout barked, mistaking Owen's knocking for a real visitor. Owen shushed the pup and patted his head.

"It's our secret knock," the women answered in unison. Their tones suggested this should be the most natural thing in the world.

He blinked at them slowly. "And ye have a secret knock because . . ."

Aileen scoffed. "Fer safety, ya dolt."

His face must've still registered confusion because Saoirse offered some clarification. "With you unconscious, and it bein' just us two lasses, we needed a way to make sure we knew who we were opening the door to." She shrugged. "If we didn't know who was on the other side, we didn't open the door."

So much for a distraction. What sort of man wasn't even able to protect his property and his women? He shook his head. No, Saoirse wasn't his woman. But she was a woman under his roof, in his charge. *Get ahold of yourself, man.*

The fact remained, they were vulnerable so long as Owen was laid up. Okay, they had been vulnerable before, hence Owen being in the state he was in. But they'd at least had a fighting chance then. His hands balled into fists, and he let out a gasp as pain shot up his arms.

The two women went to pieces, scurrying over to him. "What's the matter?"

"Are ya alright?"

"Are ya in pain?"

"Should I send for the doctor?"

Owen growled, and before he could stop himself, he exploded. "Hang it all, lassies, I'm fine! I just moved wrong. Can I not get a moment's peace?"

Saoirse flinched and stepped back a pace or two. Aileen looked hurt. Blast his short temper.

He sighed. "I'm sorry to shout. But I'm grand. I just need some time." He flung a quick glance around the small cottage. "And space."

The two nodded and shuffled off to the kitchen and busied themselves doing who knows what. Owen took the opportunity to really study his wounds—inasmuch as he could—for the first time. His right arm had gotten the worst of it, it seemed. The entire arm was wrapped in bandages. It throbbed and burned almost constantly. He had no idea how many gashes there were, or how serious, but judging from the pain and the difficulty he had in closing his bandaged hand, he assumed the injuries were fairly extensive.

His left arm also had some wounds, but they seemed less severe. The most aggravating at the moment were the ones on his abdomen and sides. Every breath was a new experience in pain, and if he didn't keep his breathing shallow enough, the gashes screamed out a reminder.

He turned his attention back to his right hand, and his mood darkened right alongside the setting sun outside the window. He tried not to entertain it, but he couldn't shake the intrusive and persistent fear that his weaving days were over. All at once, a laundry list of all that would change in his world if that were the case flashed through his mind.

Selling the farm that had been in his family for generations. Losing his flocks, his horses, Stout. Having to move to Letterkenny or, worse, Dublin. Worse still, leave Ireland altogether. He shuddered. He couldn't let those thoughts overtake him. He had to fight to hold on to what was rightfully theirs. He had to fight to keep what was left of his family together. He had to fight to heal.

And now, he had to fight to stay awake. Fatigue settled on him as suddenly and heavily as a lead blanket. His eyes refused to stay open, and when he forced them, the room began to spin. At length, he decided to escape into the recesses of sleep and hoped to wake to a better future in the morning.

Owen didn't bother lighting the lantern. He wasn't even sure he could. It was enough of a miracle that he managed to finagle the door to the weaving shed open. The soft morning light beginning to stream in through the doorway would have to suffice. He walked a slow circle around the loom. All appeared to be in order and exactly as he'd left it last. Sinking gingerly onto the stool he kept at the front of the loom, he winced as his wounds protested. He just needed a minute. The trek up the hill had nearly done him in.

Doc McGinley said you could start moving around a little, he reminded himself. Though Owen knew full well that when the man said that during his visit the day before, he hadn't intended for Owen to hike up the hill to his work shed. But Owen simply had to get a look at the place for himself. And to inspect the contraption up close. He knew every nook and cranny of this loom, having worked on it since he was a lad, but he wanted to examine it again with fresh eyes, to see if there was any way to rig things so he could still do the weaving. No miraculous solution revealed itself, however. He decided to just see how bad it would really be.

Owen bent down and picked up the shuttle from the basket on the ground. It had already been tied to the warp, and not for the first time, Owen was grateful to his past self for being disciplined enough to prepare the loom at the end of a long day so he might start as soon as he walked in the door the next morning. He was just able to pinch the shuttle between the thumb and forefinger of his right hand, but the heddles needed lifting in order for him to pass it through the strands of warp. When he pressed the far-right pedal to do so, he let out a shout, dropped the shuttle, and doubled over. *Blast*. How could a few superficial wounds on his sides make it hurt to use his legs?

A shadow darkened the doorway. "Ya know, ye're lucky I'm the one to come across ya and not your sister." Saoirse's voice was laced with humor, but he could tell by the stance of her silhouette she was a mite annoyed to find him here. She closed the distance and stood next to him. "What're you doin'?"

Owen bit back the sarcastic response that first sprang to his lips and chose instead to simply look up at her, presuming she already knew the answer to her question. Compassion and a dram of pity shone in her sea glass–colored eyes.

"Just give it a bit more time," she said.

Owen scoffed and shook his head. "There is no time. I've already lost three days—that's over sixty yards of tweed not made that should have been made."

Saoirse winced. "I know." She shrugged. "Well, I don't fully know. But I understand you're in a bind now."

"I wish I was in a bind. This"—he swept a small arc with his left hand—"this is impossible."

"Nothing's impossible." She laid a hand on his shoulder. "When is your order due?"

Owen looked past her and stared out the door. "Twenty rolls of finished tweed—in a complex pattern and color scheme—due by Paddy's Day." He wagged his head. "That's over eight hundred yards. I can weave roughly twenty yards a day. Well, I could have."

Saoirse nodded and slowly walked the length of the loom, her hand running along the frame of it. Then she bent and studied the warp, heddles, and board from which the warp was wound. She reached her hand out to touch the warp but stopped and pulled it back as if the threads were going to bite her.

She pressed her hands to her hips, sucked in a deep breath, and released it in a huff. Her gaze settled on his. "I'll do it."

9

What are you doing?

Saoirse pushed aside the question ringing in her mind. What choice did she have? The only other option was to sit back and watch as Owen and Aileen foundered in the coming weeks. Or leave and pretend they never existed.

Owen's laugh interrupted her thoughts. It wasn't a mirthful or even amusing sound, rather one of doubt. "That's kind of you to offer. But I don't think so."

He started to stand but winced and lowered himself back down. As he tried again, Saoirse rushed to his side and grabbed his elbow, but he waved her off.

"I'm being serious," she said, ignoring the doubt churning in her gut. "You can show me what to do."

At length, Owen was on his feet. He simply shook his head and brushed past her as he shuffled outside.

Saoirse followed him, squinting at the unusually bright February morning, and turned to close and latch the shed door. She watched as he slowly ambled down the hill, enjoying the view, and fighting frustration toward him in equal measure. She knew men to be a stubborn lot, but Owen Mc-

Cready was something else. Would he really let his pride get in the way of keeping his family afloat? Did he think her so incapable that she couldn't learn how to do what he did? It was weaving. How hard could it be?

You hardly know the man. Why does it matter so much to you?

Saoirse had to stop at the bottom of the hill and consider the question. She'd known Aileen and Owen for barely a week—hardly enough time to form a deep connection. Then again, she'd experienced more in the last seven days with them than she'd been through in years with her own family . . . last month's tragedy notwithstanding.

She'd gotten a front-row seat to how Aileen and Owen really and truly depended on each other. One would be lost without the other. And by caring for Owen, tending his wounds, changing his dressings, sponging his face . . . she'd managed to memorize every crease and curve. Without even trying, she could see the salt-and-pepper stubble lining his cheeks, she knew where the whiskers swirled just so near his jawline. She knew the rhythm of his breathing as he slept. She could trace the patterns of veins on the back of his hand, and her fingertips remembered the feel of his even when he wasn't there. She hardly knew the man, and yet she knew more about him than perhaps any other man she'd known, in ways she couldn't have imagined. And while it might sound scandalous to speak out loud, it was the purest form of compassion because it was born out of the complete dependence of one upon the other, the act of serving another human with absolutely zero expectations of anything in return.

Of course, Saoirse certainly couldn't say she'd fallen in love with Owen McCready as she worked alongside his sister to care for him in his time of need. But she could no longer deny the fact that she'd fallen completely in love with the idea of him, as well as the idea of bringing him back to health so he could fulfill whatever it was the Good Lord had prepared for him to do. And she was convinced that those plans did not include the McCreadys being relegated to the poorhouse because of the injustice of a sheep heist gone awry.

She rounded the corner just as Aileen met Owen in the doorway of the house.

"And just where have you been, mister?" Aileen's balled-up fists were pressed firmly to her hips.

Owen glanced behind him and met Saoirse's gaze for a split second. "Don't worry, Mammy," he said to Aileen. "Just went for a wee stroll." He shuffled inside.

Aileen pursed her lips. "Mm-hmm." She looked to Saoirse, who simply shrugged. "Well, I'd say ye've had enough excitement for one morning. Sit yerself down by the fire and I'll make ya a cuppa before I see to the sheep."

At the mention of the flock, Stout picked his head up, ears perked. "Not yet, boyo," Owen said. He sat down with a grunt, then rested his head against the back of the chair and shut his eyes.

"Aileen," he said, eyes still closed. "Did you put her up to this?"

Aileen rounded the chair, a fresh cup of steaming tea in her hand. "Did I put who up to what?"

Owen cracked one eye open.

"She had nothing to do with it," Saoirse interjected.

Aileen set the cup and saucer on the small table by the fireplace with a rattle. "Would one o' ye kindly fill me in on what ye're on about?"

"Saoirse here"—Owen lifted his head, fully awake now— "has offered to do the *fíodóireacht* for me."

Saoirse smiled and nodded. Aileen would see it her way, surely.

Aileen's eyes rounded as she looked at Saoirse. "Dáiríre?"

"Really," Owen repeated as he laid his head back again.

Aileen's puffed breath caused her lips to flap together. "'Tis a noble idea, to be sure." She sighed and wagged her head. "But I don't think ya know what ye're sayin'."

Saoirse's brows pulled together. "Well, I figured Owen could talk me through it and show me what to do as best he can. I just want to help."

Aileen crossed the room and rubbed her hand down Saoirse's arm. "I know, dearie, and I appreciate it." She lifted a shoulder and let it fall. "But weavin's far more complex than most folk realize."

"Can you do it?" Saoirse asked Aileen, in genuine curiosity. She hadn't even considered the notion that perhaps both McCreadys were skilled in the craft.

"Psh!" Aileen laughed. "No way. I do the cardin', spinnin', and help with the dyin'. The fíodóireacht is all Owen."

Saoirse sat at the kitchen table. "You never learned?"

The corners of Aileen's mouth tugged downward, and she shook her head. "Most weavers are men. I don't really know why. Maybe because the womenfolk typically tend to the home and whatnot. But I never did learn." She shrugged.

Saoirse wondered how they hadn't ensured they both were familiar with all aspects of the process—for times just like this. But if she thought about it, her family had been the same. No, they didn't run a trade craft from their home, but they each had their own roles and responsibilities.

"Well, all the more reason to teach me." She sighed and lifted her hands, palms to the ceiling. "At least let me try."

Aileen and Owen turned to each other, a whole conversation taking place with just a look.

Saoirse leaned back in her chair. "If we don't try it, you'll lose the contract for certain."

"She has a point, Owen," Aileen said.

He groaned. "Ye lassies are gonna be the death o' me."

"Seems ye've got that part down pat on yer own, brother." Aileen laughed.

Another sigh from the man of the house. "Be that as it may, I just don't see how it'll work."

Aileen rolled her eyes and crossed back over to Saoirse, then whispered in her ear, "Give me some time to work on him."

––––––––––––––––

That afternoon, the three worked together in the barn feeding the stock, mucking the stables, and the like. Owen begrudgingly sat at the rough wooden counter polishing saddles and cleaning tools—tasks he often put off for more active chores. But Aileen had forced him to either sit here and work on these tedious tasks or sit in the house while the women worked in the barn. He couldn't stand another second in that bungalow, so he opted for the lesser of the two evils. He would never give Aileen the satisfaction, but these chores were long overdue, and Owen secretly appreciated the forced time to slow down and focus on things he often swept aside.

"How did you get into weaving to begin with?" Saoirse

asked, huffing a strand of hair from her face as she tossed a shovelful of soiled straw into the wheelbarrow.

Owen rested his elbow on the counter. "Well." He paused to think back to what his parents had told him. "My great-great-grandparents on my father's side started this wee farm. Sometime after my great-grandparents took over, they took in a loom through a government scheme and began weaving."

Saoirse nodded.

Aileen stopped sweeping and rested her forearms on the top of the broom handle. "The fíodóireacht is what kept our parents afloat during the famine."

Owen bobbed his head. "And not long after that came the Glenveagh evictions in '61. Granted, we aren't on Glenveagh land, but we're just a stone's throw away. Being fairly profitable crofters didn't hurt in keeping our land then, either."

"Mammy passed from a bad flu shortly after the evictions," Aileen added. "Then Da went in a horrible accident in '89, so it's been just the two of us ever since." Aileen's eyes glistened. "Without the weavin', we'd have been sunk."

Saoirse froze, a strange expression on her face. She seemed to get lost in thought for a long movement, then she blinked and said, "Wait, ye've been on yer own for twenty-three years?" Saoirse's voice cracked. "Ya had to be just kids."

Owen dropped his gaze to the floor. "I was fifteen." He looked at his sister.

She met his gaze, sadness shining in her eyes. "Thirteen."

Saoirse pressed her hand to her heart. "So young. And ye've no other siblings?"

Owen's lips tugged into a thin line. "That's a long story."

"They'd all passed on already." Aileen sighed.

"I'm so sorry." Saoirse's sad gaze bore into Owen's.

He hated talking about these things. It made him feel weak. Vulnerable. "Ah, well"—he attempted to add a tone of nonchalance to his voice—"we've not had it any worse than anyone else in Donegal. In fact, we've fared much better than many." His gaze drifted in the direction of the weaving shed. "Thanks to the loom."

A heavy silence hung in the air, all three lost in thought for a moment. Aileen's sigh broke the quiet. "What about ye, Saoirse?"

"Hmm?" Saoirse blinked and turned toward Aileen.

"What of your family? What did they do before . . . I'm sorry, that's terribly insensitive of me."

A shadow flitted across Saoirse's face, and something Owen couldn't read flashed in her eyes. "No, it's fine. We all worked at Waterstown House in some form or fashion." She gave them a watery smile, then leaned the shovel against the wall and hoisted the handles of the wheelbarrow. "I'll go dump this."

Owen watched her hurry from the barn. As she turned the corner outside, he caught a whisper of her shuddered breath before she disappeared from sight.

———————

Once she could no longer feel Owen's gaze boring into her back, Saoirse abandoned the pushcart and fled to the field she'd hidden in on her first morning in Dunlewey. Her breath came in jagged gasps as her heart threatened to pound out of her chest. Stomach churning, she collapsed behind the low rock wall and let the sobs come freely as the faces of her mother, father, sister, and brothers drifted across her mind's eye.

Her keening echoed in the valley, but she didn't care. How long would their memory send her careening down a spiral of panic and anxiety? Nae, it wasn't their memory. It was what she'd done. And now the guilt compounded with the fear of what Owen and Aileen would do if they knew tugged her below the surface of grief and shame, suffocating her and setting her head spinning. They could never know.

And yet . . .

A part of her wanted them to know. Wanted him to know—to know and tell her it would all be okay. Saoirse desperately wanted to be free from this millstone tied around her neck, but the risk was far too great. What good would it do to confess her horrible past? It wouldn't undo what she'd done. All revealing her secrets would do is tarnish any hint of good impression the McCreadys had of her and saddle them with the weight of who they'd welcomed into their home. They hadn't even revisited the fact that she was still living in their barn and eating their food days after she was supposed to have left. She'd never even had a chance to try and find a new post. Nor did she want to. She wanted to stay here, with Aileen. With Owen. To work alongside them and do everything within her power to ensure they stayed on their farm as long as they wished. To see it handed down to the next generation.

But to do that, she had to bury her secret. To lock it up and hide it away, never to see the light of day again. The notion almost killed her.

10

The next morning, word arrived from Doctor McGinley summoning Owen to the village for a checkup.

"Can the man not make the journey to you?" Annoyance laced Aileen's voice, and Saoirse shared it. Owen was just getting used to being up and around, and now the doctor expected him to make a bumpy wagon journey who knew how far away? It seemed a ridiculous expectation.

Owen shrugged and reached over to scratch Stout between the ears. The dog responded with a single tail thwap on the floor and a lolling tongue out the side of his mouth. "I presume he's got a good reason. And it's just to Glentornan."

Aileen scoffed. "Oh, just Glentornan." She rolled her eyes and turned to Saoirse. "It's a wee village nestled in the heart of Poisoned Glen, about twenty minutes away by cart down a windy road more deeply rutted than a nun's worry lines."

Saoirse couldn't help the chuckle that bubbled up at Aileen's colorful commentary.

Owen stood—more easily than he'd seemed to so far—and stretched. Saoirse tried not to notice how his linen shirtsleeves pulled taut against his shoulders as he did so. "It could be good," he said. "We missed Sunday services. We could stop in at Friday services afterward."

"Well, now, that's true," Aileen replied. "We need to stay on the Big Fella's good side."

Saoirse nodded, but inside her heart raced, and sweat prickled the back of her neck. She'd not been to a church service since her family had died. She wasn't sure she and God were on speaking terms—and she wasn't entirely sure whose fault that was. There had been many a day since the fire that she had no interest in darkening God's proverbial door. Then others when she desperately needed His tender touch of grace. But she was certain He wanted nothing to do with a transgressor like her.

"Shall we all go, then?" Owen asked, looking between the ladies. "I can set Stout on sentry duty with the flock." At his name, the dog sprung to attention and trotted to the door, his tail eagerly expressing his opinion of that idea.

Saoirse swallowed the thickness in her throat. "That's grand, so." She decided she'd go and just sit quietly. If God wanted to show up, He could, but she'd not beg.

"I'll bring the wagon around," Aileen said and snapped her fingers. Stout immediately bolted through the door and to the northeast field.

Some time later, the three sat shoulder to shoulder across the wagon's bench. Owen had scoffed at Aileen's idea that he might be more comfortable riding in the back. He wasn't going to lounge back there like some invalid, and he wasn't going to relegate either of the ladies to that fate either. So they all crammed on the bench. Now, with part of his hip hanging off the outer edge, he wondered if his sister might've been right. The wounds on his side had improved greatly over the last week, but bracing his core still hurt pretty strongly. He could never tell Aileen that though. He'd never hear the end of it if he did.

Aileen drove the rig, Saoirse sat in the middle, and then Owen on the far end. As they bumped and rumbled along the road, he tried not to notice when his knee would brush against Saoirse's. At one point, his left hand was resting on his leg. When Aileen took a corner a little too quickly, Saoirse gripped his fingers and instantly his hand was on fire. Not so much from pain, as that wound was also beginning to heal, but from her touch.

"Sorry," she said, her cheeks pink.

When he knew she was steady, he slid his hand from her grip. "Ye're grand," he said around a tight-lipped smile. It made no sense for him to want to snatch up her hand again, but he did. He rubbed his palm against his trouser leg a few times and pushed the thought from his mind.

Slowly but surely, Fadó wound along the southern edge of Dunlewey Lough, which eventually turned into Upper Lough Nacung, where they turned right and entered the tiny village of Glentornan. About a dozen or so cozy stone buildings lined either side of the dirt road that ran through the center. Most of the buildings were homes, but one served many purposes, including where Doctor McGinley would take patients from time to time. Aileen slowed the wagon to a halt, and the three lumbered down. Even though it caused him great pain, Owen reached up with his left hand for Saoirse and Aileen to hold onto in turn as they alighted.

Saoirse excused herself to explore near the lake's edge while Aileen said she was going to check in with a friend. Owen made for the doctor's makeshift office. He squinted at the dim interior as he entered.

"Ah, Owen, good to see ya." The doctor rounded the small rectangular table that served as his desk. "Thanks for coming."

Owen nodded. "Of course."

Doctor McGinley approached, his arm extended as though he meant to shake Owen's hand. Owen lifted his still-bandaged right forearm and waved it. "Och!" The man smacked his own forehead softly. "Silly me, I don't guess we'll be shakin' hands anytime soon."

Owen didn't find the situation as humorous as the doctor did, so he just responded with a nod. He knew McGinley didn't truly think Owen's predicament was funny, but he still hated that he had little to no use of his dominant appendage.

"Have a seat." Doctor McGinley gestured to another table about the size of a small bed. "Let's see how we're progressing."

He started by having Owen remove his jumper and linen shirt in order to examine the wounds on his torso. It didn't take long for McGinley to remove the bandages from around Owen's ribs and set straight to poking and prodding. The man's hands were like ice, and Owen yelped and sucked in a gasping breath.

"Perhaps ye should treat yerself to a cuppa after this," he said when he had returned to his senses.

The doctor chuckled. "Yeah, sorry 'bout that. I've never been able to warm up these blasted hands." He moved around to check Owen's back. "But ya know what they say, 'cold hands, warm heart.'"

"Mm," Owen replied. "Nice try, Doc." The pair shared a laugh, and the physician came back around to the front of the table.

"These all look great," he said, gesturing to the wounds on Owen's sides and back. "Are they still sore?"

"A bit," Owen said, certain that his definition of "a bit" and the doctor's varied greatly.

"Well, they're comin' along nicely. And it's to be expected that they be a mite tender for a while longer." He began unwinding the bandages from Owen's left hand. "And while ya won't be tossing any cabers anytime soon, ya should be able to move pretty freely now without restrictions there."

Owen nodded, gladdened by the news, even if they'd not yet looked at the worst of it.

The last of the gauze was pulled away, and Owen's stomach churned at the sight of his jagged, stitched flesh. The sutures were well done, as far as he could tell, anyway. He'd helped plenty of ewes deliver lambs, and he'd stitched up many a gashed sheep or horse rump, so he was no stranger to a bit of gore. But something about seeing his own flesh in such a state was unsettling.

Doctor McGinley turned Owen's arm this way and that, inspecting his handiwork. After a few long minutes, he straightened. "All in all, I'm very pleased. There's no sign of infection, and it looks like ye've done a good job keeping the dressings dry. The wounds look to be healing right on track."

Owen released a sigh of relief. "Good to hear." He shifted on the chilled tabletop. "How much longer do ya think I have till I'm right as rain?"

McGinley's teeth made a hissing noise as the doctor sucked in a slow breath. "Hard to say. Another few days, maybe, for this arm." He stepped off to the side and rummaged through his bag. "The cuts on your left are much more superficial than on your right. So, you're lookin' at another week at least, plus longer after the stitches come out to continue healing."

Suddenly the door opened, and Saoirse bounded inside. "Sorry, Aileen, I got a litt—" She stopped short, mouth agape, then stared at Owen's bare chest for a long moment before blinking and slapping her hand over her eyes. "Good gracious me, I'm terribly sorry!" She turned around and bumped into the doorjamb. "Oof."

Owen couldn't help the laugh that rumbled deep in his chest.

"I, uh . . . I thought this was the house that Aileen had said she'd be in, but clearly I was mistaken. I'm so sorry. I'll just go." She finally dropped her hand from her eyes, stepped outside, and reached back to grab the door handle. She tugged the door closed, but not before Owen caught her steal another glimpse of him.

Owen turned his attention back to the doctor, who stood with a roll of fresh bandage in his hand, and the most amused look on his face. "Well . . . shall we continue?"

The frigid blast of wind that assaulted Saoirse's face as she left the doctor's office did nothing to soothe the burning in her cheeks. She lifted her eyes to the heavens and took a steadying breath. When she lowered her gaze, it landed on Aileen, who stood in the doorway directly across the street.

"Get a wee bit lost, eh?" A playful light danced in Aileen's eyes.

Saoirse fought the urge to look at the door behind her. "I may have gotten a bit turned around."

Aileen stepped aside and gestured Saoirse across the road, her shoulders bouncing in amusement. "C'mon, *a chara*."

Though they were the only two outside, Saoirse looked both ways before finally shuffling across and joining Aileen at her friend's house.

Saoirse entered the modest home and was greeted by an older woman with a lovely, genuine smile. "Bridie, this is Saoirse, the girl I was tellin' you about." Aileen gestured from Saoirse to her friend and back. "Saoirse Fagan, Bridie Sheridan."

Bridie skirted the hearth and approached Saoirse, hand outstretched. The silver streaks in her hair glistened in the muted afternoon light. "*Céad míle fáilte!*"

Saoirse shook the woman's hand. "*Go raibh míle maith agat.*"

Bridie led them into the sitting room and invited them to rest by the fire. The small room was moderately furnished, but the fire in the hearth filled the space with warmth. The three passed the time sipping tea, Aileen and Bridie catching up with one another, and asking all the compulsory introduction questions for Saoirse.

After a while, a church bell in the distance tolled five o'clock. Aileen stood. "We're heading to Friday services. Are ye and John goin'?"

Bridie laughed, the wrinkles around her eyes deepening, softening her features even further. Saoirse liked her immensely already. "Sure, what else would we do?" Bridie answered.

Aileen joined in the laughter, and Saoirse smiled.

"Well, we'll see yas there, then," Aileen said, then crossed the room and looped her arm through Saoirse's elbow. "We need to fetch Owen from McGinley's and then drive the wagon around."

"Of course, of course," Bridie said as she walked them closer to the door. It was another few minutes before they actually left, however, due to the multiple rounds of good-byes and offers of more tea and subsequent declines.

At last, they reached the end of the ritual that takes place in every Irish home upon the leaving of guests, and Aileen and Saoirse stepped out into the frigid evening.

They turned left out of Bridie's house and started up the street heading east. Heat flashed in Saoirse's cheeks when she glanced across to the doctor's office. The windows were dark, so clearly Owen was no longer there, but the image of him sitting on the table in his trousers with no jumper or shirt on was burned into her brain.

Owen was nowhere to be seen, but Aileen seemed to know where she was heading. "So," Aileen said, tugging gently on Saoirse's arm. "What d'ya think of our Glentornan? Quite the booming metropolis, eh?"

Saoirse laughed. Clearly quite a few people lived here. And she noticed for the first time that one of the buildings boasted a greengrocer sign. Across from that was a pub with orange light glowing in the windows. But otherwise, it was barely a village. "It's lovely," Saoirse replied. "Where is the closest city? What if you need a hospital?"

Aileen shrugged. "Well, Ballymann is about an hour or so that way." She pointed west. "It's a mite larger than Glentornan. They have three pubs." She puffed up her chest and nudged Saoirse with her elbow.

"And that way past Glenveagh another hour or so"—Aileen pointed toward the mountains—"is Letterkenny. It's a proper town with a cathedral, hospital, clothing shops, and the like."

As they passed the pub, Aileen waved toward the window, slowed her steps, and eventually stopped.

The door swung open, and out came Owen, his eyes dark and his expression brooding. He barely acknowledged the ladies before turning and hastening toward the wagon.

Saoirse leaned closer to Aileen. "Is he drunk?"

Aileen kept her eyes pinned on Owen's back, pressing her lips together. "Uh-uh. He doesn't drink." She studied her brother in the waning light before tugging Saoirse along. As they scurried behind him, she muttered, "Something's not right."

Once back in the wagon, the journey to the church took about ten minutes, but it felt like an hour as they rode along in silence. Saoirse kept her arms wrapped tightly around her middle, trying with all that was in her not to bump into Owen. Not only because she could not bear it after her embarrassing blunder back at the doctor's office but also because his mood had soured so much in the time she'd been chatting with Aileen and Bridie. She almost worried he'd toss her overboard at the slightest misstep—if it was even possible for one to misstep while riding in a wagon.

At last, they arrived at the church. One other cart sat outside, and a handful of parishioners were winding their way to the entrance of the stone building. The white walls gleamed, even in the muted twilight, and two large wood doors greeted them. The tower loomed tall on the opposite end of the church, its four spires practically spiking the clouds. "It's gorgeous," Saoirse said with a sigh.

"It's made of white marble and blue quartzite that was mined in the area," Aileen told her. "Such a sad story."

"Oh?" Saoirse turned her gaze on Aileen.

"Aye. Lady Jane Russell—the landlord of this parish until the late 1800s—wasn't a particularly nice lady. She and her husband doubled and tripled rent for the tenants of their land. But her husband died just three years after moving here, and she had this church built in his memory about sixty years ago."

Aileen pointed to a field just southwest of the church building. "And there, you can just see a large headstone. That is a communal grave for one of Lady Jane's daughters, her son-in-law, and four of their ten children—most of whom died before six months of age."

"How tragic," Saoirse said, her hand pressed to her throat.

"What's tragic is the hundreds, if not thousands, of people who died because of that woman," Owen said. "The only good thing she did was give us this church, then leave," he grumbled as he slipped inside.

Saoirse followed Aileen in and joined Owen on a pew about halfway up the aisle. Half a dozen others sat scattered in various places around the room. If this was anything like Saoirse's church back home, each one of them sat in those exact places every single time they attended service for no other reason than that's where their family had sat the first time they came.

The rector ascended to the pulpit, and the service began. He opened with prayer, then read two passages.

The first was from the book of Joshua, recounting the battle of Jericho. "My friends," the priest began, "God commanded the Israelite army to be strong and courageous and to march around the city for seven days." He paused and scanned the small crowd. "A full week of doing the same exact thing, with no apparent results. And yet, they marched. Then, on the seventh day, they marched silently around the city seven times."

Next to her, Owen shifted and grunted softly. Saoirse absently wondered how on earth he managed to sit on the pew so long. He must have been so uncomfortable.

"But then!" The priest's raised voice jolted Saoirse back to his message. "On the seventh lap, they shouted loudly and broke jars concealing torches. When they did, the walls protecting the city came crashing down, allowing the army to defeat their enemy and take over the city." He let his words reverberate around the vaulted ceilings, his arms stretched wide, matching his grin. Saoirse couldn't help the smile tickling her own lips in response, though in truth she wasn't entirely sure why.

At length, he lowered his arms, and his gaze went back to the large book in front of him. When he spoke again, his voice carried the hush of awe. "How incredible is that? Days upon days of nothing. Now, I wasn't there—though I know some o' yas think I'm old enough to have been." Laughter rippled through the congregation. "But I don't have to have been there to understand what many of them were likely feeling. I wonder how many of them began to doubt, began to question why God would have them do such a silly thing.

And just when I imagine their faith may have begun to falter, God reminded them of His power and might. How many of you—of us—have felt the same way? Wondering if all the motions we go through are worth it, especially when God seems silent."

Saoirse blinked against the sudden burning behind her eyes. Two rows in front of her, a young girl with ebony ringlets turned around and smiled at her. Saoirse returned the grin and offered a small wave. The girl waved back, but then her mother gently eased her back to face forward.

"And it wasn't just this once," the rector continued. "Listen to what the Scriptures say in the book of Judges." He read a long excerpt about God delivering the Midianite army into the hands of the Israelites by choosing Gideon, the most unassuming man, to lead the army. God dwindled the army's size down from ten thousand to just three hundred. He had them surround the enemy camp, shout, and break jars hiding torches. Not a single soldier carried a sword or any weapon at all, but the enemy army was defeated because they got so confused that they turned on themselves, thinking they were fighting the Israelites.

"Don't miss this, *a chairde*. Sometimes God's plans for our victories are so vastly different from our own that they don't make any sense. They may seem downright ridiculous, but it's always best to follow His lead and accept His provision and help as He provides it."

The priest then led them in a prayer, and Saoirse willed the thrumming in her chest to slow. The way the priest spoke stirred something inside her, but she wasn't sure what or why. Then, just as the closing hymn began, Owen shot to his feet and stormed outside. Both Saoirse and Aileen jumped at the sudden movement, then turned and watched him leave. When the door closed behind him with an echoing thud, Saoirse looked to Aileen, who appeared just as confused as Saoirse felt. Aileen shrugged and knelt as the final prayer began. Saoirse followed suit, dutifully bowing her head and closing her eyes. But her thoughts were nowhere else but with Owen.

11

Owen paced back and forth alongside the wagon, his chest burning. Not from his wounds this time but from anger. Frustration. He ripped his flatcap from his head and tossed it into the wagon bed. He raked the fingers of his left hand through his hair and let his head fall back as his gaze searched the sky.

The stars were veiled, and the dark expanse that stretched above him seemed a giant void. The doctor had said it was too early to tell for certain, but that Owen would likely lose the use of his right hand. The gashes had gone far deeper than he'd realized and while they'd managed to keep infection at bay, McGinley had had to stitch through several layers of tissue, working with jagged edges that had been ripped by Haggerty's less than razor-sharp blade, which tore his flesh rather than cut it. Owen's greatest fears were being confirmed. He was going to lose everything that he'd ever held dear. It wasn't enough that God had taken his parents and siblings from him, save Aileen, but He had to allow this to happen too. For Owen to lose the ability to earn any sort of reasonable or respectable living. He felt utterly alone. Abandoned.

Deep in his spirit, a voice echoed. *Be strong and coura-geous.*

Owen dropped his gaze from the sky and looked around. Strong? Courageous? What did that mean?

Before he had a chance to suss out the meaning, the church doors opened and the parishioners trickled into the night.

By the time Saoirse and Aileen reached him, Owen was at the wagon step, his one good hand ready to help them board.

The first several minutes of the journey home passed in relative silence, save for the crunching of the graveled path beneath the wooden wheels. Owen stared into the darkness ahead of them, mesmerized by the swaying light of the lantern he'd lit and hung on the front hook.

"That was an interesting message, don't you think?" Aileen's question ripped him from his stupor.

"*Go deimhin*," Saoirse replied. "I'd heard those stories many times over the years, but I'd never thought of them that way."

Aileen shifted the reins in her hand. "Exactly, I was thinking the same thing." She was quiet for a moment. "But I must admit, God's plans do often seem a bit . . . *craiceáilte*."

Owen snorted. They seemed crazy, alright. Look at the mess he was in at the moment. If this was in any way part of God's plan, it was just about the craziest thing he could imagine. Crazier still was the idea that his and Aileen's quickest way back to stable ground was to teach Saoirse how to weave. He shook his head. It took years to reach master weaver status, and the colors and patterns Murphy's wanted were extremely complex. Well, that wasn't entirely true. The barleycorn pattern Owen had perfected—and that Murphy's loved so much—didn't so much involve a complex color pattern, but rather a combining of similar colors, which blended together from afar, allowing the unique texture to shine through. Saoirse might be able to figure out a plain weave, but it would still take months, if not years, for her to become proficient enough at it to meet the high standard Murphy's required. But the barleycorn? Not a chance.

"Do ya not agree, Owen?"

Confound his sister's incessant questions. "I don't know." *Be strong and courageous.* Once again the phrase drifted, unbidden, through his mind.

Next to him, he could feel Saoirse studying his profile.

He wasn't prepared to air all his thoughts on the matter at this particular time. And he certainly wasn't prepared to foray into the potential meaning of this whole strong and courageous nonsense with his companions, so he chose only to offer, "God does move in a mysterious way."

Back in the solitude of the barn that was swiftly becoming Saoirse's new home, she stood at the small square window and stared out at the dark world. Though the inky black of night had fallen, she could still picture the rise and crest of every hill, the patchwork hem of every stone wall. She could imagine the McCreadys' sheep meandering lazily through the fields or bedding down in a cove somewhere. The scene in her mind—and, in truth, the daylight—was as idyllic as it could be. To an outsider, this might appear to be the most perfect, charming life. And yet, the flock lived in the ever-present danger of being stolen or killed for their meat and wool. Owen and Aileen had to scrape by day to day, eking out a meager living through strenuous and intensely physical work. And still they were better off than most in the county.

The McCreadys had enough beds, multiple pieces of furniture, and at least a couple articles of clothing each. So many in the area had quite literally nothing other than the roof over their heads. Children went naked, or nearly so, their wee toes freezing year-round. Many families had nary even a stool to sit on, and their hearths merely smoked instead of allowing the soft heat to burn and permeate their home with its comfort since they didn't have a way to properly dry the peat.

Just like Owen's sheep, Saoirse's thoughts meandered over hill and dale, ruminating on such thoughts until, similar to the creatures of habit they were, they wandered home to their own turf and bedded down in the memories of her family. Squeezing her eyes against the tears that were the close bedfellows of such thoughts, she pulled the plaid tighter around her shoulders. If the Lord truly was guiding each on his or her own path, the rector had been right—very little of what He did made sense. And, if she was honest with herself and with Him, most of His plans seemed downright silly. Dare she be brutally truthful and say stupid? It was almost impossible to see what God could be orchestrating with all that had transpired in the last six weeks, including bringing her here to the McCready farm only to send them into a full-on crisis.

The fleeting thought that He brought her here to be of help to them swept into her mind, but she swatted it away. Recent events had made it clear she did not bring aid or help in any way, only tragedy and despair. If she really wanted to help Owen and Aileen, she'd sneak away this very moment, never to return, and save them from her special brand of ill fate. And yet, she found herself shimmying deeper into the hay.

Once settled in, she rolled onto her side and let her eyes drift closed. A moment later, they sprang open again. She forced them shut only for them to fling wide open again. Though fatigue had long before settled on her shoulders, her mind refused to let her rest, so she lay on her side and watched the flames through the door in the stove. Each one flickered and twisted, reminding her of the Celts of old sending their petitions to the heavens through dance. And yet she had no such petitions to make, as she was certain God had no desire to listen to her pleas.

If she was going to stay with the McCreadys, she had to find a way to help support them beyond just weeding the garden and mucking out the stables. She refused to stay simply out of the selfish desire for their company only to watch them shrivel away into nothingness.

She thought back to how gracious Aileen had been since the night they met, and her heart warmed with gratitude. And then there was Owen. Though gruff and intimidating at first, she'd seen enough to know he was a sheep in grump's clothing. Underneath his hardened exterior hid a tender heart.

And what an exterior. A vision of his eyes popped into the forefront of her mind, and she sighed. Her fingers wiggled as they recalled the feel of his grip when he helped her into and out of the wagon. And then there was the doct—*No, don't think of that.*

She shook her head and flopped onto her other side, her face instantly cooling as she turned away from the heat of the stove. She pushed her attraction for Owen aside and tried to figure out what could have possibly put him in such a sour mood before the church service. Perhaps ill news from Doctor McGinley? Her heart lurched. May it not be so. And yet, it made perfect sense. He'd been in a pleasant enough mood before his visit, and the storm clouds had settled over his countenance after. Was his life in danger? He seemed too hearty of health for that. Certainly if he was on the verge of succumbing to his wounds, he'd be in poorer form. Unable to carry on as he had been.

Then it struck her—weaving. What if he was not able to weave again? Ever? No, that settled it once again in her heart and mind. She had to find a way to convince him to teach her how to use the loom.

At the breakfast table the next morning, the three sat around small bowls of steaming porridge and cups of tea. Stout had managed to find a place where he could lay on both Saoirse's and Owen's feet, with his head on Owen's and his rump on hers. Saoirse wiggled her toes and Stout responded with a single wag of his tail.

Aileen was talking about what to put down in the garden next month, but Saoirse had no idea what she was saying. Her pulse quickened as she rehearsed in her mind what she was going to say to Owen. How she was going to broach the topic of weaving again.

She opened her mouth to speak, but Aileen barreled on ahead, obviously excited about her vegetable plans. "Bridie told me about a new way of putting down carrots so that they grow better. I can't wait to try it."

Saoirse took a long draw of her tea. The interruption had somehow stolen what modicum of confidence she'd built up, and now she was back to the drawing board. She glanced over at Owen. His bowl empty and his teacup halfway so, the man stared off, clearly not listening to his sister. Saoirse's gaze flitted to Aileen, who appeared unfazed by the fact that she was the only one benefitting from her conversation—nae, oration.

Saoirse went back to rehearsing her own monologue. *So, about that weaving . . .*

Have ya given any more thought to my weaving idea?

Oi, stubborn auld man, let me weave for you.

She shook her head slightly and drained the last of her tea from the cup. Everything she thought of only made her sound daft. Or arrogant.

"Hello? Anybody home?" Aileen's voice seeped into Saoirse's consciousness. "Saoirse!"

Saoirse jumped and gave her full attention to the woman sitting across from her. "I'm sorry, I was . . . what did you say?"

A peculiar expression crossed Aileen's face, a mix of amusement and perhaps concern. "I asked if you'd meet me in the garden after you feed the horses to help me plot out the sowing for next month?"

"Ah, yes, of cour—"

"She can't." Owen's voice still held the gravelly tone of sleep. He stacked his teacup in his bowl and stood. "She's workin' with me. Both o' yas are."

Saoirse and Aileen exchanged a questioning look, then turned to Owen.

"In the shed." Apparently unwilling to expound on his

thoughts, Owen punctuated the conversation by carrying his dishes to the basin and setting them down with a thud. Then he turned and lumbered outside. Stout attempted to scamper after him, but the door closed before he could slip out.

All three—Saoirse, Aileen, and Stout—stared at the door as if they expected Owen to come back in and offer more clarification. At length, Stout huffed out a heavy breath and shuffled over to curl up at Saoirse's feet.

"Did he mean the garden shed?" Saoirse asked.

Aileen rose and gathered their dishes. "Don't think so." She shook her head. "Can't remember the last time I saw him go in there. Besides, I've no clue what there would be in there for ye to do."

Saoirse stood and poured fresh water from the kettle into the basin and began the washing up. "Could he have meant the barn?"

Aileen was silent for a long moment. "I think he meant the weaving shed."

12

Saoirse's cheeks were damp from trekking through the mist that hung in the air. There wasn't a lick of wind, which was odd for this time of year. Though technically spring, February was typically marked by pounding rain and the continued gale-force winds of winter. But not today. It was as if nature herself was making a peace offering for the turmoil of recent weeks. Either that or it was the calm before the storm. Saoirse pressed her eyes closed and pulled her shawl tight. *May it not be so.*

She squinted as she entered the dim interior of the weaving shed. Though Owen had lit a lantern, the muted morning light offered little to no help, making the inside of the shed seem almost black. After a moment, her eyes adjusted and Saoirse could finally see that Owen was leaning against the loom, his ankles crossed and his right arm laid over his left at his middle. She also realized she'd been staring at him this whole time while she waited for dark to become light.

Neither one spoke for a long moment, as his eyes bore into hers, and she wondered if he could hear her heart beating against her chest from where he stood. She couldn't tell if the intensity of his gaze was merely due to the intensity of the blue in his eyes or if his expression was as emotionally charged as it appeared to be.

"If this is going to work, you must do exactly as I say," he said at length, his voice low. Measured.

She swallowed hard and nodded.

"Alright. Now . . ." He seemed about to give his first piece of instructions when he stopped short. "Where's Aileen?"

Saoirse turned and peered out the still open door. "I'd say she'll be here any moment."

Owen's forehead creased and he said only, "Mm." He mumbled something Saoirse couldn't quite make out, though it sounded vaguely like Aileen likely finding an excuse not to come. Then, after a moment, he stooped and picked up a ball of thread. "First things first." He motioned with his head for her to join him, and she obeyed.

"The weaver's knot," he began. "The entire foundation of a good tweed rests upon a solid weaver's knot. You hafta be able to tie and release it with one hand."

Saoirse's eyes widened. "You can tie a knot with one hand?"

"Aye," he said. He pointed to the set of threads hanging up and down, perpendicular to the flat threads stretching the length of the loom. "Those are the heddles. They don't actually go into the weave. Instead, the warp"—he gestured to the flat threads—"runs through small loops in the heddles. And they are secured with weaver's knots."

Saoirse bent to get a better look. "There must be hundreds of these threads."

"Thousands," he replied. "This is a double-width loom."

She puffed a breath through her lips. "That's a lot of knots."

He nodded matter-of-factly. "Then," he continued, moving around to the front of the loom, "you attach the weft—that's the threads you actually weave back and forth with—to the first thread of the warp with the same type of knot so the yarn doesn't go all the way through when you pass the shuttle from side to side."

Saoirse's head spun. She'd tied many a knot in her day but never knew there were multiple kinds. And she'd never attempted to tie one with one hand. She didn't see how it was possible. "So . . . how do ya do a weaver's knot?"

Owen unraveled a bit of lavender thread from the shuttle and tugged one strand of warp to the side to create space between it and the thread next to it. His movements were a little stunted and clumsy, as he was working with his left hand. But he still managed to drape the lavender piece over the gray warp, and then in some strange feat of witchcraft, flipped his finger around, pulled on a loop, and suddenly there was a knot there. "See? Easy."

Saoirse laughed. "Oh, yes, very simple."

The faintest hint of a smile played on his lips. "Here, watch me again. Ya just put this purple over the gray, twist your finger around it, grab the gray with your thumb and forefinger"—his torso contorted as he tried to convince his nondominant hand to function with dexterity—"and pull."

He turned to her. "Now, you try." He pulled a spool of yarn from a shelf and unwound some, allowing it to hang down. Then he cut a shorter piece and held it out it toward Saoirse. "Best to practice on something that's not the loom."

Equal measures of confusion and amusement swirled in

Saoirse's mind, and she simply blinked back at him. Owen responded by waggling the short length of yarn in the air. At length, sighing, Saoirse took the piece from him and stepped toward the longer strand still hanging from the shelf. She glanced at him from the side of her eye. He'd put his hands behind his back and was waiting.

She took hold of the long thread in her left hand and used her right to drape the shorter piece over it. She stared at them for a long moment, trying to recall what Owen had done. Then, after a deep breath, she let her fingers fly. When she gave a final tug, the spool of thread fell from the shelf, and bonked her in the forehead before crashing to the floor with a muted thud. She held up her hand only to discover she hadn't been successful in tying the weaver's knot at all. Not even close. Instead, she'd managed to tangle both strands of yarn around her right index finger, the tip of which was turning red and was quickly on its way to a deep purple color.

"Well, that's one way to do it," Owen said. "The wrong way, but it's somethin'." A low chuckle began in his chest and built up until it burst through his mouth. His robust laughter filled the small shed, and Saoirse found it completely impossible not to join in. As they laughed, Saoirse tried to pull her finger free, but to no avail. When she bent to pick up the spool that had fallen, Owen went at the same time, and their heads cracked together, sending them into an even heavier fit of laughter.

They both fumbled through guffaws, simultaneously apologizing, asking if the other was alright, and rubbing their hands on the offending spots on their own heads. The dull throbbing in Saoirse's finger grew more intense, and her laughter died down as she tugged on the end of one of the strands. Big mistake. The vise tightened to an almost unbearable level.

"Eh, Owen," she said, her face contorted. He was still wiping his eyes. "Owen, my finger . . . it's getting cold. And I can't . . ." She found another end and started to pull.

"No, no. *Ná dean é sin.*" He reached for her hand. "Don't do that," he repeated. "Ye'll make it worse." He held her hand, palm up, and examined it as he turned it over and back again.

"Step closer to the light." He pulled her gently toward the door. "Open your fingers flat," he said, then he dragged the fingers of his left hand over her palm to move hers out of the way.

Panic began to set in. The end of her index finger had gone from cold to numb. Her breath came in jagged huffs and a tear escaped and slipped down her cheek. "Please hurry," she cried. "It hurts." She bounced her knees in an effort to keep from fisting her injured hand up against the pain.

"Hey," he said, his voice soothing, low. "I've got you." He inclined his head closer to hers so she'd meet his gaze.

When she did, the stoic calm she found there instantly released the tightness in her chest.

"Okay?"

She nodded.

After inspecting the tangled mess another moment, he gently tugged on a new strand. Saoirse sucked in a breath. "Sorry," he said, then dropped that piece.

He bent his head closer to her finger, and Saoirse could see his eyes tracing the path of the yarn. Then he set to work, and a few seconds later, one loop loosened over her finger. He continued working, the pair of them silent. Occasionally, a stray strand of his hair would tickle Saoirse's face, he was that close. His steady breathing was the only sound other than Saoirse's heart beating in her ears. She tried to watch his hand as it worked, his other one, still bandaged, cradling hers tenderly. But her eyes kept drifting up to his face. As his fingers traced the path of the yarn around hers, her gaze traced the contours of his cheeks. The strong line of his jaw. The intense azure shining through his lowered lashes.

When he looked up at her, Saoirse's breath caught. "Better?" he whispered.

She couldn't bring herself to look away or speak so she merely nodded.

Movement in the corner of her eye broke her trance, and she glanced over to see that the two pieces of yarn were dangling from his fingertips. "Oh, thank you."

Now he nodded, then bent over her hand once more. He brushed his fingertips where the thread at been, the skin a bit swollen and red. He closed his good hand around hers.

"It'll be sore for a bit, but the skin isn't broken, so ye'll be grand out before teatime." He met her gaze again, then reached up and wiped the track of tears from her cheek.

When he let go of her hand and stepped away, cold air rushed in to fill the space and Saoirse shivered.

"C'mon, then. Let's try again," he said.

Saoirse shook her head. "I'm not sure that's a good idea."

"*Tsk! Tsk!*" He wagged his head. "Ya gotta get right back up on that horse."

Sighing, Saoirse made her way back over to where Owen was returning the spool to the shelf and preparing another set of strands for her. When he handed her the second short piece, she looked at him, questioning.

"G'on," he said.

When she took the yarn from him, he sidled up beside her. "Now, put that one over the top of the longer one. That's it. Now, loop your finger over the short one. Yep, perfect." He put his hand over hers, pausing her movements. "Now, ye're gonna wind your finger around and poke it through the loop that you create."

Saoirse nodded, then turned her attention to her hand. Her tongue poked out the side of her mouth as she efforted to do exactly as he'd instructed. When she did, he continued, "Now, grab hold of the long piece with your thumb and forefinger."

She did.

He nodded. "Now, pull."

When she tugged, both strands looped around and around and then came apart again.

"Wrong."

They both erupted in a fresh fit of laughter, and Saoirse had to hold her hand to her side to quell the aching there. When they managed to catch their breath, Owen leaned his shoulder against the wall and crossed his arms over each other. "Again."

Owen filled his lungs with the damp air, savoring the chill that spread throughout his chest. Adjusting his flatcap, he blew a shrill whistle, and Stout materialized by his side.

"Away to me," Owen commanded, and Stout was off like a flash to circle the far side of the sheep two hills over in order to herd them to another one behind Owen. Stout's delighted barks echoed on the afternoon breeze, even though the dog himself could not be seen. Good grief, that dog loved his job.

Owen smiled and made his way down the eastern crest from where he was and up onto the next hillock. It had been far too long since he'd been out in creation with his flock. He scanned the horizon where the dramatic crags of the Seven Sisters rose to the sky, a ruffled patchwork skirt flowing below them in rolling fields. Without even looking, he could picture the peak of Mount Errigal behind him, tugging the clouds low like a blanket. He'd bet there'd be snow atop it in the morning. They'd not had too much snow or ice this winter, thankfully, but February was always a mixed bag when it came to weather. One day could be sunny, warm, and calm, and the next blustering with gale-force winds flinging ice around like shards of glass.

He reached his hands to the sky and stretched, relishing the ability to do so with hardly any pain in his ribs now. He lowered his arms and tugged his jumper back in place, then fiddled with an errant thread, which turned his thoughts back to the weaving shed and Saoirse. He twisted the wool around his finger, triggering a sudden guffaw as he envisioned Saoirse's first go at the weaver's knot that morning. She'd looked like a magician trying to distract her audience with fancy footwork, contorting her body this way and that, as if she could guide the thread by bobbing and weaving her arms and shoulders.

But, fair play to the lass, she didn't give up. She seemed tempted to at first, but she kept going, even after the unfortunate tangled knot incident. In Owen's mind, it wasn't too terribly unfortunate an incident, as it gave him an excuse to hold her hand in his and inhale the heather-filled earthy scent of her hair.

He stopped short and scowled. Where had that come from? He had no reason to think of Saoirse in such a way, and certainly no reason to believe she'd return the admiration. No, it wasn't admiration. It was just . . . just . . . He didn't know what it was other than a distraction.

He huffed, tugged his cap lower on his head, and quickened his pace to the crest of the hill where he knew Stout to be headed. As he walked, he tried to make a plan for what Saoirse needed to learn next. And to convince Aileen to learn the craft as well. As he'd suspected, his sister had met him with a mountain of excuses as to why she hadn't shown up. But it would really help them if she would agree to learn. There was no telling how soon he'd be able to get back to it. A thought that clinched his stomach. He glanced down at his right hand and tried to flex it. It moved but only just. *It could just be hindered by all the bandages*, he thought. *But what if that's not the issue?*

It was imperative both women were able to carry on in the craft if they were to have any hope keeping their heads above water and not get evicted. He absently wondered if Murphy's would offer an extension of any kind to give them a chance to catch their breath a bit. Surely if they knew the state of him, they'd understand. *Or they'd cut you loose for someone who can get the job done.*

No, they were best suited to just carry on with their plan and hope the ladies would be worth their salt with the weaving. They had no choice.

13

Saoirse sat at the table, tying and untying a weaver's knot on a thread she'd fastened to the leg of the table. After a couple days of practice, she'd finally mastered the process—well, perhaps mastered wasn't the right word. But she was able to create the knot with ease and speed, then tug it loose just as easily when needed.

Yesterday, Owen had shown her how to thread the four sets of heddles that hung from the bar over the loom, and she began to see just how integral the weaver's knot was to the whole operation. Each strand of warp had to be passed through the small eye of all four heddles and secured with a weaver's knot. As rain and sleet pelted down outside, Saoirse had learned how to set the heddles to lift the right threads at the right times for the pattern Murphy's had ordered. A push of a pedal or pull of an overhead handle caused the strings of the heddle to tug up or down, allowing the shuttle to pass through. Then the pedal was released and another one selected, and the shuttle was sent back. The whole process was far more involved than she'd ever dreamed. The colored thread on the shuttle had to be cut and tied off, and a new color tied on every time the color needed to change—which in this pattern was often, in order to create the speckled, haphazard design that mirrored that of the slate-and-heather-covered hills of Donegal. Saoirse hadn't done any actual weaving yesterday, but everything was now set for her to start. Once she finished her breakfast, and after a few more practice knots, she was to meet Owen in the shed for her first go at weaving.

The door opened and Saoirse curled around herself, hiding against the icy blast of air that came in with Owen.

"Muise, that wind would cut ye in half," he said as he hurried to the fire. "Then quarters."

Saoirse chuckled.

"Ah, g'on with yerself," Aileen said, mixing up a fresh batch of brown bread. "Ye've been going on for days about how ya can feel it in your waters that a freeze was comin'. Just stay there by the fire and enjoy the fruits o' your premonitions."

Owen shot a playful glare at his sister. Then a satisfied grin spread across his face. "It's good weavin' weather."

Aileen flapped a dough-covered hand. "If ya say so." She turned her attention to Saoirse. "I'm just glad it's you and not me up in that icebox." She shivered dramatically.

"It should be you in there," Owen said, crossing over to the stove and hovering his hands over the simmering kettle. "Ye both should be learning the trade."

"So ye say now." Aileen cackled. "Where was that attitude when I was a wee gairl, itchin' to learn only to be told it was men's work, eh?"

Owen rolled his eyes and poured himself a cup of tea. The perfect punctation to any Irish conversation. Saoirse smiled as she untied the thread from the table leg and wound it up to practice with later. She was just about to warm herself with one more cuppa before heading up to the shed when Stout suddenly sprang up from his spot at the hearth, sprinted to the door, and began barking earnestly.

"Oi! Quiet, you," Aileen scolded.

Owen shushed his sister, crossed the room, and tugged his coat and hat from the peg. "What is it, boyo?"

Stout whimpered and scratched at the base of the door as though he was trying to dig a hole underneath it. When Owen didn't move, Stout stilled, pinned his gaze on his master, and gave one loud, strident bark.

"It's the sheep," Owen said. "Looks like the weavin' will have to wait," he said to Saoirse as he tugged the door open.

"Will we come with you?" Aileen asked, hurrying to grab her cloak.

"No." Owen turned and jabbed his finger toward the women. "Stay here. Could be dangerous."

Aileen sighed as she latched the door behind him.

Saoirse's heart pounded against her chest and she stared at the door as if she could see Owen's form retreating over the hill. She turned back to Aileen. "Bandits?"

Aileen shrugged. "Could be, I s'pose. But it's an odd time for them to hit, what with the weather an' all."

"True." Saoirse chewed her lip. "Unless that's precisely why they would choose now to strike."

A shadow of fear crossed Aileen's face and her gaze drifted to the window over the basin. "Let's pray it's not so."

An hour later, Saoirse had helped Aileen finish the brown bread, chopped veg for their lunch stew, and practiced more knots than she could count. The wind whipped outside, and Saoirse's heart jumped with every bump and thud. Surely Owen should be back by now, shouldn't he? If it were bandits, how would he fight them off? What if he was hurt again? Or worse?

Saoirse shook her head, forcing her thoughts in a different direction. Stout's bark had sounded completely different the night the bandits attacked. He sounded fierce. Ferocious. Today he sounded . . . worried. Alarmed.

Aileen had gone to the barn to see to her chores there and to ensure the horses' water hadn't frozen. Unable to take another moment feeling useless sitting around the house, Saoirse filled a flask with tea, wrapped a few hunks of bread in a cloth, and dropped both in a satchel that hung by the door. She whipped her cloak and hat from the peg, slipped her feet in a pair of wellies, and hurried out into the elements in search of Owen.

Hunched against the wind and squinting against the ice shards stinging her face, she first glanced at the weaving shed. It was dark and closed up tight. A quick peek in the barn window revealed he wasn't in there either. Shielding her face against the elements, she scanned the horizon in a slow circle. Nothing. At last, she headed off toward the field she remembered Owen saying the sheep were being moved to yesterday.

Tromping into the wind, it took ages to crest the two hills between the house and where she knew the sheep were supposed to be. Legs and lungs burning, cheeks both stinging and numb at the same time, she finally reached the hilltop she'd been aiming for. Just down the other side, parallel to a stone wall, Owen was hunkered down, his slicker draped over him. Stout sat by his side, keeping watch over the fields surrounding him. When he saw her, the dog stood, tail wagging. His front paws did a little tippy-tap dance, but he didn't leave his master's side.

Saoirse hurried down the hill. "Hello, Stout. There's a good boy." She ruffled the wet fur behind his white ears.

Owen's head popped out from under his jacket. "I told ya to stay put."

"Is everything alright? Are you hurt?" she asked, ignoring his comment.

When he sat fully straight, Saoirse saw for the first time the ewe lying in front of him. It released a painful bleat. Saoirse sank to her knees next to Owen. "Oh, the poor thing," she said. "What is it?"

Owen stared down at the helpless creature. "She's in labor."

Saoirse's brows soared. "In February?"

"Aye." He nodded. "Some sheep lamb as early as late January, but my flocks don't usually until nearly March."

"So it's too early." Saoirse absently scratched Stout's back as she watched the labored breathing of the mother-to-be.

She looked at Owen's face. His cheeks and the tip of his nose were bright red, and his lips held the slightest tinge of blue. "You're freezing." She reached into the satchel and pulled out the flask of hot tea.

Owen eyed it for a brief second, then took it from her hands, spun the lid off, and sniffed. He took a small sip, then poured some on his hands and sank into the relief. "Thanks," he said as he tugged his slicker tighter around his shoulders and turned his attention back to the ewe. "I think she'll be fine if we can just get her to birth the lamb. But I can't get a good enough grip on it." He held up his still-bandaged right hand.

Saoirse swallowed hard, looked from the sheep to Owen and back, then scooted closer to Owen. "What can I do? How can I help?"

Owen sighed, and he studied her face for a moment. Saoirse couldn't read whatever thoughts or emotions were swirling behind his eyes, but he seemed to be at war within himself. After a moment, he moved over and gestured for Saoirse to take his place.

"Normally sheep can lamb on their own out in the field," Owen told her.

Saoirse nodded.

"But this wee fella is breech." He gestured to the ewe's backside. Saoirse could just see a pair of hooves poking out.

Her eyes widened. "Breech? Are ya sure those aren't the front hooves?"

Owen gave her a sympathetic look. His lips pressed into a line and slipped up to one side. "I'm sure."

She looked back to the sheep, her heart pounding. "How can you be certain?"

He floated her another look. This one seemed to say "Do you really want me to describe how I know?" He lifted his messy hands, and that was enough to communicate everything Saoirse needed to know.

"Oh." She swallowed hard. "Yes, I see."

The ewe cried out, and her side tensed as another contraction took hold.

"Okay," Owen said, "if you're really going to be of help, you need to do exactly as I say, when I say it."

Saoirse nodded again. She could do this. Right?

"Alright," he continued. "Grab the lamb's feet and pull straight back."

Saoirse hesitated. What if she hurt the sheep? Or the lamb? What if she did something wrong and caused them both to die?

The intensity on Owen's face deepened. "Pull now, before the contraction is over."

Saoirse grabbed the lamb's hind feet, trying to ignore the chilly, slimy mess under her fingers. She squeezed her eyes shut and tugged.

"That's it. Pull," Owen said. "Hard. Harder, but straight back."

"I am." She tried to ignore the quaver in her own voice. Despite her pulling, nothing was happening.

The ewe cried out again, this time louder and shriller. "Ye've got to really pull," Owen said.

Saoirse did, and the lamb moved a little farther out into the world, but then stopped. "It feels stuck." She started to shimmy the lamb side to side a little bit.

Owen's hand gripped her arm. "No, don't do that. It could cause the lamb to get wedged in the canal. Just pull straight back."

Saoirse did as instructed, but her hands slipped and she fell back. Scurrying onto her knees, she grabbed the lamb's legs again and pulled once more but still knew she was holding back.

Owen scooted over until he could see her face. "Saoirse, pull."

"I am!" Tears blurred her vision.

Owen shook his head. "Harder. The ewe needs help."

"I'm scared. I don't want to hurt them."

Owen sighed. "Ye're not gonna hurt them unless you don't pull. C'mon now, hard as ye can."

Saoirse clinched her eyes shut and pulled harder. The lamb moved a little more. The ewe cried out again. Saoirse joined in with her own outcry, as she pulled with all her might. "I think I'm losing it. I can't hold it."

Suddenly, warmth enveloped her back, and strong arms reached around her. Owen's left hand gripped her left wrist, while the fingers of his right did the same on her other wrist as best they could. Owen's cheek brushed up against Saoirse's as they pulled together.

"Okay, hold there," he said, his breath tickling her ear. "I need to readjust my grip. We'll go again when the next pain hits."

Saoirse nodded, her gaze trained on the animal in front of her. The ewe stirred and cried out again.

"Go," Owen grunted, already starting to tug.

Together, they pulled and pulled. Saoirse's hands and forearms burned, and her neck strained. She relaxed a little to take a breath.

"No, don't let up," he said. "He's almost there."

Taking a deep breath, Saoirse pulled again, leaning back to push against Owen's chest for leverage. Finally, the lamb's hips popped out.

"Now, pull downward," he instructed. "Toward the ewe's feet."

Saoirse nodded again, and they both adjusted their positions and pulled again. After three tugs, the lamb slid free and into Saoirse's lap. The force of it caused her to topple backward.

Saoirse looked down at the newborn lamb. Joy bubbled

up in her chest and poured out in a mixture of tears and laughter. "Hey, little fella. Happy birthday."

The baby released a hearty bleat, and Owen joined in the laughing. Saoirse cleared the lamb's face with her hand, and her head fell back, exhausted.

"Well done," Owen said, his voice still in her ear. "Very well done."

It was only then that Saoirse realized she was lying back on top of Owen, his arms still around her, helping her hold the heavy lamb. Despite the cold, she'd never felt so warm. So safe. So happy.

Eyes closed against the rain that fell on them, she fought the temptation to stay there in Owen's arms and, instead, scrambled to sit up. "Sorry," she said, then turned her attention back to her newest patient. "How are ya, wee lad?" The lamb baaed once more and wriggled free from her arms before wobbling up to stand on shaky legs. He was black as coal and bigger than any lamb Saoirse had ever seen. She was immediately smitten.

"Look at the size o' him, Owen!" She turned to him. "No wonder he got stuck!"

Owen was wiping his hands on the wet turf when his gaze finally fell on the newborn. His grin faded, and his face paled.

Saoirse looked back to the animal, who was trying to take his unsteady first steps over to his mother to feed. "What is it? What's wrong?"

"He's as dark as pitch."

Saoirse smiled. "Not a spot of white! Isn't he gorgeous?"

Owen's taut gaze met hers, something akin to fear swimming in his eyes. "Don't you know? If the first lamb of the season is black, there will be mourning clothes for the family within the year."

Saoirse felt the smile slip from her face, and the familiar pang returned to her gut. No. It couldn't be. There'd been enough mourning and loss already. Surely there wasn't any substance to the old wives' tale. "That's just an auld legend," she said, forcing a lightness to her voice.

As he lumbered to his feet, Owen pinned her with a look that said "If you say so."

14

Saoirse was in the weaving shed before Owen the next morning. All the previous night's conversations were monopolized by wee *Dubhín*—the name Saoirse had secretly given the new lamb. While hardly tiny by typical lamb standards, adding the diminutive "-ín" onto the Irish word for black just seemed to fit the wee fella with whom Saoirse was completely in love.

The moment he'd been born, Saoirse had been overcome by a sense of joy and accomplishment like she hadn't felt in ages. She was so grateful the lamb had been born safely, especially after the ordeal Owen and the ewe had been through to bring him to that point. To Saoirse's mind, Dubhín was nothing less than a symbol of God's grace. But to Owen and Aileen, he was a harbinger of death.

And while Saoirse failed to see how such a sweet wee thing like Dubhín could be anything other than a joy, she couldn't shake the impending sense of dread and doom she'd carried with her from Westmeath. She felt as though the touch of her hands first gripping his wee hooves suddenly transformed him from a fleecy white to a coal black because of her past transgressions. And with last night's conversations still hanging in the air of the house, mingling with Saoirse's own doubts, the cottage felt suffocating and oppressive. So she'd hurried out to the weaving shed as quickly as possible this morning.

She moved about the small space, lighting the few lanterns scattered in the corners of the room, and double- and triple-checking the heddles and warp in preparation for her first day of true weaving.

When Owen's silhouette darkened the doorway, equal measures of excitement and dread washed over Saoirse. Excitement to endeavor to do something new, something that she now found extremely fascinating. Dread because she couldn't live with herself if she managed to destroy what little of Aileen and Owen's livelihood remained. *God, please help me.*

Owen entered and closed the small red door, taking most of the morning light with it. It was simply too cold, wet, and windy to leave the door open. "Ready?" he asked, brows raised.

Saoirse heaved a deep sigh. "As ready as I'm going to be."

Owen scanned the length of the loom as he approached. "Me too," he muttered.

So, he held the same reservations she did. Perfect. Saoirse willed the burning in her cheeks to dissipate.

He moved around to the foot of the loom and motioned for her to join him. "Now," he began, "once this thing gets going, it'll be too loud for any talking. So, I'll have to explain now, and then you're just goin' to have to give it a go."

She nodded and fixed every ounce of focus on his hands and feet as they reminded her of the process he'd talked her through the other day. She watched the heddles rise and fall, the pedals get pressed one by one, the handle pull in opposition to the pedals, and the tapestry beater move back and forth in a dizzying dance.

"Ye'll be goin' much faster than this, of course," he was saying. "I can't do it very well with just the one hand."

Saoirse rolled her lips inward. *Of course.* "I see."

"Take it away, maestro," he said and stepped aside.

With another cleansing breath, Saoirse took her place and mumbled the poem Owen had taught her. "Pedal for the heddle, pull for the wool. Shuttle crosses over, then beater takes over."

Owen hummed his approval and nodded for her to start.

Slowly and clumsily, not unlike Dubhín had been in taking his first steps yesterday, Saoirse completed one full round of the process. After the beater had tugged and pushed the weft into place, she released the breath that had been building in her chest and looked to Owen, certain every bit of uncertainty shone clearly on her face.

His face was taut, brows pulled together as he bent to look at the first stitch she'd done. Saoirse's heart raced faster by the second. When he straightened and looked at her, his stance and visage softened. He chuckled. "Not bad," he said. "But we'll have to work on that speed."

After giving her a couple of pointers, he set her off again. When she started to look back at him after one stitch, he shook his head. "Carry on."

Saoirse continued on for about five or six stitches. Already her arms burned from pulling the handle above and sliding the beater back and forth, and her left leg protested from holding all her weight on it as her right foot worked the pedals. She stopped and shook her arms.

"You do this for ten hours a day?" she said, disbelief lacing her voice.

He smiled, light dancing in his crystal blue eyes. "Aye." He leaned against the wall and crossed his arms. "A little more involved than ye expected?"

Saoirse huffed out a laugh. "Very much so."

He shrugged and pushed himself to stand. "Ye're not doing too bad a job," he said. "But ya need to find yer rhythm."

He mimicked weaving and began to sing a song, his movements keeping the beat. Saoirse watched him. When he finished the first verse of the song, he noticed her face and stopped. "What?"

"I bet ye're a grand dancer." Heat flushed her cheeks again, and she cleared her throat. "Eh, I mean, that's great. But I can't think of any songs."

"Try the one I was just singing," he said. "Do ya know 'I Am a Wee Weaver'?"

Saoirse shook her head. "The tune seemed a little familiar, but I wouldn't be able to sing it myself."

Owen nodded and stepped closer. "Okay, I'll sing, you weave. Aye?"

Saoirse met his intense gaze. It seemed a bit odd and a little awkward to have him stand and sing over her while she tried to figure out this whole weaving rigamarole, but what choice did she have. "Aye," she said at length.

"I am a wee weaver," he began, his smooth baritone voice filling the small space. "Confined to my loom."

Grateful for her long sleeves that hid the goosebumps prickling her skin as he sang, Saoirse began again with the pedals, then the shuttle. The pace of the song was slower than she expected but just right for setting a good rhythm in her movements. But they still felt stilted. Foreign. And as the loom got going in earnest, it drowned out his voice and she lost the flow.

"Ugh." She groaned. "I'm so sorry."

"Don't be sorry," he said. "It's a lot to learn, and ye're really doing grand."

Saoirse scoffed.

"Tell me, what happened there?" He gestured to the loom.

She shrugged. "The volume of the heddles and beater drowned out your voice, and I lost the rhythm. I'm trying to remember the order of everything, and I just got mixed up."

Owen nodded and shifted his feet. "Ya hafta remember, weaving is a highly internal process."

He must've read the confusion on Saoirse's face because he chuckled, and his eyes drifted toward the ceiling.

"How can I explain it?" he said, eyes still focused upward.

Saoirse kept her gaze fixed on his profile while she waited, not wanting to miss a stitch of his wisdom.

"Right," he said at length. "Weavin' is like a heartbeat. It's a part of you. Your rhythm is gonna be different from mine. It comes from in here." He tapped his chest. "Aye?"

Saoirse mulled over his words. It made sense . . . mostly. "But how do I find it?"

He shrugged. "Ya just do it."

Saoirse turned her palms up toward the ceiling and studied her hands. Could she really do this? Did she even have a rhythm inside her?

As if reading her thoughts, he tipped his head so she met his gaze. "Ye can do this." He stepped behind her. "I'll stand a little closer so you can hear me. But I'd wager before long, ye'll have yer own way of gettin' the beat."

Sighing, Saoirse nodded. "Could I have a wee rest, first?" She rubbed her hands up and down her left leg. "I still don't see how you can do this for hours on end."

He flapped his hand. "Bah. It's like anythin' else in life. You work through the times when the task is difficult . . . when it feels impossible. And before you know it, you're able to complete it without even thinking about it." He stepped over so he was just barely behind her. "I'll take over the pedal for a bit. How's that?"

Saoirse blinked. "Is that possible?" Her question came out with a laugh.

Owen thought for a moment. "We'll find out." A chuckle rumbled deep in his chest. "If ya need, just mime the movements with your foot so ya get used to the flow of it. It's just for a few minutes to give ya a rest."

He started in on the second verse and pressed the first pedal. "As Willie and Mary roved by yon shady bower . . ." His left shoulder was pressed up against the back of her right one, and she could feel his voice reverberate through him as he sang.

She pulled the handle and threw the shuttle through. They repeated the pattern over and over. Forcing herself to ignore the feel of Owen's side pressed against her and his leg brushing against hers as he moved from one pedal to another, she worked at finding the flow and making sure she didn't mess anything up. She didn't want Owen to have to cut the cloth free and start all over again. Eventually, Saoirse let her eyes drift closed as Owen's singing and the beat of the loom lulled her into a trance of sorts. Before she knew it, they'd gone through four rounds of the full song without stopping.

Owen finished the last verse, slowed, and let the last note

hang long in the air as they naturally found a stopping place together. They stood still, silence ringing in deafening clangs around them. Neither moved for a long moment, as though they'd break the spell that had fallen over them. Saoirse's breathing was shallow, and she finally opened her eyes and let her gaze fall onto the loom. She gasped. "I did it!"

Owen's chuckle thrummed against her shoulder. He stepped to the side of the loom for a closer look. Saoirse shivered at the sudden lack of warmth but couldn't pull her eyes from the few inches of tweed she'd woven. Nae, *they'd* woven.

Owen bent until his nose almost touched the fabric. He studied the warp and weft for what felt like ages, then met her gaze again. The approval she found there warmed her to the core.

He opened his mouth as if to speak when Aileen's voice shattered the air.

"Are ye two comin' down for lunch or will ye just stand there starin' at each other all day?"

Owen blinked. Saoirse wasn't sure if she was grateful for or annoyed by the intrusion.

Aileen stood in the doorway. "C'mon, lovebirds, what'll it be?"

Owen spun and shot a glare at his sister. What would possess her to say such a thing?

"We'll be right there," Owen said, rolling his eyes at her. He glanced at Saoirse, whose cheeks burned as she fiddled with a thread on her sleeve.

"Suit yerselves," Aileen said, then turned on her heel and bounded away.

"Now, let's see that weaver's knot in action," he said to

Saoirse, pointing to the light lavender thread on the shuttle. "Can't risk anything unraveling while we're out."

Saoirse deftly cut the thread and had secured it with the trademark knot in a flash. Owen nodded his approval. "*Iontach maith.*"

She smiled. "I'll see to the lanterns."

Owen nodded and headed outside. Squinting against the midday light, he stretched, the cool air on his face a welcome change from the warmth of the shed . . . and Saoirse. Stout sat a few yards away, his back to them, staring far into the distance. That dog would rather be out on the hills with the sheep more than anywhere else. Except maybe curled up on the hearth with a leftover stew bone.

"What's he doing?"

Owen startled at Saoirse's voice next to him. She chuckled but kept her eyes on Stout.

"He's keepin' watch on his flock."

Saoirse pressed a hand to her chest. "That's the most adorable thing I've ever heard."

They were quiet for a moment, both watching the dog. His pure white head stood atop his all-black body, in stark contrast. He was a good-looking beast.

"He's a beautiful wee thing," Saoirse said, as if reading Owen's thoughts.

He nodded.

"I've never seen a collie like him." She gestured toward Stout. "Without a lick of black on his head."

Owen smiled. "That's why he's called Stout."

Saoirse looked at him, brows knotted.

Owen turned her to fully face the dog. "What does he look like sittin' there?"

"Mm . . . a dog?"

Owen laughed. "Well, okay. Aye." He nudged her elbow. "Hold yer hand up like ye were gonna grasp him around the middle—like ya would a glass."

She did and craned her neck to look up at Owen with an expression full of confusion.

"Now, what's he look like?"

Saoirse turned back to the dog, head bent to the side, and was still for a long moment. Standing behind her, Owen couldn't see her face but could imagine her squinting in concentration. Suddenly, her head popped up, and she dropped her hand. "He looks just like a pint o' stout!"

Laughter tumbled out of her mouth and echoed over the hills. Stout turned, tongue lolled happily to one side, and trotted over to them. "Well, aren't you the clever one," Saoirse said to the dog, scratching his ear.

"I'm the one who named him," Owen said, mock hurt in his voice.

"Oi! Come eat, or else don't blame me if it's cold!" Aileen shouted from the bottom of the hill.

"Away home." Stout took off like a shot, leaving Owen and Saoirse to trail behind him.

15

Sun pooled in through the two square windows on the front of the house and bounced around on the whitewashed walls inside. A welcome respite from the dark, dreary storms the past few days. As Owen finished his last bite of stew, he sat back in his chair, eyes closed, and let the light warm his face as pride warmed his chest. He couldn't believe how well Saoirse had done with her first weaving session that morning. For the first time in weeks, he felt like he could take a full breath. Not because of his injuries, but because he finally felt there was hope for him and Aileen. Hope that they were going to make it. Despite the ill omen of the first lamb of the season, all things seemed to be pointing up. He was even able to move his hand more today than he had since the attack, and hope grew that he might not lose the use of it after all.

A knock at the door jolted him out of his reverie. "Maybe it's another lodger," he said, a playful smirk on his face, and sent a wink in Saoirse's direction.

Aileen laughed but looked confused, if not a bit concerned, about his rare display of humor.

Still chuckling, he opened the door to find Tommy

O'Hanlon on the other side. "Tommy, how are ya?" The official Irish Post hat was at least a full size too big and sat awkwardly on the boy's head.

"This came fer ye today," Tommy said, his voice still cracking with youth. "They said it were really important, and I figured it might be another few days before ya got back to the village to collect yer post, so I brought it here."

Owen's smile was replaced by a scowl as he tried to imagine who would be sending him an urgent post and why. He absently took the letter from the lad's hand. "Thanks, Tommy."

When the boy cleared his throat, Owen blinked. "Oh, sorry." He reached into his pocket and gave the boy two pence—one for the price of the stamp and one as a tip.

"*Go raibh maith agat*," Tommy said, then sprinted off back toward the village.

"What is it?" Aileen asked, moving to Owen's side.

Owen tore open the seal and unfolded the letter. As he read, the familiar weight returned to his shoulders, and his hand floated to his forehead to quell the dull pounding that had accompanied his reading of the letter.

He clenched the paper, then threw it across the room with a shout. "*Dochreidte!*" Ignoring how Aileen and Saoirse jolted at his outburst, he plodded over to his chair by the fire and sank down, elbows on his knees, head in his hands.

Footsteps shuffled over, and he heard the crackle of paper as one of them unfurled it from the ball he'd crushed it into.

"It's from Murphy's," Aileen said, her voice taut. "Dear Mister McCready, it is with much sadness that we inform you that our storehouse was badly damaged in the recent storms. Several rolls of tweed were destroyed, and we find ourselves in the unfortunate position of not having enough completed fabric to fulfill our current orders and demands." Aileen stopped reading aloud and sucked in a shuddered breath.

"What does that mean?" Saoirse asked. Owen felt her presence next to his chair.

Aileen was quiet for a moment, and the sound of paper fluttering told Owen she was reading the rest. "It means . . . it means . . ." Aileen's voice cracked, and she sniffled once more.

Next to him, Saoirse moved, and suddenly she was reading. "In light of these unfortunate events, we must ask that you submit your finished rolls of tweed earlier than agreed upon. Please remit the completed fabric to us by the end of this month." Her tender hand laid on Owen's shoulder. "Oh, Owen," she whispered.

Aileen sank to the floor, her hands gripping his knee. "What're we gonna do?" Her voice, barely above a whisper, threatened to undo him. Stout scooted over and plopped down on Owen's feet, but not until he'd placed a cursory lick to his hand. Surrounded by every member of his household, being held by them, each one looking to him for answers, the load of expectation was almost too much to bear.

He shook his head, unable to voice that he had no idea what they were to do. Yes, Saoirse had made incredible strides in her first day of weaving. But not enough to produce as much as they'd been asked to make in two weeks' less time.

A weighty silence filled the cottage. The only sounds were the crackling of the fire and the occasional sniffle from one of the ladies.

Strength and courage.

Owen's head shot up at the almost audible voice.

Aileen's red-rimmed eyes met his, a tenuous hope swimming in them. "Did ya think of something?"

He ignored her question. "Did ye year that?"

"Hear what?" Aileen and Saoirse asked in unison.

Owen allowed the words to echo in his mind over and over, pulling his thoughts toward Father Cunningham's homily last week—and Owen's subsequent conversation with God. Could this be one of His plans? It all seemed ridiculous enough. Cruel, even. There was only one way to find out.

Owen stood, almost knocking his sister over. "Get dressed and meet me at the wagon in ten minutes."

The journey to Glentornan had felt hours long, as not a single one of them said a word the entire way. When Owen had ordered them all out to the wagon and left the house, Aileen had told Saoirse it was best not to ask questions when he was like that. So, they'd rumbled through the valley, questions surely swirling in each of their minds as the reality of Murphy's letter settled further over all of them.

When they rolled to a stop in front of the church, the muscles in Saoirse's neck tightened. She didn't know exactly what they needed, but she wasn't sure it was this. She offered a weak smile to Aileen, who was still lost in thought. Owen helped them each down, and as they entered the dimly lit stone building, they were met by Bridie and John Sheridan.

"Well, as I live an' breathe," Bridie said as she approached Aileen and gave her a hug. "The McCreadys darkenin' the door of the church twice in less than a *seachtain*?"

Aileen held on long to her friend. When they released, fresh tears glistened in her eyes. "Aye, well, needs must."

"Mm," Bridie replied, nodding. Her gaze searched Aileen's face, but she didn't inquire about her tears. Instead, she turned to Saoirse. "How are ya, love? Good to see ye again." She swallowed Saoirse up in an embrace. The emotion that welled up in Saoirse took her by surprise.

"You too," she finally managed to murmur.

The three women stood and chatted for a moment while Owen and John greeted one another, and then they all wandered to their customary rows. The organ played softly, and the gleaming marble walls amplified the sound until it filled up Saoirse's very soul. Her gaze drifted to the ornate wooden zigzag pattern of the ceiling. She wondered if her prayers would penetrate such a fortress or if it took the petitions of a more worthy believer to reach the throne of heaven.

What on earth was the Lord up to? Why would He have brought her all the way here just to bring disaster on another poor, unassuming family? Or perhaps He'd not brought her here at all and she was completely on her own. Sighing, she lowered herself onto the wooden pew.

She went through the motions of the hymns and prayers but struggled to quiet her soul enough to really pay attention to what she was doing. When Father Cunningham ascended the pulpit, she squinted and worked to keep her focus fixed on his message. He began reading from the Scriptures. Saoirse nodded in agreement, then paused. These verses sounded very familiar. It wasn't uncommon for the same verses to be read during services throughout the week but rare that they would be repeated the following week.

When he finished the passage about the battle of Jericho,

he began to read again from the book of Judges and the account of Gideon. Saoirse was struggling to keep her mind from wandering when a verse jumped out and nearly slapped her in the face.

"And Gideon said unto him," the priest was reading, "Oh my Lord, if the LORD be with us, why then is all this befallen us? and where be all his miracles which our fathers told us of, saying, Did not the LORD bring us up from Egypt? but now the LORD hath forsaken us, and delivered us into the hands of the Midianites."

When he finished reading the full account, ending with Gideon defeating the Midianites, Father Cunningham paused and scanned the small crowd of fewer than a dozen attendees. "My friends, I know most in this room live less than comfortable lives. Tragedy befalls this community, this country, more than most—or so it seems. But we can see here in God's own Word, that His wisdom reaches far beyond our own."

He then went on to speak about all the ways God works in our lives, all the while giving examples from the Holy Scriptures, of ways and times God's actions made no sense. From Moses and Aaron to Joshua, Gideon, and on down to Mary and Joseph, and even to His own son, Jesus. All down through the history of the world, God used ordinary people to do strange and wonderful things. And they all started with a plan that made no sense—and some of those plans seemed downright foolish.

Saoirse couldn't help but agree with what Father Cunningham was saying. But how did it apply specifically to her? What was God's plan for Saoirse Fagan?

———————————————

At the end of the service, Aileen and Saoirse walked out to the wagon together while Owen lingered inside, head low as he sat in the pew. Bridie approached and looped her arm through Aileen's.

"Come on down fer some tea, will ya?" Bridie asked.

Aileen sighed and glanced at Saoirse, who shrugged. She couldn't deny that the company sounded wonderful. While she'd grown to love spending time with both Aileen and Owen, she couldn't help but feel a buffer of sorts was needed. Especially today.

Aileen chewed her lip. "I dunno."

"It might be just the thing," Saoirse offered.

Bridie nodded, a wide smile lighting her face. "John's in there workin' on yer man." She hitched her thumb back toward the church. Saoirse followed the direction just in time to see John and Owen exit through the large wooden doors. John clapped a hand on Owen's shoulder.

"I talked him into it," John said as they approached. "C'mon, woman, *ar aghaidh linn*."

Bridie flapped her hand at her husband playfully. "I'm comin', I'm comin'." She turned to Saoirse and Aileen. "We'll see ya in a wee sec."

They waved and nodded, then turned to get into the wagon.

"Eh," Owen said, "I thought we'd walk?"

Aileen's gaze flitted to the sky, and Saoirse followed suit. Hardly a cloud blocked the view of the stars, and the wind was unusually calm.

"Seems a lovely night for a stroll," Saoirse said, the lightness she tried to infuse in her voice failing to reach it.

Owen moved between the two women and extended his elbows.

"Oh, such a gentleman," Aileen quipped, humor dripping from her words.

"Ye're more than welcome to walk on yer own, dear sister," he retorted with a laugh.

Aileen rolled her eyes and hooked her arm through his. "Just don't let me fall, aye?"

He flashed her a look and said, "That's kind of the point," and then he turned his attention to Saoirse, waiting.

She slipped her right hand into the crook of his elbow, noting the warmth of his rough woolen jumper almost immediately. Owen tucked his arm in slightly, and the trio set off toward the center of Glentornan.

The dirt path was deeply rutted from years of wagon and donkey use, not to mention the thousands of free grazing sheep that had traversed it over the centuries. There was just enough star- and moonlight to make out two or three feet in front of them.

"Did anyone else find tonight's message a mite . . . interesting?" Aileen asked, drowning out the crunching of gravel and dirt beneath their feet.

"How so?" Saoirse swallowed back the twinge of guilt at not readily agreeing with her friend.

"Well," Aileen answered, "I've been goin' to that church since I was a wee gairl, and I've never felt like Father Cunningham was talkin' directly to me."

Next to her, Owen nodded. "And ya did tonight?"

Aileen scoffed. "Didn't ye?"

Had all three had the same experience tonight? "I wonder wha—" Saoirse's ankle rolled on the lip of a rut, and her foot slid out from under her. In a flash, Owen's hand grasped hers and pulled her toward him.

"Easy now," he said, his grip tightening as Saoirse struggled to right herself. "Ya alright?"

"Oh, Saoirse, are ya okay?" Aileen added.

Saoirse swiped an errant ringlet from her face. "I am, thank you." She rolled her foot around in a circle and winced.

Owen's gaze drifted to her feet. "Your ankle?"

Saoirse nodded, and carefully shifted some of her weight onto it. Sore but not painful. She breathed a sigh of relief. "It's grand. Just twisted it a bit, but no real harm done."

His eyes met hers. "Ya sure?"

"Aye. Let's carry on. Bridie'll be waitin' on us."

As they turned back in the direction they'd been heading, Owen didn't release his grip on Saoirse's hand. Instead, he tucked it under his arm, next to his chest. Warmth flooded her cheeks even as she relished the feel of his masculine, workworn hand holding hers, and she chided herself for taking such delight in his touch.

He means nothing by it, she told herself. Surely he was just trying to prevent another slip or, worse, a fall resulting in further injury to any of them, keeping them from finishing the tweed order even more. The weight of their reality settled once again on her shoulders, and in her soul, as they rounded the walk leading to the Sheridans' house.

16

Soft orange light spilled from the doorway as Bridie welcomed them inside. Owen stepped back, allowing Saoirse and Aileen to go ahead. As Saoirse brushed past, he thought he caught her glance at him from the corner of her eye. Owen curled his fingers into a ball, the absence of Saoirse's hand far too noticeable. He didn't know why he never released his grip after she nearly fell. He told himself it was in case she tripped again, but the tingling that remained on his skin said otherwise.

He greeted Bridie and John and followed them to the sitting room where a hearty fire roared in the hearth and a tray of tea and biscuits awaited them on a small table.

"I thought it'd be a wee bit cozier in here," Bridie said.

As the women exchanged pleasantries and small talk, Owen watched the flames dancing in the grate, a verse the priest had read rattling around in his head.

*"If the L*ORD *be with us, why then is all this befallen us? and where be all his miracles which our fathers told us of . . ."*

Owen had never related to anything in the Good Book so

much. Had he not asked similar questions himself? Though instead of the Midianites, Owen felt abandoned to the hardships of this world and the thieves who had all but destroyed his livelihood.

"So," John said when the conversation had reached a lull, "what's goin' on with ye?"

Owen drew a long breath, weighing how much to share. "Oh, y'know, same ole, same ole."

John chuckled. "Right."

"Owen Sean McCready, what're ye like?" Aileen scolded, then turned toward John. "There's more than we likely have time to tell ye."

John reached over, poured himself a fresh bit of tea, and waited.

"We had our first lamb of the season," Aileen began.

"That's a mite early for ye, isn't it?" Bridie asked. "Did it go alright?"

Owen nodded. "Mostly."

Aileen grimaced. "A wee all-black lamb. Desperate."

"Och." John scoffed. "Ya don't buy that whole malarky about death followin' the family if the first sheep is black, do ya?"

Heat flashed in Owen's cheeks. As a man of faith, he should discredit such superstitions. And yet, they were difficult to ignore. After all, those beliefs endured because there had to be an element of truth to them, or they'd have died out long ago, wouldn't they?

"Come now," Bridie crooned, "ya canna tell me that the Creator of the universe is going to be derailed by a wee lamb because of the color of its wool?"

Owen chuckled. "It does sound silly when ya put it that

way." He took another sip of his now lukewarm tea. "Anyhow, that isn't really what's weighin' on me."

"Right, then." John leaned forward and rested his elbows on his knees. "*Amach leis.*"

The corner of Owen's mouth twitched in amusement. Never one to mince words, John's request that he come "out with it" landed more as a command than an invitation. Owen appreciated his direct approach. "A letter arrived from Murphy's today."

"Ya have another order. Aileen came back with it before the attack, aye?" Bridie asked.

Owen bobbed his head. "But their storehouse was damaged in the storms, and they lost a good bit of tweed." He scratched the back of his neck. "They've pushed up my due date by two weeks."

"*A thiarcais!*" John mumbled. Next to him, Bridie tsked.

"And with this"—Owen lifted his right hand—"it's nearly impossible. It was nearly impossible as it was. But now . . ." He wagged his head.

The revelation hung in the air for a heavy moment. Bridie sucked in a sharp breath and turned to Saoirse. "Did ya not say ya were learning the craft? Can ye be of help?"

Saoirse's cheeks pinkened, and her gaze fell to the floor. "I'm hoping I will be. I'm still very green at the loom though."

Bridie and John looked to Owen, as if to ask if that were true. "She's a natural, in all honesty," he said. Saoirse shot a surprised look at him, and he offered a small grin. "But she's not ready to take on that amount of demand just yet."

"Well, Owen McCready, if anyone can make it happen, it's you," Bridie replied. Owen wasn't sure what gave her such confidence in him, especially in his current state. He had to have a woman he just barely knew take over several of his jobs because he wasn't able to cope.

Aileen sighed. "I'm not sure even Owen can meet this demand." She turned sad eyes toward her brother.

Owen had no argument against the statement. And yet, hearing it out loud stung like lemon juice in a scratch. Especially since Owen wasn't sure he'd ever weave again, let alone with the speed and superior quality he was known for. He drained the last of his tea, the tepid liquid doing little to soothe his raw spirit.

John took his pipe from the ashtray on the table, lit it, and sat back, his arms crossed over his chest. The pipe smoke swirled around John's head like a halo, the sweet aroma of the tobacco mingling with the earthy scent from the fire. "What aren't ye tellin' us, lad?" he asked around the pipe-stem.

Owen blanched. "I'd say that's about the worst of it," he said, absently wiggling the fingers of his right hand.

John's eyes narrowed into slits, and his gaze bore into Owen's. How could the man tell he was holding back? He'd not told his sister or Saoirse what the doctor had said about the prognosis of his dominant hand. What good would it do to work them up into a lather until they knew for sure?

"Owen." John's voice held the same tone Owen's did when he was trying to coax Stout into giving back a scone he'd grabbed from the table.

Owen tugged the flatcap from his head and raked his fingers through his hair. He really didn't want to have this conversation. Not now—or ever, really, if he was honest. But it was clear John wasn't going to let it go. Sighing, Owen came out with it. "The healing on this hand isn't goin' quite as well as I would like."

"What?" The shock and fear in Aileen's voice confirmed Owen's reasons for not wanting to broach the subject.

"What did the doctor say?" Saoirse's voice was more even, but concern swam in her eyes.

"The wounds are far deeper here than they were anywhere else. It will be a longer road until we know what lasting effects there might be." There. That should hold them. It wasn't a lie, but it wasn't the entire truth either, which Owen was fine with.

Saoirse's gaze dropped to Owen's hand, along with every other eye in the room, it seemed. The shadow behind Owen's eyes suggested he wasn't being entirely open about what the doctor had said. Not that she could blame him. If time was needed in order to know what lingering effects there might be from his injuries, Saoirse presumed that meant there was at least a chance that his use of it might be greatly hindered. She hadn't even considered the notion that he might not be able to use his hand again. She blinked the thought away and tried to focus on what they could control in this moment— which seemed to be very little at first glance. However, she was learning to weave and would do whatever she could to ensure the order got finished in time.

"We'll figure something out," she said at length. "I'll weave all night if need be."

The smile Owen offered her in return held little confidence.

"Aye," Bridie chimed in. "And we'll do whatever we can as well. We canna weave for ya—as much as I wish we could." She turned to John. "I've always wanted to learn how to weave. Anyway"—she shook her head—"we can help with other chores and the like. Whatever will help ye the most."

Aileen reached across and took hold of Bridie's hand, silent tears shining in her eyes.

Owen shifted in his seat, clearly uncomfortable. He stood and tugged his hat back on. "*Go raibh míle maith agaibh*," he said. "Well, we should be goin'."

Aileen and Saoirse shared a glance before rising to their feet. Saoirse suppressed a sigh, but Aileen released hers, eyes fixed on Bridie.

"Right, of course," Bridie said. She and John stood as well. "We'll be prayin' for ye. Do let us know what we can do."

Aileen nodded and hugged her friend. "We will. T'anks."

"Thanks for the tea as well," Saoirse said as she flung her cape across her shoulders.

As they stepped out into the chilly night, Aileen rushed to catch up with Owen, who was already several feet ahead of them.

"That were a bit rude, wasn't it?"

Owen slowed and looked at his sister, confusion plastered on his face. "Ah, they're just tryin' to help. It wasn't rude for them to offer."

"Och!" Aileen scoffed. "It wasn't rude of them, ya eejit. *Ye* were rude."

He stopped. "How do ya figure?"

Aileen tossed her hands. "They made a verra generous offer, and you just dismissed it out of hand."

Shaking his head, Owen started plodding back toward the wagon again. "Aileen, they have their own duties to see to. They don't have the time or the resources to spare to help us take care of our own farm."

Saoirse jogged to catch up with the two, who apparently walked faster the more heated the discussion.

"Hang yer pride, auld man," Aileen said. "Don't you think we ought to let Bridie and John manage their own time and resources? Ya know ye'd do the same fer them if the tables were turned."

Owen spun on his heel. "But they're not!" he shouted. Both Saoirse and Aileen flinched at the sudden outburst. "Don't ye get it? I should be able to provide for my household! John's not the one whose hand might never work right again, or the one who can barely feed his family. I am! And I'll not accept any more charity. I won't."

Aileen stared hard at her brother for a long moment before a sob choked out. "That's the spirit," she said, then she brushed past him and continued up the hill.

"Aileen, wait!" he called after her.

Saoirse caught up to Owen. She lifted her hand to place it on his shoulder but hovered it there for a moment, unable to decide if she was going to actually follow through. At length, she tenderly laid her hand on his arm. He startled at her touch and whirled around as if he'd forgotten she was there.

His posture softened, and he scrubbed his hand down his face. "I'm sorry for yellin'."

She pulled in a deep breath, the scent of damp earth, cold air, and the earthy smoke from turf fires pouring from the chimneys of Glentornan bolstering her courage. "I know how hard this is for you."

Owen's head hung low. "Do ya?" His voice held a deep sadness and sense of resignation.

"Well, maybe not exactly, but I understand how much you want to be able to stand on yer own two feet. And that's admirable. Too many folk want to take the easy way out."

Owen puffed a laugh through his nose and shook his head.

"And I do know how hard it can be to accept help from other people . . . especially if you feel you don't . . . what I mean is . . . do you think getting some help from the Sheridans might be one of those weird plans from God that doesn't make sense?"

Owen's gaze drifted to the sky and he slowly wagged his head back and forth. The soft light from the moon and stars filtering through the drifting clouds set his skin aglow. "Y'know, I might be startin' to regret going to mass tonight." He leveled his gaze on Saoirse's, and the sadness and confusion swimming in his eyes gripped her with ferocity.

Her first instinct was to comfort him. To tell him it's always best to seek God in the midst of the unknown—or the known, for that matter. And, yet, she could relate to his sentiment in the very core of her being. She smiled. "I know." She shook her head slightly. "Sometimes it seems like it would be so much easier if God would just reveal what He's up to, so that it all makes sense from the beginning."

A single guffaw puffed from Owen's lips. "Wouldn't that be nice." He lifted his right hand and studied it, his gaze tracing the swaths of bandages winding around it. "Then again, I'm not sure I would've agreed had He done so."

The corners of Saoirse's lips slid upward. She gently grasped his fingers and nodded, even as the faces of her family members drifted into her mind's eye. She understood completely.

17

Stout's howls reached the wagon long before the dog could be seen.

"What's that auld coot on about now?" Aileen said, annoyance lacing her voice.

Owen stared hard into the darkness ahead of them, the light from the wagon lantern barely reaching more than a foot or two. "Somethin's not right," he muttered. "He doesn't bark like that for no reason."

Snapping the reins, he shouted a command for the horse to speed up. Beside him, Owen could hear Saoirse murmuring something indecipherable. But from the cadence and intensity of her words, he gathered she was praying.

Stout met them on the road about twenty yards from the house. He sprinted alongside the wagon, and when Owen tugged them to a stop, Stout hopped in three circles and barked once more.

Owen sprang down and knelt to the dog's level. "What is it, boyo?"

Stout yapped again, then ran into the shadows.

"Oi, come 'ere, Stout!"

The collie returned to Owen with something in his mouth. Owen carried it over to examine in the lanternlight. A swath of gray frieze had been torn from something. Owen balled it up in his fist, recognizing the scrap. "Haggerty," he ground through gritted teeth. He sprinted toward the field where he'd left the sheep that afternoon, ignoring the calls of Saoirse and Aileen behind him.

As he trudged through the darkness, he couldn't help the smile tickling the corner of his lips, despite the dread swimming in his gut. He was curious if Stout had been able to take a bite of anything more than Haggerty's trousers, and he bargained that Haggerty might think twice before hitting Owen's flocks again after taking a blow in the backside twice in a row.

The muted trotting of Stout next to him as he crested the hill settled a strange comfort over Owen. But as he climbed over the stone wall hemming the flock in, the smile fell from his face, and his gut twisted. Nearly half his sheep were gone. He wandered the field, taking stock of which animals were left. The wee black lamb and his mother were gone, along with a few dozen of his best sheep.

Anger seethed in his gut, threatening to set him ablaze as his teeth clenched, and he paced with ever-quickening speed. A guttural scream built up in his chest, and he finally released it as he kicked a metal feed bucket that had been used to supplement the winter grass. His shout echoed in the night, the bucket flew and tumbled down a small knoll, and searing pain flashed in his foot. That was all he needed, a broken toe to add even more insult to injury.

Owen scolded himself for his outburst even as the pain tempted him to lash out once more. He chose, instead, to sink onto the stone wall. Ignoring the damp chill seeping through his breeches, he let his head fall into his hands. What else could go wrong? What was he supposed to be learning that he wasn't grasping? Was God trying to show him something but Owen was too thick to see it, and therefore God sent more calamity his way?

Owen's head wagged slowly back and forth. None of it made a lick of sense and, if he was honest, he wasn't sure how much more of this he could take. Wiggling his toe in his boot, he was relieved to find that, while sore, it did not seem to be broken. *Thank God for small miracles.*

An ice-cold nose on the back of his hand jolted Owen out of his contemplation. Stout had positioned himself between Owen's knees and tipped his head up to look at his master. A nervous whine squeaked from his throat.

"It's alright, boyo," Owen said, scratching Stout's head. He knew every one of the dog's sounds, and this whimper was not one of pain or injury, or even impending danger, but rather concern over Owen's well-being. "I'm alright."

Owen scanned the field once more. The fleece of his flock shone softly in the silvery moonlight as he counted them each again. Eighty head, from what he could tell. Just over half his flock remained. Pulling in a deep breath, he allowed the musty scent of the livestock, the earthy aroma of the grass and bog, and the damp sea-laden air to fill his lungs and bolster his spirit for the journey back. His heart sank again.

He was going to have to relay yet another one of his failures to the two women who mattered most in his life. Pausing, he let that thought roll in his mind, examining the idea from every angle. Could he truly say Saoirse was one of the most important people in his life? The past few weeks with her passed before his mind's eye like a moving picture. Owen watched the phantom images, realizing just how much Saoirse had worked her way deeper and deeper into their home, family, and, indeed, his heart in a very short amount of time. Aye, he would give just about anything to avoid having to tell her about his latest foul-up. But he also knew nothing good came of lies and half-truths, so he gathered his courage, wishing he had a wee dram of whiskey to help with the task, and mustered his wits for the conversation that was to come all too soon.

He released a shrill whistle—the wordless command to Stout to head home—and started back down the hill. The journey over far too quickly for his liking, he stood outside and stared at the door for a long moment, trying to figure out if there was any way he might come out of this situation not looking like a daft fool. Before he could solve that puzzle, the door flew open.

"Owen Sean McCready, what in all creation is the matter wit' ye?" Aileen grabbed his arm and tugged him inside. "Ya rush off in a flurry, leavin' me and Saoirse to our own worries, and then ya just stand out here like nothin's going on?"

Owen opened his mouth to tell her that he was alright, and everything was fine, but shut it again and grimaced. While physically unharmed, he was far from alright. "Sorry, kid." He brushed past her. "Is the kettle on?"

Her sharp *tsk* echoed against the walls of the house. "O'course it is."

Owen glanced at Saoirse as he hung his hat and coat on the peg. The light in her eyes when she saw him warmed him to the core.

"Thank God ye're okay," she said. "Is everyth—" She met

his gaze again and paused. She must've read the heaviness in his eyes because she instead asked, "What happened?"

Aileen slipped a steaming cuppa into his hand as he paced the room. Saoirse and Aileen's gazes trailed him like Stout watching his sheep. He adjusted his grip on the cup to wrap his hand around it, hoping the heat would both thaw his chilled fingers and infuse him with courage. He finally settled himself in front of the fireplace.

"Haggerty struck again," he began, his voice low, his stare trained on the floor. The fire crackled behind him as weighty silence filled the room. Owen absently wondered if he could simply slip away and hide in the blaze, pulling its flames over him like a blanket. He forced himself to look in his sister's eyes when he answered. "He got 'em this time."

Aileen's hand flew up to her chest. Saoirse rose and stood next to her. "All of them?" Aileen asked.

"No," he said around a mouthful of tea, "but he got away with about half."

A quiet sob slipped from Aileen's mouth, and she slowly sank. Saoirse managed to slip a chair from the dining table under her so she sat on it instead of landing on the ground. Saoirse stood behind her, rubbing her hands in comforting swipes up and down Aileen's shoulders and upper arms.

"Which ones?" Aileen asked with a sniffle.

Owen rattled off the ones he knew for sure were gone. "The ewe and her lamb—"

"Not Dubhín!" Saoirse cried.

Owen blinked and confusion pulled his brows together. "Du—what?"

Saoirse shrugged. "It's what I'd named the wee lamb," she said, looking a mite sheepish herself.

Owen couldn't help the smile that tickled the corners of his lips. Not only had she named the lamb as if it were a dog, she'd come up with the most childlike name on earth. "Ah" was all he managed to eke out. He was afraid if he said more, he'd end up pulling her to him, kissing the spot on her forehead where her worry showed the most, and holding her tight. He took two big chugs of tea, ignoring the searing heat as it trailed down his throat. He needed to get ahold of himself. Not only did he have no business having those kinds of thoughts about Saoirse, he certainly had no business entertaining such thoughts at a time like this. Half his flock had just been heisted—a catalytic event that would lead to devastating losses in their weaving next season due to lack of wool for the yarn, among other things.

"We've got to alert the gardaí," Aileen said, shooting to her feet.

Owen held his hand up. "We will, we will. But I'm not leavin' ye two here at night while I ride back into the village in the pitch-black. It's not safe for you lot to stay here alone, and I'm not riskin' life and limb on that road. If Haggerty's clan doesn't get me, the drop-off the side of the road into the Poisoned Glen surely will. We'll handle it tomorrow."

"But—"

"What is Sweeney goin' to do right now, anyway? Eh?" Owen crossed the room and set his empty cup on the counter with a thud. "He can't very well look for clues or follow tracks in the dead o' night, can he? We'll summon him tomorrow. That's all we can do."

Aileen huffed and stomped to the kitchen. "It's just not right, I tell ya. Not right 'tall." She shuffled dishes and pots around the kitchen under the guise of tidying, muttering her discontent all the while. She'd retreated into herself, her words nearly unintelligible, but Owen knew she was giving Haggerty a piece of her mind, and it was in Owen's best interests to just leave her be. After one final clang of the large stew pot on the stove, his sister blustered her way back through the sitting room and into her bedchamber.

Owen stared after her, even as he warred with the temptation to throw caution to the wind and head into town. He knew it would do no good. Even if he managed to reach the guard station safely, all Sweeney would say is he'd be out first thing in the morning.

"I'm really sorry, Owen." Saoirse's voice shattered his thoughts. "It's awful." Warmth radiated along his side as she came up next to him.

"Aye, 'tis." He glanced down at her. "And thanks."

"But I'm really glad it wasn't worse."

He looked at her, questioning.

She gestured to his right hand. "If ye'd have caught him in the act, it could've gone much more badly this go-round."

Owen hadn't even thought of that. He raised his right hand and studied it.

"How is it?" She faced him.

Sighing, he concentrated, trying to get his fingers to obey his command. They moved but only just. "Still mending."

Saoirse cradled the back of his hand in her palm and ran her fingers over his, much like he'd done when she'd knotted herself into the thread. Fire shot up his arm at her touch, but not pain. A blazing, wonderful sort of heat that he never wanted to end. "Well . . ." She continued to study his hand, then drew in a long breath. Owen wondered if she was weighing what she wanted to say next. She licked her lips briefly in thought, and he couldn't tear his gaze away. "It's still relatively early days yet. We'll keep praying for God's complete healing."

Her eyes floated from his hand up to meet his gaze.

With great effort that Owen hoped didn't show on his face, he managed to bring his thumb down to brush the backs of her fingers that still rested on his hand.

"Ye'll be alright," she said, her voice barely above a whisper. Her gaze swept over his face.

Owen's other hand drifted up and rested on her forearm. He wanted to thank her, but words refused to form in his brain. All he could do was nod.

"Will she?"

Owen blinked quickly, the spell broken. "Will . . . who?"

Saoirse lowered her hands and jutted her chin in the direction of Aileen's room.

It was only then that Owen realized his sister was still stomping around, as was her habit when she was so angry she didn't know what to do. A low chuckle rumbled in his chest. "She will be. She just needs to get it out of her system." He leaned closer to her ear and added, "Stout does the same thing when I forget to save him the bones from my chicken."

Saoirse laughed. "Good to know." The clock on the mantel began to chime. "I should be going. It's gettin' late." She stepped around him and headed for the door.

He hurried to reach the door before her. "Goin'? Where?"

"I'm tired," she said, tugging her cloak from the peg. "I was going to go to bed."

Owen pressed his lips into a line and shook his head. "I don't think it's a good idea for you to be stayin' out in that barn alone after all that's happened." He tried to ignore the guilt gnawing at his gut that he hadn't just invited her to stay in the house from the very beginning.

Saoirse flapped a hand. "I really think I'll be fine." She reached for the handle, and his hand landed on top of hers. He noted that she didn't pull away.

"Not after all that's gone on. It's not safe." He closed his eyes and drew in a deep breath. "I should've never had you sleepin' out there. You can share Aileen's room. It'll be a bit tight, but ye'll both be safe, and that's what matters." He lowered his voice. "I'd never forgive myself if somethin' happened to you. Promise me you'll stay in here with us?"

Her eyes were trained on their hands, both still on the handle. She looked up and met his gaze, searching his for something he couldn't decipher. "I promise."

18

"Thanks for sharing your room with me," Saoirse said as she unfolded the blankets she'd been sleeping on the last two weeks. Owen had gotten them out of the barn and shaken them out for her. He'd apologized profusely for not having more bedding things in the house to use, but Saoirse didn't know anyone other than the very wealthy who had extras of anything. In fact, many lacked even the basic necessities for living.

Aileen laughed. "Are ya jokin'? I was chuffed he finally came around and let ya get out o' that dank barn!"

"I really didn't mind it," Saoirse said as she bent down to spread out her pallet on the ground. "It was warm, quiet, and comfortable. I'd managed to make a wee little home for myself back there." When she straightened, Aileen had pinned her with such a look of incredulity that Saoirse burst into laughter. "What?"

"Can ya hear yerself?" A mixture of humor and disbelief laced Aileen's voice. "Ya can't tell me ya actually liked livin' out there?"

Saoirse pushed her lips up and bobbled her head. "Wasn't

so bad. Certainly better than the alternative." She yawned and stretched. "Though I must say I prefer the aroma in here to the one in the barn," she added, laughing.

Aileen joined in. "And I'll tell ya, you can thank me fer that! If it were just my brother livin' here, this place would reek to high heaven. It'd make the barn seem like a perfumery."

Saoirse's jaw fell open, and she playfully tossed a pillow at Aileen. "You're awful!"

Aileen shrugged. "I know he seems all knight in shining armor to ye, but I assure ya, he's just a regular man . . . with all the regular man smells." She made a face that reminded Saoirse of when her younger brother had tasted *carrageen* for the first time. She pulled the covers on her bed back and slipped underneath them.

But as she considered what Aileen had said, heat flashed up her neck. "I'm not sure I understand. Knight?"

Aileen raised up on her elbow and rolled her eyes, the soft lantern light accentuating the playful gleam dancing in them. "Och, please. The whole wairld can see ya think he hung the moon."

"I do not!" Saoirse scoffed. "I'm just grateful to both o' ye for a place to stay and a way to earn my keep." The burning in her cheeks reminded her that, perhaps, that wasn't all there was to it. And not for the first time, she was thankful for the low light that hid the intense blush no doubt coloring her cheeks. Her argument was weak, she knew, but she hoped her friend would buy it.

Aileen studied her for a long moment, a smirk playing on her lips. At length she said, "I don't see how anyone could be smitten with that auld codger out there."

Saoirse's gut tightened. Clearly Aileen knew him better than she did. Why might she say such a thing? She efforted to keep the tone of her voice neutral when she asked, "Why's that?"

"He makes eatin' lemons seem like a joy." Aileen then mimicked her older brother, rattling off some of his most oft-used phrases.

"Tsk. You're awful," Saoirse teased. Though she couldn't deny the woman's impersonation was spot-on. Aileen winked and lay back down, pulling the covers up under her chin.

Saoirse chuckled and settled herself on her own makeshift bed. She looked up at Aileen, who appeared to be halfway to *Tír na Nóg* already, then smiled.

"Wha'?" Aileen asked, her voice thick with fatigue.

"Nothing." Saoirse shook her head. "Just bein' in here with you reminds me of sharing a room with my sister back home."

"Mm." Aileen lifted her brows and nodded. "I always wanted a sister. Were ye close?"

Saoirse pulled in a long, slow breath and released it, the subtle scent of hay, tea, and turf comfortingly familiar. "Aye, we were."

She let her gaze drift around the cozy space. In many ways, she felt even more at home now than she had since leaving her own home to come to Donegal. She'd never spent so much time alone until she came here. Her family had all lived in a small house, not terribly unlike Owen and Aileen's, and she'd shared a bed with her younger sister her entire life. It had taken her several nights to adjust to the quiet and solitude of the barn. She'd missed the extra body heat terribly, but even more so, of course, the company of her sister—something she would never have the privilege to experience again.

So, lying in this tiny room now, Aileen's breathing already slowing, and the sound of Owen's soft snores floating under the closed door, was like having a favorite blanket wrapped around Saoirse's shoulders. She hadn't realized how much she'd missed being part of a family, and living in a real home, until this moment. And in this moment, she was immensely grateful to have that again. Yet it brought with it such an agonizing ache for her own family that she struggled to breathe. She remembered the time she had set out to make dinner all on her own for the first time. She'd burned the fish to the skillet so badly, more of it was left charred onto the cast iron than had ended up on their plates. That's when her less-than-fortunate streak really became a running joke in their house. The fact that she'd done things exactly as her mother had done her whole life but ended up with disastrous results made for constant lighthearted jabs at Saoirse. A sudden and overwhelming longing washed over her, to be able to return back to that simpler time when her bad breaks only resulted in a smelly sitting room and family jokes.

Tears stung her eyes, and she rolled onto her side, her back to Aileen's bed. Once the first tear slipped from the corner of her eye, across the bridge of her nose, and onto her pillow, a floodgate was opened. Unable to quell the tide, Saoirse let the tears flow but choked back her sobs so as not to wake Aileen. What she wouldn't give to have her family back—Mammy, Dadaí, Grainne, Seanín, and Mícheál. And, of course, the family dog, Finn. All gone in a flash.

Flash. Saoirse flinched at the word. It was an all-too-accurate description of her family's last moments. And, as was the case every day since, suffocating guilt accompanied the memories of her beloved family. But the heaviness was joined by a new addition—paralyzing fear that the Mc-Creadys would rescind their welcome once they knew the truth of it all. As far as she knew, the gardaí weren't after her for payment of her crimes, but with the looming involvement of the law enforcement to bring justice to Haggerty and his men came the fear that her own justice might be awaiting her as well. The thought sickened her, though she knew she wasn't deserving of arrest and didn't even know if anyone was looking for her. Just the thought that perhaps someone might be was enough to set her heart racing and gut churning.

She didn't know what Owen would do if he ever learned the truth. A vision of his face floated into her mind. His piercing blue eyes saw right through her facade and into her heart. She could deny her feelings to Aileen all she wanted, but there was no more denying to herself that her friend was right. Saoirse was, indeed, besotted with Owen McCready. No, it was more than that. She cared for him deeply—more than she had anyone outside of her family. And if he found out what she'd done . . . no, she couldn't bear the disappointment she'd see in his eyes. But more than that, if she was no longer welcome in the McCready home, Saoirse didn't know what she would do. The thought itself was suffocating, and she determined, once again, to do whatever she needed to ensure he never found out.

Swallowing the new tinge of guilt at the idea of keeping secrets from Owen, she rolled to her other side, closed her eyes, and prayed for the sweet release of sleep.

Owen unlocked the weaving shed and took a deep breath, letting the heady, earthy scent of the wool yarn, the wood from the loom, and the tangy scent of the oil in the lantern wash over him. It was his favorite place to be, outside of being on the hills with his flock.

Saoirse would be joining him any minute to get back to the weaving. It felt like ages since they'd worked the loom side by side even though it'd only been a day. At any rate, they were already dreadfully behind. As he lit the lanterns and checked the warp and stock of spools, he went over that morning's conversation with Sweeney. They'd gone out and walked the field and found the tracks leading off in the direction Haggerty had taken the stock, but there was little to be done. Sweeney said two other farms had been hit last night as well, and while they were working to track the bandits down, the chance of recovering the sheep was slim to none. The real hope was capturing Haggerty and his men, putting them in jail, and bringing this thieving nonsense to an end. When Owen shared the news, Aileen had been livid, insisting there had to be something more the gardaí could do. Saoirse had been strangely quiet the entire time and almost seemed to shrink into the background as soon as Sweeney had arrived.

Owen couldn't say he wasn't frustrated himself, but what else could he do? There wasn't enough time to get the weaving done and chase down a mob of sheep bandits, so he had no choice but to let Sweeney and his men do their job while he did his. His jaw tensed.

Let Saoirse do yer job for ya, more like.

As if summoned by his thoughts, Saoirse's frame darkened the doorway. "Sorry. I'd have been here sooner, but Aileen needed my help in the barn."

Owen shook his head. "Not a bother. Ye're here now."

She crossed the small space and began inspecting the threads on the loom. "Will she not be joining us?"

Owen sighed. "*Níl.* I tried to convince her it's best if she learns too, but you know Aileen."

Saoirse chuckled as she scanned the dim interior. "All set here?"

"Aye."

She straightened and her gaze met his. "I'm sorry things didn't go better this morning."

He shrugged. "They went about as well as they could have. Nothin' more to do but let the guards do what they do best."

She rounded the front of the loom and grabbed the shuttle. "I suppose. I'd just hoped they'd be able to get your sheep back."

Owen took a spool of dark-red yarn from a shelf and handed it to her. She loaded it onto the shuttle like a seasoned weaver. "They may yet, but I figured it was a long shot. I'll be happy if they can get Haggerty and his ilk off the hills."

Saoirse secured the new yarn to the first strand of warp and got the shuttle set for the first throw.

"Anyhow," Owen said, "I'd trust Sweeney with my life, so I know he'll do all he can."

Saoirse tensed slightly and she blinked, keeping her eyes fixed on her work. "Ye're good friends?"

"Well." Owen gestured to the pedal she needed to start with. "He was there for me more than anyone else when my da died—other than Aileen, of course."

She looked at him, sadness in her eyes. "I'm glad you had someone to lean on."

Owen offered a small smile in return, unsure how to respond. He fought to keep his memories—and anger—at bay. If he let himself, Owen could still feel the grief and anger as fresh as it was the day of the accident. The fact that someone could be so careless—

"Okay," she said, her lighter tone jolting him back to the present, "am I all set to start?"

The weaving. Right. He took a steadying breath and nodded. "Think ye're ready to go solo?" he asked, ignoring the disappointment swelling in his chest at the thought of not weaving together as they'd done the day before.

She blew out a breath. "I'd like to try. I'd hate for you to have to hold my hand forever." Her cheeks pinked, and she averted her eyes. "I mean . . . if I'm going to learn to weave, I should learn it properly, y'know?"

He nodded. "Ya remember the song?"

She grimaced slightly, her nose crinkling around her freckles in the most delightful way. "I think so."

He started the first verse, keeping the pace a mite slower than he would've for himself, and watched as she pulled the handle, pressed the pedal, and threw the shuttle for the first pass.

19

Saoirse stifled a yawn as they rumbled down the path into the village. She and Owen had worked in the shed for several hours the past two days, and she was exhausted. Her body ached and her mind was numb after such intense focus for so long. She had been looking forward to the time with him, but the task required such concentration, especially as her speed increased, that they'd hardly spoken the whole time. Now, with the wagon rocking from side to side, it was like Naomh Íde herself was singing a lullaby just for her, making it almost impossible for Saoirse to keep her eyes open. Every now and then, a rut or rock in the road would jolt the rig and shake her back to her senses—for which she was grateful. If she fully gave in to the pull of sleep, she'd either fall over the side of the wagon or end up lying on Owen's shoulder. Not that leaning into his strong form, his warmth wrapping around her as he secured an arm around her waist, didn't sound enticing. Heat spread up her cheeks, and she was grateful no one else could read her thoughts.

She had almost declined when Owen said they all needed to head into town. The thought of catching a quick nap in the quiet by the fire had sounded like just what the doctor ordered. But Owen insisted she come.

"I'm not about to leave ya here to yer own devices with those scallywags terrorizing the county like they own the place," he had said. "You and Aileen can go for a walk, visit the church to pray, or call on Bridie. Ye're just not stayin' here alone."

So, the three of them crammed onto the wagon together as it rolled down the hill now, past the church, and into Glentornan. Owen had a doctor's appointment to check his right hand and arm. Saoirse snuck a glance at him from the corner of her eye. His gaze was trained forward, his expression neutral. Except that the muscles in his jaw were taut, and the creases between his eyebrows were just a mite deeper than usual. She fought the urge to reach for his hand and encourage him that everything would be alright.

Suddenly he turned, and his eyes met hers. Apparently her glance had turned into staring. She offered a shy smile. "Don't be nervous," she said.

He scoffed slightly. "I'm not."

On the other side of him, Aileen snorted. "Aw, sure, and what's there to be nervous about, eh? Ye're just about to find out if yer livelihood is in danger or not."

Owen swatted his sister's arm playfully at her attempt to defuse her own fears or discomfort.

"Alright," he said, turning back to Saoirse. "I might be a wee bit nervous."

Saoirse smiled and bumped his shoulder with hers. "It'll be fine. I know it."

He returned her smile, and his gaze dipped briefly to her mouth before bouncing back up to her eyes. "Thanks."

The wagon rumbled to a stop, and the trio alighted. Owen made a beeline for Doctor McGinley's office.

"It's just yer arm he's lookin' at, aye?" Aileen called after him.

Owen stopped and turned back. "That's right."

"Right." Aileen huffed a determined breath and tugged her shawl tighter around her shoulders. "I'm comin' with ya."

Owen started to protest, but Aileen brushed past him and was at McGinley's door before he could form an argument. He sighed. "Suit yerself." He offered a sheepish grin to Saoirse and shrugged.

"Good luck," she said, then she watched the siblings disappear into the darkened interior of the doctor's office.

Saoirse spun in a slow circle, once again taking in her surroundings, as she tried to decide what to do with herself for the next while. She looked to the northeast, in the direction of the church. Time in solitude and prayer sounded lovely, but she wasn't sure she wanted to trek back up the hill alone to do it. Turning more northward had her looking in the direction of Bridie and John's home. While she thoroughly enjoyed their company, she'd also experienced their hospitality, unannounced, twice now. And she did not feel like she knew them well enough to simply call on them, especially knowing that Bridie would insist on filling her with tea and biscuits. Saoirse couldn't, in good conscience, consume any more of their much-needed supplies. Finally, she faced due west and decided to follow the winding road through the village. Dunlewey Lake stayed on her right, its unseasonably calm waters reflecting the sky and peak of Mount Errigal like a mirror.

A dozen or so stone houses lined both sides of the narrow street, and no one else was about. Saoirse figured most were working indoors, or out in the fields. At the end of the road, tucked up against the foothills, stood another stone building with a thatched roof. Muffled singing floated up out of the chimney, mingling with the turf smoke as it curled lazily in the still air of the late afternoon. A small stone sign next to the door read "*Scoil Mhic Dara.*"

"Saint MacDara's School," Saoirse muttered to herself. "Interesting." While it was not uncommon for schools to be named after saints, Saoirse found it interesting that one in this part of the county was named after the patron saint of seafaring and fisherman. Though, if legend was to be believed, MacDara's first name, *Síonach*, was an old Irish word referring to stormy weather. That alone made sense, as this part of Donegal was known to get some of the worst squalls on the island.

The sound of church bells shattered the air. The door of the school burst open, and half a dozen children ranging in age from five to ten erupted into the fresh air. The form of a tall, slender gentleman filled the doorway and called out some sort of instruction or parting word to the children, but Saoirse couldn't make out what he'd said. She had to jump to the side of the road to avoid being run into by the squealing students as they sprinted past her.

"*Tá brón orm*," the man called and waved.

Saoirse waved back, smiling to let him know she accepted his apology and wasn't cross.

"Those wild Donegal children'll kill ya if ye're not careful."

Saoirse yelped and spun around. Aileen stood there, grinning like the cat that ate the canary. Saoirse pressed a hand to her chest. "I think you'll be the death o' me first, Aileen."

Aileen laughed. "C'mon, doc's all done with Owen."

Saoirse studied her friend's face, searching for any sign of how the visit had gone. But Aileen was looking past Saoirse, staring at the school, her face like a stone tablet, revealing nothing except a slight blush in her cheeks. "How'd it go?" Saoirse asked.

Aileen turned and started walking back toward the wagon, shrugging a shoulder. "Well, the stitches are out and he doesn't have to wear the bandage anymore, but it's still too soon to know how much use he'll have out of it." Her tone was flat, matter of fact. Saoirse couldn't tell if she was holding anything back—either news or emotion.

Up ahead, Owen was walking to the wagon, his pace just barely slower than a jog. Saoirse's stomach clenched. Her gaze dipped to his right hand. The bandages were indeed gone, but otherwise the limb hung nearly lifeless at his side as he hurried toward the rig.

When Aileen and Saoirse finally met up with him, Owen's stiff posture and the darkness in his eyes made Saoirse pause. He extended his left hand toward her, his gaze fixed on some distant point behind her. She took his hand and allowed him to help her into the wagon, but she could not relish the touch of his roughened skin against hers as her heart thrummed against her chest, worry for him swirling in her gut.

The ride back was silent—an experience that was becoming all too common for Saoirse's liking. Time and again, she opened her mouth to ask Owen what the doctor said, but fear caused her to clamp it shut again. She wasn't afraid of his reaction but rather the words he might say. If he had, in fact, lost most of the use of his hand, she wasn't sure she could bear the weight of the news alongside everything else that had happened of late.

Next to her, Owen shifted and turned his palm up. Saoirse watched silently as he studied his palm before his fingers slowly and stiffly curled inward a mite and then relaxed. He let his hand slide down until it rested on the edge of the rough bench seat, right next to Saoirse's. The side of his hand bumped up against hers. He shifted, mumbled an apology, and tucked his arm closer to his side. Saoirse studied his profile for as long as she felt able to without drawing his gaze back to her, wishing there was more she could do to ease the burden weighing on his shoulders. He hunched slightly in the seat, as though the physical weight of all he carried was literally pulling him down. She slid her hand in his direction and draped her pinky finger over his.

He didn't move or look in her direction. But he blinked, and after a long moment, he curled his little finger around hers and shifted so the sides of their hands pressed fully together. His stature softened ever so slightly, and Saoirse couldn't be sure, but it sounded like a shuddered breath rumbled in his chest, much like the ones that had shaken her as she tried to hold her tears at bay so many times.

Saoirse's eyes drifted closed, the sheer pleasure of his touch warring with the worry burdening her heart for him. *Lord, please help.*

20

When they finally arrived back at the house, Owen sent the ladies inside while he put the wagon and horse away.

"I need to feed Fadó, then I'll be back down," he'd said.

As they shuffled inside, Aileen went straight to set the kettle on and started slicing the brown bread she'd made earlier that morning. Meanwhile, Saoirse saw to the fire. She'd have much rather swapped roles with Aileen—if she never tended another fire in her life, it would be too soon. Though, restoking the embers and adding a few new spates of turf was far better than ensuring the flames were died down enough to safely leave the house without letting the fire go all the way out. It was widely believed that to let a home's fire go all the way out would cause the soul of the home to flee, allowing bad luck to be ushered in. However, in Saoirse's experience, it seemed to be just the opposite. And because of that, she was thankful that Owen had seen to the task of readying the fire for their absence this afternoon—something she would avoid doing for the rest of her life, if possible.

"Ya alright there?"

Saoirse blanched at Aileen's voice. She turned to her and smiled. "Grand, so."

Aileen leveled a look of disbelief at Saoirse. It was only then that she realized tears were streaming down her face.

"Fer a girl who's alright, ya sure do a load of cryin'," Aileen said, crossing the room with two steaming cups in her hand. She lowered herself into one of the high-backed chairs and handed a cup to Saoirse.

Saoirse swiped at her cheeks, embarrassment and anger swirling in her chest in equal measure. Embarrassment at having her emotions so on display, and anger at herself for not being able to even think of her family in passing without tears automatically following suit. "It's nothing." She sniffled.

Aileen tsked and shook her head. When she met Saoirse's gaze again, nothing but compassion shone in her eyes. "Look," she said, gesturing for Saoirse to take the other seat. "I know I'm not yer sister, or yer mam, but I do feel like we've become friends, aye?"

Saoirse nodded, her gaze dropping to examine the liquid swirling in her cup.

"I also know ya must've been through somethin' fierce to wind up out here in the wilds o' Donegal all on yer own." She paused, her eyes boring a hole into the side of Saoirse's face.

Saoirse took a sip, refusing to look at her friend directly.

Aileen sighed. "All I'm sayin' is, ya live here with us, help provide for us, share our resources. I've heard ya crying in the night, and while I can't imagine what ye must've been through, I just want ya to know ye can share yer heart too." She slurped her tea. "That's what family does."

The stinging behind Saoirse's eyes forced her to squeeze

them shut, new rebellious tears spilling over as she did. Drawing in a long breath, she filled her lungs with the comforting aroma of the tea and the strident scent of the fresh turf as it caught the flames and forced her emotions to steady. When she opened her eyes and finally met Aileen's gaze, she was overcome with a sudden urge—nae, a need—to tell her everything. Carrying her secret was proving to be far more burdensome than she'd expected, and she hated the way it felt hiding such a big piece of her story from the people who'd been so generous to her. At the same time, overwhelming fear gripped her. What if they hated her for it? What if they kicked her out?

In the back of her mind, another voice whispered, *What if they don't?*

She wrapped both hands around her cup and lifted it to her mouth, the hot, creamy tea bolstering her courage as she allowed herself to recognize just how tired she truly was. Not how exhausted she was from her labors on the farm or in the weaving shed. But how weary her spirit was from carrying a burden she was never meant to carry. Her soul was thin and sheer, like a banshee blown about on the gales, haunting her every move. Would sharing her load bring freedom or more pain? She couldn't wait any longer to find out.

She drew in one more long, deep breath, then released it with a sigh. "On my last day back home—"

The door slammed open, and Owen stomped in and over to the stove. He tried to lift the kettle with his right hand, but it went crashing to the floor. He released a guttural shout and pounded the table with the side of his other fist. "Hang it all!"

Both Saoirse and Aileen shot to their feet. "Are ya alright?"

"Did ya burn yerself?"

"I'm fine!" He sank into one of the wooden chairs at the table and dropped his head into his good hand.

Both women rushed to his side. Aileen carefully scooped up the kettle, leaving the small pool of water seeping into the packed-dirt floor, and set it back on the stove. Saoirse laid a quiet hand on Owen's shoulder.

"Give it time," Aileen said.

Owen's hands flopped to the table, his head remaining low. "There is no time," he said, punctuating each word with a bounce of his hands. He swiped under his nose as he stood and crossed over to the fireplace. "I don't know how many more times I can have this conversation. There was barely enough time before all this"—he swung his arm in an arc. "There's more and more obstacles at every turn, each one stealing even more time than the last."

Aileen tossed her hands. "Well, I dunno what ya want me to tell ya. I'm not goin' to blow sunshine up yer . . . I'm not gonna lie and say, 'Sure, it's grand, now. Go on and do all yer things.'"

"No one is askin' ya to," Owen replied.

Aileen turned and wiped the already clean counter with a rag. "Coulda fooled me," she muttered under her breath.

Saoirse's glance flitted to Owen. Either he didn't hear his sister's remark or was choosing to ignore it.

She joined Owen at the fireplace, the gentle heat warming her feet as she approached. "I can't imagine how frustrating all this must be for you—the injuries, the missing sheep, an' all." Her gaze dropped to her feet. "And doin' it all with an extra mouth to feed." She picked at a thread on her sleeve. "But," she continued, "you are not in this alone. Aileen and I will do all we can. And I know you know that."

Owen's head bobbed. "I do." He rubbed his right wrist. "I just hate havin' to rel—" He shook his head. "I just hate this." The rubbing continued.

Saoirse laid a hand on his forearm, and he stilled. She waited until he met her gaze. "It'll come."

He nodded and thanked her, but the shadow behind his gaze belied his doubt, and the sadness keeping the smile from reaching his eyes tugged at Saoirse's heart.

It would come, wouldn't it? It had to. Right?

"*Siúil ar aghaidh iad.*" Owen punctuated his command for Stout to walk the sheep forward with a shrill, quick whistle. Stout took off, his excited pants leaving puffs in the chilly air. Owen watched the dog do what he did best. His body was pressed low to the ground as he sprinted toward the herd, his breathing a rhythmic huffing that expressed his joy at working. As a younger pup, Stout would get so excited while working that he'd terrify the sheep into running away, and they'd be almost impossible to corral. But he'd also been eager to learn and took great pride in a job well done. Now a seasoned professional at the tasks he was asked to perform, Stout knew exactly when to slow down and creep around the back or side of a group, when to sprint at them head-on, and when to use a combination of trotting and barking or yipping to get the stubborn sheep to yield to his will.

Owen absently wondered if God were to work like Stout, what tack was He currently using in Owen's life? If Owen was honest with himself, the Lord felt awfully absent lately—napping back at the shed, perhaps. Owen grimaced briefly as his gaze drifted to the sky—part in fear that a bolt of lightning was on its way to end Owen's life for such disrespectful thoughts, part in a sheepish shrug. "Can't blame me though, can ya?" he spoke to the clouds with a chuckle.

In all honesty, however, Owen felt very much like one of the herd who had been allowed to drift away. And for the first time ever, he wondered if that was how his own herd felt when he let them roam free for long stretches of time. He sighed and flexed his right hand. Or, at least, tried to. The cold air had stiffened it even further. A brisk wind whirled around him, flinging water from the branches of the ash trees overhead, turning his mind once again to things above. Of course, he still believed in God, in His power, and in His goodness. Owen swallowed. Perhaps the goodness part was a bit of a stretch at the moment, if he were honest. The goodness bit had been vexing him most. If God was so good, why was Owen in the predicament in which he currently found himself?

"Good dog. Time now." Stout obeyed, slowing his pace. His open mouth, with the corners pulled back, made it look like he was smiling. "Good. Walk up." Stout slowed further and approached the three sheep taking refuge behind a gorse bush, then coaxed them into the larger fold of sheep. In fact, Owen usually let them roam more freely than this, but given recent events, he worried every second they were out of his sight. He wondered if they were annoyed at his increased presence of late, or if they'd even noticed. Before long, Stout had all the remaining sheep gathered and was looking to his master in expectation.

Owen whistled a pattern. "Come by." Stout rounded the herd clockwise. When he reached the back of the group, Owen added, "Now home."

Stout barked once and set to work. wrangling the herd home to the field Owen most commonly used as a pen when the sheep weren't allowed to roam freely. As they trudged over the hills, Owen's thoughts returned to matters of faith. He allowed his mind to mull over the last two messages Father Cunningham had given and tried to imagine the scenarios surrounding the battles he'd spoken about, but it all felt muddled now. Owen couldn't remember who fought at Jericho or why Gideon was so afraid. All he could recall with clarity was the idea that God's battle plans often made no sense. Before now, that idea had comforted him, but now he found it deeply unsettling.

He jogged ahead of Stout and the herd to open the rustic wooden gate blocking the entrance to the field. Stout deftly ushered the herd inside and looked expectantly at his master. Stout's eyes were bright with pride and excitement, and his tongue lolled off to one side, tail wagging. "*Sin é.*"

Stout barked and ran to Owen's side, rubbing against his leg. "Good boy," Owen said, scratching Stout's head. "Good dog." Stout grunted once, then turned and began trotting toward the barn and home.

21

Relief washed over Owen as the final hymn ended and the priest offered his departing blessing to the congregation. All of yesterday afternoon and evening, after bringing the herd in, he couldn't stop mulling over God's goodness, struggling to reconcile it with his current circumstances. He was anxious to come to church this morning and hear a fresh word, and to connect with the Almighty alongside others. However, the longer the service went on, the more his chest tightened and his gut twisted. The potent incense that usually brought him comfort had, instead, weighed him down and caused his head to swim with its pungent aroma. Every song had been about God's grace and provision. But rather than bolster his faith, he found they only fed his doubts. He hurried down the aisle and burst into the fresh, brisk air, taking it in gulps.

Somehow Aileen had beat him outside and was already setting up the picnic lunch. The unseasonably calm weather allowed them to take their cold lunch out of doors rather than hurrying home after service. Several other families were following suit, including John and Bridie, who had spread their plaid out near Aileen's.

As he approached, Aileen gestured to where she wanted him to sit. Lowering himself to the ground, he greeted the Sheridans again. Saoirse handed him a basket of sandwiches from her place on his right. Owen took two and passed the basket to his sister on the other side of him, who was reaching across and handing Saoirse a flask of tea. He had just picked up a triangle of sandwich when Bridie stopped him.

"Eh, shall we ask the Lord's blessing on the food?" she asked.

Heat crept up Owen's cheeks, and he set the food back down on the blanket. "Of course."

Bridie took hold of John's hand and reached for Saoirse's. Aileen took John's other hand and grabbed Owen's left one. He reached for Saoirse. She smiled shyly and slipped her smaller hand into his. Equal parts mesmerized by the feel of her skin and frustrated he couldn't wrap his fingers fully around hers, he forced himself to focus on the prayer of thanks and blessings John was offering.

When the prayer ended, Saoirse squeezed Owen's hand gently and slowly slid hers back to her side. The group tucked into their simple but delicious meal. The food was tasty and satisfying, and the company delightful. However, Owen kept looking over his shoulder. It was as though the stones of the church walls were beckoning him. Despite his discomfort and doubts during the service, he couldn't help feeling there was some unfinished business that awaited him inside the house of worship. Anytime he looked away from it, he could feel its pull on his back in that uneasy feeling of being watched. When the group had finished eating, Bridie passed around a small tin of biscuits. Owen politely declined, stood, and excused himself.

"Everything alright?" John asked.

Owen nodded. "Aye. Just need to stretch my legs."

John bobbed his head in understanding, and Owen headed away from the group. He feigned as though he was going to go for a walk, but when he was certain no one was watching, he slipped back inside the church. The air was cool and damp, and it was so quiet that his breathing seemed to echo among the stone walls. Owen stood in the center of the aisle at the entrance and let his gaze trace the room. The interior was dim compared to outside, but soft light flowed in from the tall windows lining the length of the sanctuary. The glow of candles at the prayer stations at the front and back of the room added a warm radiance. The air was scented with damp, turf, and the faintest hint of incense.

At the end of the aisle stood a large table that usually displayed the elements for communion, long since put away by the priest after service. In the center of the table, on a heavy stand, stood a massive Bible splayed open, with a red satin ribbon draped down the middle. With slow and reverent steps, Owen made his way to the book. It was opened to Psalm 23. Owen skimmed the text and then divided the pages on the left side roughly in half and flipped them over. He had to turn a few more pages, but eventually landed on the Old Testament book of Joshua. Skimming once again, he stopped when he finally found the section he was looking for—the battle of Jericho.

According to what he read now, the battle had occurred because God was leading His people to take possession of land He had promised them long, long before. And when they arrived at the city of Jericho, it was highly fortified. The battle—if one could call it that—consisted of Israelite soldiers and priests marching around the city once a day for six days, in total silence. On the seventh day, they marched around it seven times. On the seventh lap, when the priests blew their trumpets and the soldiers shouted, the walls around the city fell down. Then the army invaded the city and killed everyone.

Owen shook his head. It made no sense. How could marching and shouting cause massive walls to fall down? His thoughts drifted to the stone walls slicing through the countryside all over Ireland. Many had been established thousands of years earlier, withstanding gales, storms, and all manner of other torrents. How could those stone walls last through centuries, but massive city walls fell with only shouts?

But he realized he'd gotten some of the things Father Cunningham had read mixed up. Jericho wasn't the story he really wanted to look at. He flipped a few more pages and landed in the book of Judges. He ran his finger down the columns of text until he found the verses that spoke of how the people of Midian had overtaken Israel and were oppressing them. One verse practically jumped off the page and bit Owen on the nose. It read, "And they encamped against them, and destroyed the increase of the earth till thou come unto Gaza, and left no sustenance for Israel, neither sheep, nor ox, nor ass."

Owen's jaw tensed. That was exactly what Haggerty had done to them, just on a smaller scale. His chest burned as he continued to read about how a man named Gideon was tasked with defeating the enemy army. When he read how Gideon begged God for clarification because he was the weakest member of the weakest family in all of Israel, Owen blinked, trying to clear the burning that sprang up behind his eyes. He'd never felt so weak before, and it seemed more and more of his own strength was being stripped from him at every turn. Just like God had dwindled Gideon's army down to ten thousand from over twenty thousand and, eventually, to just three hundred, Owen's resources had been stripped down to the bare minimum—including having a novice weave the expertly crafted tweed he'd been contracted to create. And every time Gideon asked God if He was sure, or mentioned how scared he was, God's reply was, "I will be with you."

Owen couldn't hold back the sarcastic laugh when the enemy armies began fighting each other out of confusion. He envisioned himself, Saoirse, and Aileen sneaking up on Haggerty's camp with lanterns, jugs, and tin whistles. The notion was so utterly ridiculous, the heat of embarrassment flooded his face just thinking about doing such a thing.

"Ah, there ya are."

Owen spun around to see John walking up the aisle of the church. "We thought the banshees had absconded with ya," he said with a laugh and a wink.

Owen snorted. "That might've been more desirable."

A shadow of concern swept across John's face before his good-natured grin returned. "Things goin' that well, are they?"

Owen huffed a breath and shook his head. "'Tis been a season, alright."

John stepped up next to him and stared down at the yellowed pages. Nodding, he inhaled slowly and let the air slip from his lips. "Ye've had a mite few difficulties of late, to be sure." He gestured to the Bible. "Gideon, eh?"

"Aye." Owen turned and leaned against the table, crossing his arms over his chest. "I've not been able to stop thinkin' about that story since Father Cunningham spoke of it last week."

John matched Owen's stance. "Well, that's not surprisin'."

Owen's brows pulled together. "Why d'ya say that?"

"Well." John shrugged. "Ye're basically livin' his same life."

Owen looked at John from the corner of his eye. Had the auld man's mind started slipping already? "Last I checked, the Almighty hasn't asked me to lead an army into battle to save His people."

John's eyes rolled playfully. "It's a metaphor, lad."

Metaphor? Apparently, the man's faculties were fully intact. Owen thought for a moment. There were a few similarities, he supposed. But beyond God's plan for both men not making a lick of sense, Owen couldn't see much else they had in common.

"Lookit," John said, pushing off the table to face Owen. "Gideon was faced with an impossible task. In his case, it was defeating a massive army with limited resources and no soldiering background. For you, it's gettin' the weaving done on time and keepin' yer farm up and goin'."

Owen's brows lifted, and he bobbled his head. He hadn't really thought of it that way before.

"And," John continued, "God required Gideon to do it with the bare minimum of manpower and supplies." He shrugged and laid a hand on Owen's shoulder. "He reduced the size of Gideon's army down to next to nothing. And from where I stand, He's doin' the same fer ye."

Owen's hand floated up and absently scratched at the stubble on his chin. When it was laid out like that, it really did seem like he and Gideon had somewhat parallel lives. "Well," he said after a pause, "when ya put it that way."

Both men chuckled.

"I just wish I knew my story would turn out as well as his," Owen added.

The corner of John's mouth made a clicking sound, and he nodded. "Well," he said, "I reckon that's why it's called faith."

Owen closed his eyes and shook his head. The man sure had a way with words. Owen wondered for a fleeting moment if John had ever considered joining the priesthood. Then again, Owen wished that perhaps his friend wasn't quite so intuitive. His remark about faith had hit Owen like a splash of cold water on a winter's day. No warm, fuzzy platitude there. Only cold, hard reality. "Well," he said slowly, playful sarcasm lacing his voice, "don't sugarcoat it fer me, John. Give it to me straight."

John guffawed and slapped his hand on Owen's back. "Don't blame me fer that one, boyo. That one's all Him." His gaze flashed upward to the ceiling.

They walked quietly toward the exit for a moment and then John broke the silence. "Och! I almost fergot!" He pressed his hand to his own forehead. "The whole reason Bridie sent me in here was to invite you, Aileen, and Saoirse to our *Máirt na hInide* celebration next Tuesday."

"Well, that's very kind of ye. Go raibh míle maith agaibh!" Owen smiled and shook his friend's hand. "Is it really Lententide already?"

John's head bobbed. "Indeed, it is." He turned to look at

Owen, a twinkle in his eyes. "And ya know Bridie won't let it start without a grand to-do. I do hope ye'll come."

Inside Owen, a war raged. While he wanted nothing more than to celebrate with his friends and family, they were still dreadfully behind on the weaving, and he hated leaving his farm unattended and so vulnerable after all that had transpired.

"Owen." John's voice interrupted Owen's reverie. He pinned a look on Owen not unlike his father used to do. "Faith, lad. Faith."

Could the man read his mind? Or was Owen just that bad at hiding his thoughts? Either way, Owen still couldn't shake the sense of dread swimming in his gut. "We'll try," he said at last.

When John's gaze intensified, Owen held up his hands as if in surrender. "I promise," he said, laughing. "We'll try. We really will."

22

Saoirse hummed to herself as she worked the loom pedals and threw the shuttle back and forth. The whole process was coming much more easily to her now, though she still had to keep her focus completely on what she was doing. If she let her mind wander too much, something would go awry. Stout lay not far from her feet, the loud din of the weaving not bothersome to him in the slightest. Saoirse supposed he was used to it after years of his master's labors. Owen had left her to weave alone for an hour or so while he saw to the sheep. They were in the field next to the barn this morning, so Stout wasn't needed. Saoirse couldn't tell if the dog was grateful for the day of rest or pouting at being left behind.

Either way, she was grateful for the company. Owen's absence loomed large in the shed, and Saoirse had to force herself not to imagine him behind her, singing, the warmth of his body pressed up against her back.

"Saoirse!"

Saoirse jolted, stopping the loom, heat flashing to her cheeks. "What, I didn't do anything."

Aileen burst into the small shed, breathless. Confound

that woman and how she always managed to scare the tar out of Saoirse at the most inopportune moments. "Guess what, guess what?" Aileen said between huffs, oblivious to Saoirse's pounding heart. "We're goin'!" she announced.

Saoirse knew exactly what she was talking about. The last day and a half, Aileen had done nothing but pester Owen about attending the Máirt na hInide celebration at the Sheridans'. Saoirse had tried to stay out of the way, though secretly she was dying to go as well. Aileen and Owen's bickering had reminded Saoirse of her younger brother and sister who used to argue over just about anything. One could say the sky was blue, and the other would find a reason to disagree. It used to drive Saoirse crazy, but what she wouldn't give to hear them nagging one another now. Seemingly unable to escape the memories of her family that had been assaulting her more and more of late, she hoped the party would be a very welcome distraction. Three times already she'd almost told Owen everything as they worked together in the weaving shed and as she helped him muck out the stables.

"Did ya hear what I said?" Aileen closed the distance and shook Saoirse's shoulders. "I said we're goin' to Bridie and John's tonight!"

Saoirse pasted on a smile. "Buíocihas le Dia," she said, laughing.

"Thanks be to God, indeed," Aileen replied. "It's about time that man came to his senses."

Saoirse shrugged. "Well, I can understand why he wouldn't want to go. There's so much to be done here." She made one final pass of the shuttle before cutting the thread and tying it off. "We've made good progress on the tweed, but there's loads more to weave."

Aileen scoffed and flapped a hand. "Ye can make up a few hours some other time. Pancake Tuesday comes only once a year, and I'm not goin' to start my Lenten fast without a proper celebration first."

Saoirse wondered if Aileen knew how insensitive she came across sometimes. But she also knew where her friend was coming from. Máirt na hInide was a time to indulge but also a time to be responsible—to use up all the forbidden items before Lent, so as not to let them go to waste.

"Don't just stand there." Aileen grabbed Saoirse by the elbow. "We've got to get ready."

Back in the house, Saoirse hadn't much to do to prepare. She cleaned her face and hands and removed her apron, then she twisted her ringlets up in a simple style, with strands falling around her face and neck.

Aileen, on the other hand, spent an inordinate amount of time weaving her hair in an intricate pattern of plaits circling her head. She then donned a lovely dress Saoirse had never seen before. Given their financial state—much like everyone else in the county—she suspected Aileen reserved it for any and all special occasions.

"You look absolutely lovely," Saoirse said when Aileen joined her in the living room.

"Aw, t'anks," she said, waving a dismissive hand, though her smile belied her delight at the compliment.

Suddenly, doubt crept up Saoirse's spine and her face flushed. "Will this suffice?" she asked, standing and shaking out her skirts. Not that it mattered if it wouldn't. It was all she had.

Aileen smiled and crossed the room to join Saoirse at the hearth. "Ah, sure, ye're grand." Aileen patted her own hair self-consciously. "I just felt like . . . makin' tonight special."

Saoirse nodded, but something about the way Aileen's cheeks held a hint of pink and her eyes twinkled with anticipation made Saoirse think perhaps Aileen was holding something back.

You're in good company then. The errant thought shocked Saoirse, and she shuffled to the kitchen to put the kettle on to distract herself from blurting out the secret that was hovering ever closer to the surface of late.

Just then, Owen walked in. Stout stood from his spot by the hearth, stretched, and trotted over to greet his master. "Hello, auld boy." Owen bent to scratch the dog behind his ears. When he straightened, his gaze fell on his sister. "Well, aren't we the pretty picture?"

"Why, thank you, good sir," Aileen said, then she dipped into a sarcastic curtsy.

Owen scoffed. "I mean it. Ya look nice, Aileen." He turned and held on to the doorframe as he worked to pull his feet from his wellies. "I just need to clean up and we can head down," he said, his voice muffled against the wall. When he turned back, his eyes met Saoirse's and widened for a split second, then he blinked rapidly.

Saoirse warmed under his gaze, as hers dipped to the floor.

"Doesn't Saoirse look nice too?" Aileen asked, a knowing tone in her voice.

Saoirse turned wide eyes toward Aileen. If she was closer, she'd have swatted her friend on the arm.

Owen cleared his throat, his gaze dropping to the floor. "I, uh . . . that is . . . I hadn't noticed." He glanced back up at Saoirse. "But, aye—ahem—she does."

He scurried to the wardrobe on the far wall, his head down, and rummaged through its contents. Then he snatched some clothes from a drawer and hurried down the hall. "I won't be a minute," he mumbled.

Aileen snickered as she shuffled toward the front door. "I'll go get the wagon ready. Saoirse, will you see to the fire?"

Saoirse's heart thudded in her chest as all the heat drained from her face. "I, uh . . . I'll get the horse and wagon."

Aileen floated a strange look at her. "It's no bother. I'm already halfway out the door."

Saoirse stared into the flames for a moment before blinking and turning her attention back to Aileen. She moved in her direction. "No, no. We can't risk you snagging your dress or mussing your hair."

Aileen started to argue, but then stopped and pursed her lips. Twice she opened her mouth as if to speak, and then snapped it shut. Finally she said, "That's very kind of ye. T'anks."

Saoirse smiled. "O'course." Then she swept through the door. As she trudged up the hill to the barn, she wondered if the thought had also crossed Aileen's mind that she had just as much chance at sullying her clothing while tending the fire as she did hitching the horse to the wagon. Heaving the heavy barn door open, she forced herself to shake the thoughts aside. Tonight was not the night to wallow in guilt and self-pity. She needed some fun, and to hear Aileen tell of it, the Sheridans' party promised to be great *craic*.

Rolling the wagon from its stall into the center of the barn was easy enough. But the McCreadys' horse, Lir, had other ideas. Named after the king of old, Lir seemed to think he was sired in the same line as the sovereign and conducted himself as such. Meaning, he didn't interact kindly with anyone he deemed below his station, and it had become clear early on in her time with the McCreadys that Lir definitely held himself in higher esteem than Saoirse. He would mind Owen, and even Aileen most of the time, but with Saoirse, he turned as stubborn as a mule. She'd have much rather hitched up Fadó, but he was too old to pull the wagon with three passengers so soon after the last journey.

As Saoirse tried to lead him out of the stall to hitch him up to the wagon, Lir dug his hind hooves into the ground and pulled in the opposite direction. She crooned, she commanded, she used all the same phrases she'd heard Owen say, but to no avail.

"What have I ever done to ya, eh, boy?" Saoirse asked through gritted teeth as she tugged the reins.

He tossed his head, pulling the reins from her hands, and whinnied.

"Don't ya wanna go down into the glen?" she asked.

He stamped his foot. She took the leads again, tugged gently, and clicked three times.

"C'mon, boy. Let's go." She tugged harder, and once again he leaned in the opposite direction. She pulled harder still, and he did the same until she was leaning with almost her full body weight, at which point he relaxed, causing her to fall to the ground. His whinny sounded like laughter.

Saoirse groaned and puffed a stray strand of hair from her face. "I like Stout better than you," she mumbled under her breath. A low grunt rumbled in Lir's chest as if to say that the feeling was mutual. When Saoirse finally managed to get to her feet, frustration overwhelmed her. She gritted her teeth, her face screwing up tight. If she didn't let out her annoyance, she feared she might burst. She didn't want to yell and risk spooking the cantankerous beast, so instead she hauled off and kicked the wall of the stall.

"Easy there, lass. My dad built this barn," Owen said, laughter bouncing his words.

Saoirse's head fell back, and she sighed. Of course he would walk in right then. "Sorry. It's just . . ."

"Lir, are ya bein' difficult?" Owen stepped up and stroked the horse's nose. Lir snorted. Owen turned back to Saoirse, his gaze on her foot, which she refused to lift up to rub. What had she been thinking, kicking a wooden wall? "*An bhfuil tú ceart go leoir?*"

Saoirse offered a tight-lipped smile. "I'm fine."

"Let's go," Owen said to Lir, then he gave the slightest tug on the reins. Lir sauntered from his stall and dutifully took his place in front of the wagon. Saoirse couldn't be sure, but she was almost certain the horse had given her a side-eyed glare as he walked past. If horses could sneer, she had no doubt he would have.

Saoirse joined Owen at the front of the wagon, and the pair worked together to hitch Lir up. Owen grabbed the heavy yoke from a sturdy peg on the wall and slid it over the horse's head. As he buckled the leather straps on one side, Saoirse worked to do the same on the other.

"Did you help him?" Saoirse asked as she tossed a leather strap over Lir's rump.

"Help who?" Owen asked without looking up from checking Lir's hooves.

"Your dad," she replied. "To build the barn."

Owen straightened, and a shadow darkened behind his

eyes. "Not as much as I should have." He stared off into the distance for a long moment.

Unsure how to reply, Saoirse finished her tasks and double-checked that all the fastenings were secure.

"He died here." Owen's voice was so low that Saoirse almost missed it.

She met his gaze, and the sorrow swimming in his eyes made her ache. "I'm so sorry." She rounded Lir and stood next to Owen.

He shrugged a single shoulder. "I wasn't here that day." He sniffled and looked away. "And he died."

Instinctively, Saoirse laid her hand on his arm. "How awful." She took a half step closer. "But it wasn't your fault."

"No," he ground out through clenched teeth, "it was O'Malley's fault. But if I had been here, it might not have happened. So, in that way, I am to blame."

Saoirse's heart clenched, and she fought the urge to wrap her arms around him to try to comfort him. He didn't readily offer the details surrounding his father's death, and Saoirse wasn't sure she should ask. She hadn't offered more details about her own family's fate when she first spoke of it. And she still hadn't been able to bring herself to do so. He'd offered this much already. If he was ready to share more, he would have. She opted, instead, to say, "You don't know that it would've turned out any differently if you had been here." She paused and took a deep breath. "And if things still happened the same way, you'd have to carry that memory around with you, which, I imagine, would be a much heavier weight."

She imagined witnessing a tragedy and having no control over it would be an even heavier burden to bear. But the weight of guilt was heavy enough—a burden that very nearly suffocated her on a regular basis. She assumed Owen's burden was the same.

"It's no matter," Owen said, snapping Saoirse from her thoughts. "What's done is done." He took the reins and led Lir outside before sliding the large door closed.

Just then, Aileen rounded the corner, smiling a mile wide. Saoirse couldn't help but smile in return, trying to muster the hope that this evening held as much promise as Aileen seemed to think it would.

Owen stood next to the wagon step and held his hand out to Saoirse. "Shall we?"

23

As they rolled along the path toward the village, Saoirse's thoughts kept drifting back to what Owen had said about his dad. She ached for the burden he carried, but for all the empathy she felt for him, Saoirse couldn't help the realization that he was bearing a load similar to that of her own—the unwieldy burden of responsibility for the death of someone he loved.

Of course, their situations weren't exactly the same. Saoirse shouldered far more direct blame than Owen ever would, but a tiny ember of hopefulness flickered deep in her soul that if he ever learned the truth about why she left Westmeath, rather than shun her, he may just relate to all she'd been through.

The wagon hit a rut, and Owen and Saoirse bumped into each other. He looked at her and offered a small smile. She responded with a grin of her own as her eyes searched his for a brief moment before turning away again. For the first time since that fateful day, she pulled in a free, deep breath that filled her lungs to their fullest. She smiled as she released it and let her gaze drift to the western horizon. The sun had set the sky ablaze in a wash of brilliant oranges, pinks, and purples, as though nature herself shared in Saoirse's newfound hope.

The wagon turned off the main road and onto the path that would lead them into the heart of the glen. The glow of a bonfire could already be seen, and laughter carried on the air as they approached.

When the wagon came to a stop, Aileen hopped down and lifted a basket of eggs and flour from its bed. Saoirse hadn't even noticed her put them in there. Owen alighted next and extended his good hand up to Saoirse. She slid her fingers into his gentle grasp and forced her attention onto the step rather than let herself get lost in his bright blue eyes, which had been set aglow by the sunset behind her.

As they approached the house, Bridie came out to greet them. "Oh, I'm so glad ye came!" She bussed Aileen's cheeks and took the basket from her before turning her attention to Owen and Saoirse.

"It's not like I had much of a choice," Owen said, laughing.

Aileen shrugged, a look of innocence plastered on her face. Saoirse noticed her friend scanning the area as though searching for someone. Aileen finally turned back to Bridie. "So," she said, sidling up even closer to the woman. "Who all is here so far?"

Bridie looked over her shoulder, her lips twisted up as she thought. "The usual *plód* so far."

Aileen's shoulders fell ever so slightly, and she nodded.

Bridie looked to Owen, questioning, but he only shrugged, clearly as confused by the conversation as the rest of them.

"I hope yas are hungry," Bridie said as she ushered them all into the house.

The small bungalow was chock-a-block with a mass of people, the air in the cozy space thick and damp. The group passed through the house and into the back garden where the bonfire roared. Several other smaller fires were scattered around for people to cook on. In the distance, cheers rang out and the church bells clanged.

"Wha's that for?" Aileen asked.

"Tommy O'Hanlon and Deirdre O'Friel just got married," Bridie called over her shoulder.

Saoirse grinned and Owen's head spun in the direction of the celebratory sounds. "Wow, they didn't waste any time, did they? And so young!"

Bridie stopped next to a fire where John sat with several pans. She set down the basket from Aileen, then picked up a bowl and began mixing its contents. "Well," she said with a shrug, "I s'pose when ya know, ya know. Besides, with weddings banned during Lent, I'd wager they just wanted to get on with it rather than havin' to wait another forty days or more."

Owen gestured for Saoirse and Aileen to each sit on one of the stumps that had been placed around the firepit before he lowered himself onto the one between them.

"Aileen, c'mon up here," Bridie said before Aileen could sit, a small scoop in the older woman's hand. "You get the first flip."

Aileen's mouth fell open, and she shook her head. Saoirse beamed at the honor being offered to her friend. Aileen looked to each person in the group before turning her attention back to Bridie. "I couldn't. It's not my place."

John's lips flapped as he blew out a puff of air. "Non-sense."

Bridie elbowed her husband's arm playfully. "Seein's how we don't have an oldest daughter to fulfill the tradition, we want you to do the honors."

Saoirse pressed a hand to her chest, an ache of awe and sadness mixing beneath her touch. Sadness as she missed her own mother so terribly, and awe at the beautiful scene unfolding before her.

Aileen looked to Owen, mouth still agape, eyes wide.

"G'on then," Owen said, swinging his hand in a small arc toward Bridie and the pan she held in her hand.

With slow, marked steps, Aileen brushed her hands down the folds of her skirt and did as Bridie bade.

"Ya know the tradition, aye?" John asked.

Aileen licked her lips and nodded. "Aye." Her voice sounded small—a little scared, even. "It's never gone well for me."

Owen laughed. "Well, that's the truth. Last year was the worst. I never thought we'd scrape the batter off the ceilin'." His shoulders bounced with intensified laughter. Clearly he was reliving the memory.

"Och!" Aileen swung her hand to swat Owen's shoulder, but he leaned out of the way.

"Well, who knows," Bridie said, holding the batter and cup out to Aileen. "'Tis a new day. A new year."

Tentatively, Aileen took the cup from their host and scooped it into the batter. She looked slowly from Saoirse to Owen and then to the pan, which John now held out to her. Taking it from him, she poured the batter in and rolled the pan around to spread the batter in a thin layer.

Aileen gave one last look to the group. Saoirse smiled and nodded in encouragement. Finally, Aileen held the pan out over the fire, watching intently for the exact right moment to flip it.

"Easy now," Owen said. "Remember, there's no extra points for height." His shoulders started bouncing again, and he covered his mouth with his hand.

Saoirse laughed and rolled her eyes. "*Tsk!* You're terrible." She waited for Owen to catch her eye, hoping he could see the playful glint in them. "G'on, Aileen. You can do it! It's your year now. I can feel it."

"Hear, hear!" Bridie and John cheered in unison.

Aileen jiggled the pan, then jostled it forward and back a few times. Finally, she stuck the tip of her tongue out of her mouth in concentration and stilled. Then, suddenly, she popped the pan upward. The pancake flung up, flipping twice in the air before landing back in the pan, perfectly flat. Her mouth popped open again in surprise. "I did it!"

John clapped, and Bridie wrapped an arm around Aileen's shoulders.

"Well done, Aileen," Saoirse called, joining John in the applause.

"Well, wonders never cease," Owen said, a look of sheer surprise on his face.

"Owen Sean McCready, you just stop that right now." Aileen's words were scolding, but her voice was laced with delight.

"I'm only messin'," he said, joining the crowd standing around Aileen. "So," he continued, "who's the lucky lad?"

Bridie patted the air. "Now, now, the superstition only

says she'll be lucky in love and likely wed before the year is over. It says nothin' about who she'll marry."

Aileen still stared at the pan in disbelief, her mouth bobbing open and closed. "I still can't believe I did it after all these years! Mine always land in a crumbled-up heap."

"If they land in the pan at all," Owen whispered in Saoirse's ear. She clapped a hand over her mouth to stop her giggle.

John thrust a plate at Aileen. "Well, yas better eat it afore it gets cold and all the luck runs out of it." Aileen turned the pan over and plopped her prized pancake onto the plate. She stepped over to a makeshift table housing butter, sugar, and sliced lemon so she could doctor her cake to her liking before tucking in.

"Right, Saoirse, your turn." John waggled the pan in her direction.

Saoirse waved her hands in front of her. "Oh, I'm grand. No thanks." She couldn't fully explain the panic that had seized her chest in that moment. As the eldest daughter of her family, she'd flipped the first pancake of Máirt na hInide plenty of times. And she wasn't sure she even believed the old wives' tale that if the pancake landed unruffled in the pan, she would marry within the year. But she wasn't sure she didn't believe it either. And for some reason, the thought of flipping errantly in front of Owen made her want to run and hide.

"Ah, g'on, g'on," Bridie and John were both saying.

"Sure, what d'ya have to lose?" Aileen asked around a mouthful of pancake.

Her gaze flitted to Owen, who was watching her, waiting for her response. At length, the corner of Saoirse's mouth pulled up, and she shrugged matter-of-factly. "The tradition only works for the first pancake of the night."

John lifted a finger, ready to protest, but he stopped, looked to Bridie, and dropped his hand. "Oh muise, she's right."

Bridie sighed. "Oh well."

Saoirse nodded, just in case they still needed convincing. Though John looked so disappointed, she almost caved and took the pan from his hands.

Bridie also looked disappointed for a wee second before her telltale joy returned. "But just because ya don't flip 'em doesn't mean ya can't eat 'em."

"Allow me." Owen stepped over and scooped a cup of batter. When he took the pan from John, it almost fell from his hand. He glanced at Saoirse, frustration in his eyes. But before she could jump up to his rescue, a loud cheer rose from the front of the house.

"Is that the pancake race?" Owen asked, eyes alight like a schoolboy at Christmas.

"I believe it is," John answered.

"Oh, I can't miss that." Owen carefully set the pan down and handed the scoop back to Bridie. "C'mon, girls." He hurried them back through the house and out the front door just in time for the start of the first race.

Four women were lined up across the street, each with a pan in hand.

"Right," Father Cunningham was saying. "I want a good, clean race, ladies. Remember, you must cross the street, touch the lintel post of the house, and cross back over to this side of the street all while flipping your pancakes."

The crowd cheered.

208

"If you drop your pancake, ye're out," the priest continued. "If ya deliberately cause an opponent to drop her pan or cake, ye're out."

The crowd booed.

"The first one back across the line wins!"

More cheers.

"What about the flips?" someone asked.

"Oh, yes." Father Cunningham nodded. "There will also be a prize for the lady who crosses the finish line with the most successful flips of her pancake!" The crowd cheered again, and the priest had to wait for them to settle back down.

"Are we ready?" he asked the contestants. They all nodded and exchanged good-natured threats of defeat to one another. Father Cunningham rubbed his hands together. "Right, then. Ready. Steady. Go!"

The ladies took off, pancakes flying in the air. One woman's landed on the ground after the first flip, much to the delight of the onlookers. A second tripped and dropped her pan just after touching the doorframe. The final two were neck and neck until the very end, when the older one just barely reached the finish line before the younger one.

Joyous chaos erupted as the winners were congratulated and the number of flips were tallied. Father Cunningham conferred with a tall, slender gentleman. Saoirse squinted through the dusk light and eventually recognized him as the schoolteacher she'd seen in the village the other day. At last, they announced that Nora Boyle had been declared the winner of both the race and the flips. She was presented with her prizes—a pint of stout and an extra stack of pancakes. She downed the stout in one go before scurrying over and feeding the cakes to a gaggle of children sitting under a nearby tree.

"Alright," the schoolteacher called out, "who's next?"

Next to Saoirse, Aileen's hand flew up into the air. "Me! Me and Saoirse'll go!"

24

Saoirse looked at Aileen, eyes wide. "What are you doing?" she hissed. "I don't want to do that."

Aileen gripped her friend's arms, eyes pleading. "Ah, please?" She glanced over her shoulder to the teacher, then turned back to Saoirse. "For me?"

Saoirse followed suit and looked to the tall man who was trying to wrangle two more contestants for the race, then back to Aileen. The imploring on her face was almost more than Saoirse could bear. She presumed looking foolish in a silly pancake race was the least she could do for the friend who'd taken her in when she had no place to go. Sighing, she rolled her eyes. "Fine."

Aileen squealed and clapped her hands, then grabbed Saoirse by the elbow and pulled her to the start line. They were both given a pan with a cold pancake already in it. The rules were repeated and then the race began. With intense focus fixed on her pan, Saoirse flipped the cake over and over, all while taking small, swift steps to avoid any jarring movements that might cause her to drop either the pan or the cake. She and Aileen reached the doorframe at the same time, touched it, and turned back. From the corner of her eye, she watched Aileen—a wide grin lighting her face—as she scurried toward the finish line. Saoirse slowed her steps a tad, allowing her friend to finish first. Raucous cheers erupted from the onlookers, and the teacher congratulated the victor, then handed her a stout as her prize. Saoirse was declared to have had the most successful flips and was thus bestowed with the honor of a stack of fresh pancakes. After one more round of racing, everyone settled down in groups to eat. Saoirse couldn't remember the last time she'd been so full. The whole meal was utterly delicious, with pancakes, brown bread, steamed puddings, and more. Hearty conversation accompanied the meal, and Saoirse enjoyed sitting back and watching Owen in his element, chatting with the neighbors he all too rarely got to spend time with.

As the meal began to wind down, the haunting whine of uillean pipes filled the air. After a few notes of adjustment, the piper jumped right in to a lively jig tune. Owen leaned forward, squinting. "Well, as I live and breathe."

Saoirse matched his posture, straining through the darkness to see what Owen saw.

"That's auld Charlie MacSweeney," Owen said.

Saoirse's brows soared. "*An Píobaire Mór?*"

Owen nodded. "The world champion Big Piper himself."

The crowd listened to the song, toes tapping, relishing the opportunity to hear someone of MacSweeney's caliber play. Eventually, no longer able to contain himself, an older gentleman stood up and shimmied onto the makeshift dance floor the Sheridans had set up and began dancing. Song after song, man, woman, and child took turns showcasing their talents in the jig, *céilí*, and reel. There was a lull in the action when Charlie took a break for a cup of tea, but when he returned, he had a broom in his hand.

"Who'll give us a *damhsa bruscar*?" Charlie held the broom up to the delight of the crowd. But no one volunteered.

Suddenly someone shouted, "Owen McCready, g'on up and give us a dance!" The rest of the onlookers erupted in applause, and calls went up all around for Owen to dance. Saoirse turned to him, delight swelling in her chest. Owen waved off the requests, but when his eyes met Saoirse's, she nodded at him. "G'on," she said. "Please?"

He studied her for a moment and finally relented. As he approached the dance floor, more musicians joined Charlie. Now, in addition to the pipes, there was a concertina, a fiddle, and a tin whistle.

Owen took his place on the dance floor and laid the broom flat on the ground, then stood behind it. After another quick tune-up, the band began an upbeat song. Owen's toes tapped for a bar or two and then he set off dancing. He tapped out rhythms with his feet and danced in a square all around the broom. Then he crossed his right leg over the handle and back, then his left at half tempo. After a few beats he repeated the steps at double time, every now and then using a stomp or double-footed jump to accentuate the downbeat. After dancing around the broom one more time, he bent and picked it up. Whistles went up from the crowd.

"G'on now."

"Get it, Owen!"

He kicked one leg up and passed the handle of the broom under it, letting it land between the thumb and forefinger of his right hand rather than grasping it. Then repeated it in reverse. After four passes, he made the sign of the cross, eliciting guffaws from the crowd, and repeated the kick steps again in double time.

Saoirse watched, a hand pressed against her chest. She remembered thinking he must be a good dancer, given the coordination needed to run the loom, but she had no idea he would be this good. She couldn't help the wide smile that spread across her face as he finished the dance with a flourish, broom under one foot, both hands raised in victory. The crowd went wild.

Saoirse turned to Aileen. "I had no idea."

Aileen chuckled. "Oh, aye, weavers always make the best dancers."

When the applause had died down and Owen returned to his seat, breaths coming in heavy puffs, John took center stage. "Well, I don' think anyone's gonna top that, aye?"

"No!"

"Níl!"

"Not a chance!"

John nodded and patted the air to quiet the crowd again. "Right. Let's get everyone out here, then. Four tops, let's go!"

Saoirse wondered how odd this whole ritual must seem to an outsider. Clearly none were present, though, because the group dutifully divided up into groups of eight and formed squares with two people on each side. Owen stood, caught Saoirse's eye, and inclined his head to the dance floor. Next to him, John and Bridie beckoned her and Aileen to join them. Saoirse nodded and stood, taking her place next to Owen. John and Bridie took their place at the top of the square, with Owen and Saoirse to their left. The couple on the left of them were another local farmer and his wife. Across from Saoirse, Aileen stood alone.

It was difficult to tell by the firelight, but Saoirse was certain tears pooled in Aileen's eyes. She turned to go, but John caught her elbow. He craned his neck and scanned the crowd. His eyes landed on someone, and his face brightened. "Hugh," he called, waving his hand. "Goitse!"

A moment later, the schoolteacher jogged up and took the place next to Aileen, who looked like she'd just seen a ghost. Saoirse and Bridie stole a glance at one another, grins playing on both of their lips. Did John know about her interest in Hugh, or was it just happenstance? Just as Hugh got settled in his place, the musicians began playing the "High Cauled Cap," one of Saoirse's favorite dances. But it had been ages since she'd been to a céilí and done set dances, so she was disappointed when she missed a few steps. Whenever she'd get confused, Owen's hand would land on the small of her back and gently guide her where she was supposed to be.

After several more set dances, the band shifted to play partner dance songs. Bridie and John were off without a second thought, as were the farmer and his wife. Hugh bowed slightly at the waist, offering his hand to Aileen, who giggled, curtsied, and accepted his offer. Saoirse turned to go sit down, but ended up facing Owen, who opened his arms to her.

"May I have this dance?" he asked.

Saoirse paused, heat flushing her face—partly from the boisterous dancing but more so from the idea of being embraced by him. Finally, she nodded and slid her hand into his and placed her other one on his shoulder. He wrapped his free hand around her waist, and they set off in a quick, two-hand polka.

Owen held Saoirse close as they whirled around the dance floor, grateful that his right hand was on her waist and not trying to hold her hand. It had been ages since he'd done any dancing, and if he was honest with himself, he'd missed it. He'd never give Aileen the satisfaction, but while taking a spin on the dance floor with Saoirse in his arms, he was overcome with gratitude that they'd chosen to come tonight. He'd gotten a glimpse of Saoirse during his brush dance, and the delight that shone in her eyes had swelled his chest with pride, and he was absolutely sure he would do whatever he needed to do to put that look on her face over and over again.

After another polka, then a reel, the tempo slowed to a gentle waltz. Several couples left the floor to rest a spell, but Owen gently pulled Saoirse closer, held her hand to his chest, and let their feet carry them away with the mournful tune. Almost immediately, her head lowered to rest on his chest, and his eyes drifted closed at the sensation. The light scent of lavender wafted up from her hair as she slid her arm farther up his shoulder and around his neck. His pulse quickened at her nearness, and he absently wondered if she could hear his heart thrumming against his chest. They made a couple of trips around the floor and eventually settled in the corner, swaying back and forth. Owen's cheek rested on the top of her head, and he resisted the urge to press kisses onto the ringlets tickling his nose. Instead, he rubbed his thumb back and forth over her fingers and smiled as she pulled in a deep breath, releasing it with a sigh of contentment.

When the song ended, neither one moved for a long moment—both seemingly not wanting the moment to end.

"Woohoo!" one of the musicians yelped, jolting both from their trance as another fast-tempo song began.

Saoirse lifted her head and stepped back. Even in the dim light, Owen could see the blush coloring her cheeks.

"Thanks for the dance," he said, his voice thick.

She nodded, her gaze holding his for the most deliciously long moment before fluttering to the ground. He cleared his throat. "Tea?"

"Oh, yes, please." Her shoulders relaxed as she headed for their seats.

A few minutes later, Saoirse sipped her tea and watched the couples still twirling around the dance floor. Owen took advantage of the opportunity to study her profile. More ring-lets had fallen down, framing her face in a golden halo of sorts. The gentle slope of her nose was silhouetted against the firelight, tracing down to the outline of her full lips. When they split into a wide grin, he followed her gaze. At the far end of the dance floor, Aileen and Hugh spun in a circle, both laughing heartily. Owen couldn't help the smile that slid up one corner of his mouth. It did him good to see his sister so happy—and to get his thoughts off Saoirse's lips. Drat. Now he was thinking of them again.

He gulped his tea, hoping the scalding liquid trailing down his throat would pull his thoughts to more proper topics of rumination.

"Right, folks, it's the last song," Charlie called out, "so if ya didn't dance with the lass ye've had yer eye on, it's now or never."

Disappointment flooded Owen's chest. He wasn't ready for this night to be over. And yet, it was probably good that things were wrapping up, the way his thoughts were running wild, envisioning holding Saoirse in his arms forevermore. Even still, he wasn't going to pass up the chance to hold her again tonight.

A throng of people shuffled out to the floor. Owen stood and held his hand out to Saoirse. "May I have this dance?" He chuckled and added, "Again?"

She studied his hand for a long moment. Then she stood, avoiding his gaze, and said, "I'd better help Bridie clean up." She scurried off to where their host was dunking dishes in a tub of water.

Her rebuff stole his breath, as though he'd been socked in the stomach. Had he misread things? Had he overstepped his bounds? He thought back to all the dances they'd shared, and his mind settled on the waltz. His arms tingled as he remembered the feeling of her pressing into him, laying her head on his chest. He remembered her sighs and how she'd melted into his embrace. Everything pointed to her enjoying the moment just as much as he was, but it seemed he'd somehow scared her away.

He couldn't very well stand there staring at her the rest of the song, so he returned to his seat. He scanned the mob on the floor but didn't see Aileen or Hugh. Trilling laughter caught his ear, and he turned toward the sound. His sister and the schoolteacher each sat on a stump a few seats away from him, deep in discussion, clearly very amused with their conversation. Owen smiled at the scene but couldn't keep his gaze from bouncing back to Saoirse. She was drying a plate and smiling widely at Bridie, who was telling a story with wild animation. Then, as if she felt him watching her, Saoirse swung her gaze toward him. Owen quickly turned away and pretended to watch the dancing, but not before he wondered one more time what had gone wrong.

When the last few notes died out, the crowd cheered, and rounds of thanks were shouted to the Sheridans for hosting such great craic for the evening. Saoirse helped Bridie carry a stack of dishes into the house, then came back out, wiping her hands on her skirts. Owen watched as she scanned the crowd and found him, shadows darkening under her eyes. "Ready?" she asked.

He nodded, noting he suddenly felt as tired as Saoirse now looked. It had been long since anyone in his house had stayed up past midnight, and he was not looking forward to having to wake in a few short hours.

A gust of wind blew past them, and Saoirse shivered, then tossed her shawl around her shoulders and pulled it tight. Aileen and Hugh walked up, still laughing.

"Thanks for a lovely evening," Aileen said, admiration shining in her eyes.

Hugh bowed slightly at the waist again. "Likewise," he said. "The most enjoyable time I've had in a great long while."

After one more round of goodbyes, several more offers for tea, and just as many declines, Owen, Aileen, and Saoirse loaded into the wagon as the wind picked up and tiny drops began to sprinkle down upon them.

25

Rain pelted the windows and fell in muted thuds onto the thatched roof of the house. Saoirse stood at the basin, staring out the window. Or, rather, pretending to stare out the window. The rain was so strong, it distorted the view beyond the sheet of water. Behind her, Aileen stood at the stove, frying some fish for their breakfast while humming a tune from the previous night. The same tune Saoirse desperately wanted to get out of her head. The slow, mournful air that she'd danced to with Owen had haunted her all night. Her eyes drifted closed, and she swayed gently back and forth, suddenly back in his arms. She could smell the wool and leather wafting from him and hear his heart thundering in his chest. Her scalp tingled where he'd laid his head, and her lips buzzed with the desire to reach up and brush them against his.

A loud clank shook her back to reality. *You're supposed to not be thinking about that.* She turned to Aileen. "Do you need any help?"

Aileen, who seemed equally far away in a daydream of her own, blinked slowly. "I'm sorry. What was that?"

"Can I do anything to help?" Saoirse asked again.

Aileen shook her head and slid two pieces of fish onto two plates. Saoirse glanced back toward the window. "Owen already ate," Aileen said, answering Saoirse's unasked question.

"Right, of course." She sat down and filled their teacups.

They ate in relative quiet for a long while until Aileen broke the silence. "'Twas great craic last night, aye?"

Saoirse nodded, studying her friend's face. "You definitely seemed to have a grand time," she said at length, a knowing smile tickling her lips.

Aileen blanched. "And what's that supposed to mean?"

"Well," Saoirse said, shrugging, "first, there was the first pancake."

Aileen blushed and dropped her gaze to the table, a wee giggle escaping her lips.

"Then ya won the pancake race," Saoirse continued. "And then, of course, there was the dancin'."

"I'd say I'll be the reigning pancake race champion for years to come," Aileen said on a laugh. "As for the dancin' . . ."

Saoirse smiled. "It seemed you and Hugh really hit it off."

"Och." Aileen stood to clear their dishes and refill their tea. "We just needed to round out our set. And Mister McDonagh needed a partner." Aileen shrugged and Saoirse noticed how she avoided her gaze.

"Oh, right. Yes, of course." Saoirse stood. "And I suppose it would've been rude to leave him without a partner for all the couples dances." She winked at her friend, enjoying immensely how it made Aileen blush even further.

"Indeed," Aileen said, her voice threatening to crack with laughter. "Besides, if ya wanna talk about couples dances, ya should be talkin' about yerself and me brother." Aileen pinned Saoirse with her own knowing look.

Now it was Saoirse's turn to have heat flush her face. Her pulse quickened. She liked it much better with the tables turned the other way round. "Let's not talk about that."

Laughing again, Aileen nodded. "Ah, so she can dish it out, folks, but she can't take it."

Saoirse rolled her eyes and moved to the front door. She started pulling on a pair of wellies, then tossed a shawl around her shoulders.

"Ah, c'mon," Aileen said, closing the distance between them. "It's just a bit of fun."

Saoirse forced a lightness into her voice that she didn't feel. "Oh, I know. I just need to get a wiggle on in the shed."

"Mm." Aileen searched her face for a moment, not looking the least bit convinced. "If ye're sure."

"Aileen," Saoirse said, laying a hand on her friend's shoulder. "I'm made of sturdier stuff than that. I assure you, it takes a lot more than a wee joke or two to offend me."

"Alright." Aileen relaxed, and an easy smile spread across her face. "Owen said he'd be up to the shed after he saw to the sheep."

Saoirse nodded and opened the door just as a bolt of lightning streaked across the sky, followed almost immediately by a deafening crack of thunder.

"*Ádh mór,*" Aileen called into the melee.

Saoirse hurried out into the storm, grateful for Aileen's wish of good fortune as she weathered the elements. The ground almost ran like a river, and the hill behind the house looked like a waterfall. It would appear she'd need all the luck Aileen could wish her. The fleeting thought sprang to her mind that it seemed a miracle the house wasn't flooding. But she pushed it from her mind as she tried to figure out the best way to get up to the shed. The road path had a good inch or so of water running down it, covering thick mud, no doubt. But the path cutting through the grass behind the house was cascading like Glenevin Waterfall. She decided to take her chances on the muddy road.

Several minutes later, soaked to the bone, with mud covering her wellies almost to the top, she arrived at the weaving shed. She unlocked it, went inside, and made quick work of lighting the lanterns. She wished, not for the first time, that the shed had a small hearth in which to light a fire, in order to lend more heat to the space. Alas, she would have to hope working the loom would suffice in warming her up. She removed her cloak, shook the excess water from it, and hung it on the peg by the door. As she waited for her eyes to adjust to the dim light, she hovered her hands over one of the lanterns and rubbed them together, thankful for even the modicum of heat it provided.

She waited until she was certain her sleeves and hair were dry enough that they wouldn't drip all over the thread as she wove. Granted, tweed was known for the protection it provided against the elements. It was a great natural barrier from the rain. However, the majority of that protection came from the tight weave of the cloth, rather than the yarn fibers themselves. And she didn't want to do anything to risk the quality of the weave or cause the colors to bleed.

As she set to work, humming the song Owen had taught her, the storm outside raged on and grew more and more intense. Before long, she could hear the maelstrom over the din of the loom, which set her nerves on edge. If things got much worse, she wouldn't be able to make it back down to the house. Or worse, Owen wouldn't make it up to the shed and would possibly end up stuck out in the fields with the sheep if visibility got to be too poor.

Suddenly the door flew open and, as if summoned by her thoughts, Owen appeared. The wind tore the door from his grip and slammed it against the inner wall of the shed. He rounded it and leaned his entire weight against it, but the squall was an equal foe. Saoirse ran over to help. Rain lashed around the edges of the door and against her face, blurring her vision as the gale tore her hair from its place atop her head and plastered it to her face. Above them, the branches of the birch trees clacked together as though trying to join in the thunder's torrent. They fought against the elements for what felt like hours. It was as if Finn McCool himself was pushing against them. Finally, feet slipping against the wet ground, they at last wrested the door closed and latched it.

They both leaned back against the door still, enjoying the relative quiet that now enveloped the small interior of the weaving shed. Their breaths came in heavy puffs, and water dripped down their faces and clothes.

"Thanks," Owen said at length, his chest still heaving from the exertion.

Saoirse nodded, then closed her eyes and swallowed in an attempt to regain control of her breathing.

After another long moment, Owen pushed against the door to stand, then pulled off his soaked slicker and hat. He hung them on the peg with Saoirse's cloak and then rubbed his hands back and forth over his head, trying to clear the water from it.

"My kingdom for a fireplace in here," he mumbled.

Saoirse chuckled. "I'd had the same thought."

Owen turned and eyed the western wall, as though trying to decide if it would be possible to put one in. At length, he spun and picked up a lantern. Hovering one hand over the top and wiggling his fingers in the warmth, he approached the loom. "Let's have a look at how things are goin', aye?"

Saoirse stepped around him and pointed out the length she'd been able to complete so far today. The room was dim at best, and the details of all the different specks of color, as well as the quality of the weave, were almost impossible to see.

Owen held the lantern aloft and bent until his nose was almost touching the tweed. "Not bad," he murmured. When he lowered the lantern and tipped it forward, Saoirse's breath hitched, and she clapped a hand over her mouth. She turned away, the fear gripping her chest nearly suffocating her.

"Are ya alright?"

Saoirse rolled her lips together and squeezed her eyes shut. "Mm-hmm."

She heard Owen's footsteps scuff over to her. "What is it?"

She opened her eyes and could just make out the glow of the lantern light, sending chills skittering up her spine and down her arms. She shivered to try to clear them. She attempted to force a lightness in her voice as she chuckled. "It just made me nervous . . . you leanin' over the tweed with the lantern."

When he didn't respond, she looked over her shoulder at him. His face was stoic, concern shadowing his features. "Fire makes ya nervous, doesn't it?"

Her eyes popped wide for a split second before she righted them. Was it that obvious?

"And why wouldn't it, with what happened to yer family?" He stepped closer, warmth radiating off of him and spreading across Saoirse's back, despite the damp. "Want to talk about it?"

In a flash, she could see the charred rubble, smoke still wafting up from it. Screams she'd never heard echoed in her mind—what she imagined her family's last moments sounded like. She shook her head. "I just had a bad experience, is all," she said around the lump threatening to choke her.

His silence stretched long like the strands of warp running the length of the loom. Saoirse couldn't decide if she wanted him to press her on it or not. She wanted so badly to be free of this burden but was also terrified at the thought of losing him—and Aileen—were he to learn the truth. Not to mention the rest of the community she was coming to love so dearly.

When he returned to studying the fabric on the loom, Saoirse released a breath that had been burning in her chest.

"Well done," he said, nodding at what she'd completed so far. "Let's keep it up. I'll work on bundling up the completed rolls. Try to protect them in case the roof leaks or somethin'. You weave."

Saoirse's head bobbed as she reclaimed her place at the front of the loom. As she settled into her weaving pattern, she stole glances at Owen from time to time. She could see his shoulders flexing even under his jumper as he held the finished tweed aloft and folded it. When that task was completed, he started reloading the basket next to the loom that held the skeins of colored yarn that would be used on the shuttle.

The hours rolled by, and the storm raged on. At one point, it seemed to be dying out, but then the winds picked back up with such ferocity, Saoirse feared the whole shed might be swept away.

When the current skein of weft yarn was nearly spent, Saoirse cut it free from the shuttle and tied it off to the warp. She then straightened and stretched her arms high overhead and twisted back and forth. Taking a deep breath, she rolled her head from side to side and front to back.

"It's tiring, isn't—" A massive crash interrupted Owen. Something thudded heavily on the roof, then rolled down and crashed in front of the shed. The window to the right of the door exploded, knocking the lantern that had been sitting on the sill to the ground. The reservoir holding the oil shattered and the fuel spilled across the floor. Flames erupted and instantly spread across the path the oil had left.

Saoirse shrieked and collapsed into a ball on the ground. She covered her ears, unable to stand the sound of her own screaming but also unable to stop as, even from across the room, the heat washed over her back and the flames licked up the fuel from the floor.

Owen shouted, and his footsteps rushed toward the blaze. Saoirse remained curled up, eyes squeezed shut, hands pressed over her ears. But after a minute or so, the intensity of the heat began to wane, and it was only then she became conscious of the scuffs and thwaps that repeated over and over again.

A chill filled the air once more and then warm hands rubbed across her back. She jolted at the touch and curled even tighter.

"Easy now." Owen's voice was hoarse as he coughed.

"Let's get you out o' here." He hooked his arms underneath hers and pulled her to her feet. She couldn't fully support her own weight, so she leaned into him. He wrapped one arm around her waist and helped her to the door. Rain poured in through the broken window, dampening the smoke that had filled the room.

Owen reached for the door, then paused. "Actually, it's too bad out there. We'll need to stay until it dies down."

Unbidden, sobs shook Saoirse's body once more.

"Shh, shh," Owen crooned in her ear. "It's alright. We're alright." He pressed a kiss to the side of her head and held her close. After a moment, he turned them back toward the loom. "Let's get ya settled over here out of the elements." They shuffled behind the loom, and he helped lower her down to sit.

"I'll be right back," he said and headed to the door.

Saoirse hugged her knees to her chest and buried her face in them. Her whole body shook, and her tears continued to flow. Sudden warmth drew her attention to her right side as Owen slid down next to her. One arm reached across her shoulders and pulled her to lean against his side.

"You're shaking," he said, his voice still raw. He softly squeezed her closer, and she buried her face into his shoulder. "It's okay. Ye're safe. I've got you."

Sitting there, wrapped in his arms, Saoirse felt safe for the first time in weeks. And the relief of it pushed all the pain and heartache to the surface. Fresh sobs wracked her body.

He shifted to wrap both arms around her, cupping her head with his left hand. He held her and let her cry for a long moment, and yet her sobs didn't slow. The storm inside her nearly matched the intensity of the one raging outside.

"Hey, hey," he said, his voice low and laced with concern. "It's alright." He pressed his lips against the top of her head and held them there for a beat before resting his cheek against the same spot.

At length, she began to calm, her breath hitching every now and then. He leaned back and brushed the hair away from her cheeks. When she met his gaze, his face crumpled. "Oh, *peata*." He kissed her forehead, then pulled back to look at her again.

They held each other's gaze for a long moment. When her breath shuddered again, he leaned in and kissed one cheek, then the other. Saoirse pressed into his kiss, eyes fluttering closed at the feel of his lips against her skin.

He reached up to brush her cheek with his right hand, but she noticed when his gaze fell on his scars, he made like he was going to drop it. Saoirse caught his hand, held his gaze, and brought his palm to her lips so she could press a slow, tender kiss to the wound that had slashed across it. "I kiss the hurt that brought you to me," she whispered.

Owen's shoulders relaxed, and he brushed his thumb across her mouth. His gaze flitted to her lips then back up to her eyes, and the air between them stilled. It seemed even the gales outside quieted as electricity buzzed in the air. He leaned forward slowly, his eyes searching hers. When his lips brushed against hers, feather light, it was as though he was asking permission to continue. Butterflies erupted in Saoirse's stomach as she considered briefly the consequences if she were to give in to his kiss the way she so badly wanted to.

But sitting here, in his arms, feeling safe and secure for the first time in ages, with him looking at her that way, she wanted nothing more than to be consumed by his embrace.

When their lips first met, the kiss began slowly, melting gently like ice in the sun on the first day of spring. It was as if they both wanted this moment to last forever and were unhurried, sinking deeper and deeper into one another, their lips speaking together all the things their words could never say.

When they finally pulled away, he pressed his forehead against hers. "Well, eh . . . thank you for that."

They both laughed nervously, and Saoirse playfully rolled her eyes. "My pleasure."

Owen sat back against the wall, still studying her face. "But really, are ya alright?"

She searched his gaze, a new war waging in her heart. She took his hand in both of hers, her thumbs rubbing arcs on the back of it, his scars rough against her skin. While his wounds hadn't actually brought him to her, they had allowed her to stay and get to know him. And now, after that kiss, it cemented in her the desire to be fully open and honest with him. If they were going to be romantically involved, she couldn't imagine fully giving herself over to him without giving him everything—including her guilt-laden past. She swallowed down the terrifying unknown of how Owen would react and then took a deep breath.

"My family died in a fire."

His brow creased in pity. "I know. I'm so sorry," he said. The light through the window had begun to turn from black and silver to bluish gray.

She shook her head. "But there's more. Lots more."

26

"Och, Saoirse." He squeezed her hand. What he wouldn't give to take away the pain that weighed her down so. "How much you've had to carry. Tell me about it."

She shook her head, her gaze fixed on their hands, fingers still intertwined. "'Twas a terrible accident."

Flashes of his father's fate sparked in Owen's memory. "I hate that we have that in common."

She met his gaze at last, her brow furrowed. Suddenly, realization seemed to dawn. "Oh, right. Yer father."

He nodded, his jaw tense as his anger toward O'Malley bubbled just below the surface. But he forced his features to soften, lest she mistake his rigidity as being directed toward her.

"It was careless, really," she began.

Anger boiled over in his chest. Irresponsibility had caused his father's death. And now it had cost Saoirse everything as well, it seemed.

She glanced up at him and paused, her eyes widening slightly.

He shook his head. "I'm sorry. I hate that you're having

to suffer the consequences of someone else's lack of care or attention." He sighed. "I know that pain firsthand. Jimmy O'Malley had been my best friend. He was helping us build the barn. I'd gone out to see to the sheep, and Jimmy and my dad were working on tying the rafters. Jimmy let himself get distracted by a pretty face when my sister walked in. He lost his grip of the rope, sending the rafter careening down. It knocked Da off the ladder and landed on him."

Saoirse tightened her grip on his hand. "Oh, Owen. That's terrible. I'm so sorry." She laid her head on his shoulder.

He smiled at the sensation of her so near, leaning into him for comfort. He cleared his throat. He wanted her to know he would always be there for her. That he would do everything in his power to protect her from ever having to suffer such hurt again. "As far as I'm concerned, taking the life of another because of one's own carelessness is the only unforgiveable sin, aside from blasphemy."

Owen felt Saoirse stiffen slightly. She was quiet for so long after, he began to wonder if she'd fallen asleep. Suddenly, she sat up and craned her neck to look out the small window above them. The morning light was growing brighter with every passing moment.

"Ya alright?" he asked her.

"The storm seems to have passed." She lumbered stiffly to her feet, the atmosphere between them having shifted somehow. "We'd best be getting back." Then she headed to the door without looking back at him.

"Saoirse?" He scrambled to his feet. "Was it somethin' I said?"

She pulled the door open to reveal a large birch tree had fallen over and blocked the entrance to the shed. Before

Owen could do anything, Saoirse scrambled over the trunk, climbed through the branches, and out into the foggy damp of a gray and dreary morning.

Owen stared after her, confusion swirling in his gut. Was she regretting their shared moment? Had he said something to offend her? Surely commiserating with her loss wouldn't have struck a nerve. This was the second time she'd suddenly turned colder after they'd connected on a deeper level. Could she simply be scared?

He made his way to the door. With much more difficulty, Owen struggled through the branches, having to stop several times to free a snagged sleeve or trouser leg. As though wanting to keep him trapped in the shed, the branches caught his foot as he broke through the last bough. He fell onto the soaked earth, mud splashing up on his face. *Perfect.*

He'd just begun to feel dry after the lashing he took last night, only to have to start the process all over again now. Muttering to himself, he clambered to his feet, swiping his hands down his legs. When he straightened, what he saw froze him where he stood. Debris and rubbish were strewn all about the hillsides. His gaze drifted to the thatched roof of the weaving shed. There was a large section of damage on the corner that had taken the brunt of the tree's fall. It was a miracle the roof hadn't leaked overnight. Turning, he surveyed the roofs of the barn and house. Both looked fairly intact, though any farming tools that had been left outside were no longer anywhere near where he'd left them. Pools of standing water littered the view as far as the eye could see. Carefully, he trudged forward and sloshed down the hill to the front of the house. The mud was easily two-feet thick, and he had to take care not to lose a wellie with each step.

He opened the door but stood on the threshold as he pulled his feet from his boots. Aileen almost knocked him over with a hug as she exclaimed, "T'anks be to God ye're alright!" Then she landed a hearty slap on his arm.

"Ow!" He rubbed the spot she'd hit. "What was that fer?"

Aileen scoffed. "Fer makin' me worry m'self sick last night, that's what."

Owen sighed as he crossed to the stove. He couldn't get a cup of tea in his hand fast enough. "It's not like I could do much about it. We tried to come down but were trapped."

"We?" Aileen's brow furrowed.

"Saoirse," he said, rolling his eyes. "Did ya not speak to her when she came in?"

Aileen's countenance darkened slightly, and she shook her head. "The gairl just burst in here and went straight to the room and closed the door." She tsked. "Tracked mud all over m'floor too."

He stared toward Aileen and Saoirse's room as though he could see what Saoirse was doing through the walls. Was she crying? Packing to leave?

Aileen came up next to him, sighing. "What'd ya do?"

Owen's jaw dropped. "Why d'ya assume it was me who did something?"

Leveling a look at him, his sister crossed her arms over her chest. "'Cause ye're the auld man who's not had a lick of experience dealin' with smitten ladies, that's why."

He started to argue but stopped short. "What d'ya mean smitten?"

Before she could answer, Aileen stopped and held up her hand, indicating for Owen to be quiet. Then she inclined her head as if straining to hear something. Moving to the front door, she opened it and waited. The faint sound of church bells drifted on the heavy air. She met Owen's gaze, fear glowing in her eyes. "Somethin's wrong," she said.

Owen nodded. It wasn't a mass time, nor a feast day. That meant the bells rang out in call for aid from any able-bodied man, woman, or child.

"We'll have to walk," he said, already on the doorstep tugging his boots back on. "The wagon'll just get stuck." His gaze bounced in the direction of the ladies' room. When he looked at his sister again, the expression on her face suggested she believed he'd committed some egregious error. But they didn't have time to get into it now.

He sighed. "You get her"—he flicked his head toward the ladies' room—"I'll get some shovels."

Saoirse's gaze pierced the ground ahead of her as they plodded down the mucky road toward the village. She absently wondered if she could bore a hole in the ground that would open up and swallow her were she to stare long enough. Sighing, she lifted her eyes to the horizon. The journey to Glentornan would take at least twice as long on foot, if not more so, given the conditions. Thankfully, the rain had completely stopped, and the clouds, while still hovering low overhead, had thinned quite a bit. The heavy moisture in the air dampened the clanging of the church bells, which still tolled on incessantly, growing more strident the closer they got.

From the corner of her eye, she could see Owen's head pop out from his place on the other side of Aileen. Though she could feel his gaze burning into the side of her face, she pretended not to notice and kept her stare fixed forward. She pulled in a deep breath, hoping the chilly air in her lungs would steady her nerves as she replayed all that had happened in the shed during the storm.

Her cheeks warmed at what others might think if they knew she and Owen had spent the night alone in the weaving shed. Granted, most of it had been a horribly awful experience—from the freezing cold to the tree collapsing onto the building to the fire Owen had extinguished, she learned after the fact, by beating the flames down with his coat.

Not all of it was horrible though. Her lips tingled at the memory of Owen's kiss. She could almost feel his arms around her again, his lips searching hers so tenderly, so earnestly. As though he was reining in Lir, holding him back from a full gallop. Her pulse kicked up as she remembered how deliciously they had melted together in the kiss. But the sizzling memory faded as she recalled the conversation that had come next. She'd been prepared to tell him everything about the night her family died, and he'd stopped her cold. If she could force herself to be objective about it, she'd guess he was trying to be supportive. He just had no idea how his comments had had the exact opposite effect.

"Taking the life of another because of one's own carelessness is the only unforgiveable sin, aside from blasphemy." His words reverberated in her mind like the church bells echoing off the peaks of the Seven Sisters forming the valley in which Glentornan lay. How on earth was she supposed to tell him that she was responsible for the fire that killed her parents, brothers, and sister—even the family dog? It

was her carelessness that had sparked the blaze. If only she hadn't been in such a hurry. To add to her irresponsibility, she'd woken late the morning of the fire, which added to her rush. Had she not overslept, she convinced herself, her family would still be safe and sound today.

As they rounded the final bend in the road before they reached the church, the ground in front of her blurred, and she lifted her gaze to the sky, blinking quickly in an attempt to force the moisture not to fall.

The clanging from the tower was almost intolerable when they joined the growing crowd gathering in front of the house of worship. Father Cunningham and Hugh were organizing people into smaller groups and assigning various tasks. Saoirse, Owen, and Aileen were asked to join a group with Bridie and John.

Their group waited while a few more people came up the path. Finally, blessedly, the bells fell silent, and the crowd breathed a collective sigh of relief.

"Right," the priest began, "there's been a landslide at the far west side of the village."

Aileen and others gasped. Saoirse lifted shaky fingers in front of her mouth as Aileen settled in closer to her side.

"Hugh, Tommy, and I did a quick search for survivors. Wee Brigit Doherty was pulled from the rubble. She'll need some time, but she'll be alright." The group murmured relief mixed with concern. Only now did Saoirse notice that Father Cunningham, Hugh, and several others were completely caked in mud. "Sadly, our own Doctor McGinley was killed when his cottage collapsed."

More gasps flew up from the crowd, and a few sobs could be heard from several townsfolk. Aileen slipped her arm through Saoirse's and pulled her close, then did the same with Owen on the other side.

Saoirse's free hand clasped her chest as she tried to wrap her head around the fact that Doctor McGinley was gone.

Hugh stepped forward. "Ye each should know yer tasks. McCreadys, Sheridans, and Saoirse, ye'll be workin' with me to clear the school." They all nodded gravely. The teacher spoke to a couple of other groups who'd just arrived and assigned them their posts.

After Father Cunningham offered a prayer of safety for the souls of those departed and of rescue for any others who may be trapped, the group silently set off for the village.

They passed John and Bridie's home, and Saoirse noticed Bridie crossing herself and offering thanks for sparing their house and their lives. Before passing the doctor's office, Saoirse paused. Had he only been there instead of at home, the doctor would be here now, safe. Sadly, his home was on the far end of the village near the school. Saoirse's heart sank at the thought of the school. *Thank God this didn't happen during the school day.*

As they reached the heart of the village, groups periodically peeled off in different directions to see to their various tasks.

Everyone in Saoirse's group slowed their steps when they approached the school.

"Muise." Bridie tugged a hanky from her sleeve and dabbed at her eyes.

"*A Mhaighdean.*" John slid the flatcap from his head and held it over his heart.

Saoirse gripped Aileen's arm tighter while she took in the sight before her. Half of the school building was completely destroyed and buried under a mountain of muck. The other half was missing its roof.

"Careful now," Hugh said, and he gathered everyone closer. "We need to clear the mud but take care. We don't know what's under there."

"Oh, heavens." Aileen's hands clapped over her mouth. "You don't think . . ."

Saoirse patted Aileen's hand, and both women looked back to Hugh.

He shook his head. "No. As far as we know, no one was inside." He looked to the rubble and back. "At least, they shouldn't have been. Just be mindful of yer steps. There could be sharp wood and rocks just below the surface."

Owen stepped forward, handed one of the shovels he was carrying to John, and turned to Hugh. "Where do we start?"

27

Owen tried not to stare at Saoirse as she chatted quietly with Hugh and Aileen in the portion of the schoolhouse that was still standing. By the way Hugh was pointing at things around the space, Owen guessed they were making a plan for cleaning and salvaging what they could. He watched as Saoirse nodded, then turned to grab some tags from a basket Bridie had brought over. Her gaze caught Owen's for a split second before she looked away a little too quickly.

Owen's brows pulled together, and his jaw tightened, matching the tension of his work while he jammed the shovel into the muck filling the other half of the school. He had no idea what had happened, or why Saoirse was suddenly so distant, but he determined to let the clean-up work distract him from his woes. Next to him, John was pushing a wheelbarrow up next to the building for them to shovel the mud and sludge into. Some of it would eventually be used in gardens or pens, but most of it just needed to be moved out. Thankfully it wasn't bogland behind the village or the main fuel source for the area would've been completely lost, not to mention thousands of years of history destroyed in an instant. Instead, the mixture of mud, slate, and remnants of bushes that had once lined the hillsides would eventually grow back.

Suddenly shouts erupted from the remains of a collapsed building across the street.

"They're alive!" someone called, desperation lacing their voice. Owen, John, and the rest of their group rushed over. John and Hugh scurried to the base of the mound where a few people worked. Owen scrambled up the rubble and caught sight of a shock of hair.

"We're comin'! Hang on!" he called, then began digging through the debris with his hands. He pulled a split board aside, and a woman's face came into view. Still pinned down by all manner of rubble, she looked to him out of the side of her eye, fear glistening in her stare. She blinked and took a shuddering breath.

Owen's heart thudded to a stop. He recognized her as Nora Boyle, the woman who'd won the first pancake race just two nights ago. The woman with enough children to form a football team.

"It's alright, we're gonna get you out," he told her. "Lads, come help me," Owen said.

In a flash, Hugh and John were by his side, digging and removing obstacles. Saoirse appeared next to him and wiped the woman's face and eyes with a damp cloth. The tenderness with which she worked sent Owen's heart reeling. *Focus.*

At last, all the rubble was cleared. Owen, Hugh, John, and Father Cunningham gingerly lifted Nora out and carried her down to the street where Bridie had a chair and a cup of tea waiting.

Murmurs went up throughout the crowd that had gathered.

"Thank God she's alive."

"Hang in there, Nora."

"God be praised. The children still have their mother."

Without Doctor McGinley, they had no way to know for sure if the woman was truly alright, but the local midwife looked her over and assured them that beyond some cuts and bruises, she appeared to be fine.

After a few minutes, Bridie took the woman to her house to get her a spare set of clothes and let her warm up in front of the fire before she reunited with her children. No one could figure out how they'd gotten out of the house in time, but praise God they'd been found wandering in search of their mother earlier that morning. The others returned to clearing out the school. Aileen, Owen noticed, was never too far from Hugh and always seemed to have a question for him. A pang of jealousy pricked Owen's heart. How he longed for Saoirse to talk with him again, to let him know what was bothering her. But every time he looked up to say something, her head spun in the other direction. He wasn't sure if she'd been looking at him too, or if he always just managed to look up at the exact moment she was turning somewhere else. Whatever it was, it weighed on him heavier than the mud trying to pull his boots from his feet. Perhaps if he kept digging, he might find the answers to his questions somewhere in the mess in which he was standing.

A few hours later, the debris was cleared from the crushed side of the schoolhouse, and Hugh and the ladies had created a system for sorting through all the supplies that had been inside when the landslide hit. That part of the process would take quite a bit longer—much like the process of sorting through the rubble Owen found cluttering his heart and mind.

Slowly, the crowd who had come from the hills started snaking their way back to the churchyard where they'd left their wagons and things. The journey was just as quiet as when they'd come into town. No more survivors had been found, but two more casualties were discovered. Old Man Mackey and his wife—the oldest couple in the parish—had died in each other's arms, and spirits were heavy as what was left of the community trudged up the hill.

Once at the church, John draped an arm over Owen's shoulder. "I know just what we need."

Owen looked at the man. "What's that?"

His arm still around Owen, John began walking toward the church. The rest of the crowd followed suit and filed silently inside the house of worship. No lanterns blazed, and no organ music filled the air. Rather, the mournful shuffling of exhausted feet served as their processional as one by one, each family filed into their customary rows. All was quiet for a long while until Hugh began singing.

"*Rop tú mo Baile . . .*" His full, tenor voice filled the sanctuary. Slowly, voices began to join him as people rose to their feet.

By the third verse, Owen had joined in. "Be Thou my battle shield, sword for the fight." But when he got to the next stanza, tears choked him. Sinking to his knees, he let the lyrics wash over him as tears silently poured down his cheeks.

Be Thou my Dignity, Thou my Delight;
Thou my soul's Shelter, Thou my high Tow'r:
Raise Thou me heav'nward, O Pow'r of my pow'r.

Riches I heed not, nor man's empty praise,
Thou mine Inheritance, now and always:
Thou and Thou only, first in my heart,
High King of Heaven, my Treasure Thou art.

High King of Heaven, my victory won,
May I reach Heaven's joys, O bright Heav'n's Sun!
Heart of my own heart, whatever befall,
Still be my Vision, O Ruler of all.

Owen began to see that he had been keeping all his focus on his hardships, not on his source of strength. Digging through the rubble of the landslide today, hearing of the discovery of the Mackeys' bodies and the loss of Doctor McGinley painted all too clear a picture that not one person is guaranteed tomorrow. The only guarantee is that one day our time on this earth will end, and we will stand before our Creator. So, we'd better make the best use of the time we have. Kneeling now in this sanctuary, with the sounds of worship and praise echoing around him in the wake of such a disaster, Owen started to gain clarity on what he needed to do.

Since God was the only constant, the only guarantee in life, Owen's energy was best spent in worship and praise of Him, in believing He would do what He promised. Owen lifted his face to the cross hanging at the front of the room. He may never have an easy life. He might not finish the tweed. He might not fully use his hand again. He might lose his farm. But if any of those things happened, it would not be because God caused them but rather because He, in His infinite wisdom, allowed them.

Pulling in a deep breath, Owen slowly rose to stand, his

eyes still fixed on the cross. "I believe," he whispered. "Please help me believe."

Saoirse stood at the back of the church, heart pounding. The spontaneous singing had taken her by surprise, and she'd needed some air. When she came back inside, she couldn't force herself beyond the back row or two. It was as though the ground had gripped her feet and was holding her fast to where she stood. So much heartache and pain had befallen the people she cared about—starting with her own family, then Owen and Aileen, and now the entire village of Glentornan. She was no expert, but she wasn't sure they'd be able to recover from this disaster. Guilt settled on her shoulders like a set of stocks in the town square. Tension crept up her neck and her breath caught in her chest.

She was foolish to think she'd be able to start over, to escape the consequences of what she'd done. It seemed her fortunes had been changing for quite some time, and once she caused the demise of her family, her ill fate was beginning to spread to others. And now, dozens more were having to pay the price for it. Never mind the fact that Owen might never be able to support himself or his family fully again. Last night's landslide felt like confirmation that she carried with her a terrible brand of bad luck and was destined to spend the rest of her life alone in order to spare anyone else from having to share in the effects of it.

You should go. At first, she tried to shake the thought free, but soon she realized it was the only way to protect those she loved from further harm. Especially with what Owen had said the night before. He'd never look at her the same way once he knew what she'd done. She needed to leave. She could sneak out now and get back to the house to gather her few things and then disappear before Aileen and Owen got home. Turning, she tiptoed out the door.

Pulling her shawl tighter around her shoulders, she set off for home—nae, the McCreadys' house. She glanced behind her once to make sure she wasn't being followed, then hurried up the road.

It would take days for things to dry out from the deluge the night before, and the trek back was just as bad as the one there, if not worse due to the need to go uphill this direction. The journey took far longer than she expected, and the last few hundred yards, she looked back every few minutes, certain she'd find Owen and Aileen coming around the last corner.

A gust of wind kicked up, swirling her hair in front of her face. Fighting against it, she pulled her hair away and glanced to the sky. *Please, God, don't send more rain.*

The area couldn't handle it—the ground was already saturated. Plus, Saoirse had no place dry to stay. She had no idea where she would go. The fleeting thought of heading back to John and Bridie's popped into her head. She knew she'd be welcome, but they would have their hands full housing at least some of those who'd been displaced when their homes were destroyed. Never mind the fact that she was trying to protect them from herself too. She would most likely be sleeping outside tonight, under a tree if she was lucky, and needed as mild weather as the Good Lord saw fit to provide. The irony of asking God's blessing of good weather was not lost on her, given how He seemed to be punishing her for all she'd done.

At the thought of being on her own, knowing bandits frequented the area, her confidence began to falter. But as the McCreadys' house came into view, she steeled herself to follow through with her plan.

Stout trotted down the hill beyond the house, tail wagging and tongue dangling out to one side. He came up and nosed Saoirse's hand.

"Good boy," she murmured as she scratched his head. "Ya take good care o' them, alright?"

He looked up at her, eyes bright and happy, tail going double time.

"I'll take that as a yes." She smiled at the dog and made her way into the house. Closing the door, she leaned against it, drinking in the place that had so quickly become her home. The mild scents of tea and dried herbs hanging in the air mingled with all that was distinctly Owen. His nightshirt hanging on the post of his bed, his favorite teacup sitting next to the basin, his flatcap on the peg by the door. She lifted it from its place and ran her fingers over the tweed, absently wondering if he'd woven it. She pulled the cap to her nose and inhaled. The earthy smell of the wool combined with Owen's own unique scent overwhelmed her, and she doubled over with a sob. How could she leave him? Not only did he still need her help finishing the tweed, but she was fairly certain she'd fallen in love with him. Memories of their tender kiss, followed by images of all their time together the past few weeks, flooded her mind. Owen rescuing her when she'd caught her finger in a knot—and the first time she felt his skin against hers when he worked to free her from the tangle. The first time they worked the loom together, his quiet strength as he stood behind her and his baritone voice singing softly.

His robust laughter filling the house while they sat around the dinner table like a wee family of three. Walking the hills with him after helping deliver wee Dubhín.

Sobs choked her and she cried out, "Oh, God, help me!"

Forcing herself to straighten, she scanned the room a final time, looking for something with which to bolster her courage. The kettle caught her eye, but there was no time for a cuppa. When her gaze fell upon the hearth, she stilled, chills prickling her skin at the sobering reminder of why she was leaving. It was for Owen's good. For Aileen's protection. And for the protection of all those she'd come to care for so deeply in the village.

Slipping Owen's hat back onto the peg, she tugged the bodice of her dress and tightened her apron strings. With determined steps, she passed the fireplace, then went down the short hallway and into the room she'd shared with Aileen. In minutes, her bag was packed and she was back at the front door.

Scanning the cozy home once more, she blinked away fresh tears and stepped outside.

28

"She didn't tell you where she was going?" Owen asked Aileen as they rounded the final bend in the road before home.

Aileen shook her head. "I thought she'd said somethin' to ye."

Owen ground his teeth, which didn't help the dull ache that had taken up residence between his temples ever since they realized Saoirse was missing. They'd swept back through the village before leaving, but she wasn't there either.

As the house came into view, the roof of the weaving shed caught Owen's eye. "Maybe she's in the shed." Perhaps she was just as antsy to finish the weaving as he had been earlier. "I'll go check there. You check the house, Aileen."

She nodded.

"I'll check the barn," Hugh said. "Just in case." With the shortage of usable houses in Glentornan for those displaced, Owen had agreed to let Hugh stay in the barn.

Owen mumbled his ascent and trudged up to the shed. The massive tree still blocked the entrance, and the windows were dark. He'd expected the one to the left of the door to be dark, since he'd shoved some scrap material to block where the branches had broken in, but the other windows also held no light. "Saoirse?" he called.

He wasn't sure why he was bothering to call out to her though. She clearly wasn't in there. There was no way she'd attempt to weave in the dark. Never mind the fact that all was silent—no raucous din of the loom polluting the air. Still, he couldn't stop himself from cupping his hands around his eyes and pressing his face to the glass, just to be sure. As he suspected, only the sight of an empty room and still loom greeted him.

Frustration and worry continued to mount in his chest, but he forced himself to breathe. She was probably back in the house sipping a cup of tea and chatting away with Aileen.

But when he arrived at the house, he found Aileen pacing the floor, hands wringing as Hugh stood by watching helplessly. Stout trotted over and stood expectantly at Owen's side.

"Any luck?" Owen asked, though he knew the answer. Aileen shook her head, her eyes full of worry.

Hugh stepped forward. "Could she have gone to visit a friend?"

"She doesn't know anyone except us and those in the village," Aileen said, her voice thick. Suddenly she turned wide eyes to Owen. "Ya don't think Haggerty got 'er, do ya?"

He hadn't considered that possibility until now. He pulled his lips into a thin line, wagging his head. "No." He shook his head more firmly. "No, I really don't. That's not really Haggerty's way. He's after stock he can sell at market, not another mouth he has to feed."

"Would she have gone out to the sheep?" Hugh asked.

Owen and Aileen looked at one another, tentative hope lighting their faces.

"I hadn't thought of that. Maybe." He opened the door. "I'll check the far field. You lot check the ones beyond the barn." He hurried from the house, Stout tight on his heels.

As they crested hill after hill, Owen's gaze swept from horizon to horizon, but there was naught to be seen but sheep, the odd building or two, and about a thousand different shades of green, save the one shade he truly wished to see— the nearly blue shade of sea glass that filled Saoirse's eyes.

When they'd walked so long that Stout began to fall behind instead of trotting ahead, they turned and headed back home to check in with the others. The light had begun to fade by the time they arrived at the house to learn that Hugh and Aileen had had the same sort of luck finding Saoirse as him.

"There's not much else we can do until the morning," Hugh was saying as he helped Aileen dish up a meager dinner of steamed fish and veg.

Owen's chest burned, and his lips screwed up to one side. "Are you suggesting we leave her out there all night?"

Hugh shrugged, but his eyes held compassion. "It'll be pitch-black out there soon." He listed off the same litany of reasons it would be foolish to go after her now as Owen had given Aileen about not chasing Haggerty when the sheep had gone missing.

"And she's out there alone in it!" Owen yelled, pointing his outstretched arm toward the door.

Aileen settled weary eyes on Owen. "He's just sayin' that it's not worth riskin' both of yer lives searching in the black o' night, is all." Aileen set a plate down at Owen's spot at the table and gestured for him to sit. Removing his hat, he raked his fingers through his hair and wrestled with what to do.

"At least get a wee somethin' in yer stomach," Aileen crooned. Her tone reminded Owen of how he would talk to a spooked horse. It irked him to no end.

"I'm not a child," he ground out through gritted teeth.

Aileen scoffed. "Coulda fooled me."

Owen tossed his hands. "I'm not being petulant, Aileen. I'm worried sick because the woman I lo—" He cleared his throat. "A woman is lost out there all alone, with little knowledge of the land or dangers hidden within it."

Aileen's eyes glinted, and she laid her hand on Owen's shoulder. "Ye're right," she said, flitting a glance to Hugh then back. "I'm sorry."

Sighing, Owen picked up a fork and jammed it into the food but couldn't bring himself to eat a single bite. Stout sat at the door, his nose almost pressed into the crease between it and the jamb, and whined. When no one responded, the dog rounded and looked at each of them, his front feet tippy-tapping on the floor as he continued to whine.

"I know, boyo," Owen said. *Me too.*

Owen's leg bounced uncontrollably under the table as he looked back and forth between his sister and Hugh—both of whom were nearly finished with their food. How could they eat when Saoirse was out there, who knew where? How could they sit in this house, safe and warm, when Saoirse could be hurt or in danger? His jaw ached, and the smell of the fish, which was usually one of his favorite aromas, churned his stomach.

"I can't take this anymore," he said, and he stood so fast

his chair fell backward. Stout barked once and pawed at the door.

Hugh sighed and rose as well. "I'll go with you."

"No," Owen said, holding his hand out, palm facing Hugh. "I don't want Aileen here alone. Plus, someone should be here in case Saoirse comes home."

"Take *an laindéir mhór*," Aileen said, crossing the room and pulling down the large lantern that hung overhead in the middle of the sitting area.

Owen pressed his lips together in a soft smile and nodded as he took the light from her. "T'anks."

After stopping by the barn for an extra blanket, he headed out in the direction of the shed. He had no idea where to begin looking, but his trek to the east had been a bust, so he went in the first direction he thought of. When he passed the weaving shed, he glanced once more in the windows. Still dark.

As he wandered, his parting words echoed over and over in his head. *"In case Saoirse comes home."*

How had it come to feel like her home in such a short period of time? And how was it that the place he'd lived his whole life somehow now felt less like home without her in it? And what would he do if the worst had happened and Saoirse was no longer with—*No.* He couldn't think like that.

He began to hum a tune to keep his mind occupied, stopping every few bars to call out Saoirse's name or to stoop and shine the lantern into a copse of trees or under a bush. When he realized the tune he was humming, it was a punch to the gut. It was the same song they'd just been singing a few hours earlier in the church. He was reminded once again of the commitment he'd made—to worship and praise God, no matter what.

He lifted his face to the heavens. "God, please let me find her. Lead me to her." He stopped short of adding "before it's too late."

––––––––––––––––

The sky was just beginning to fade from black to gray. Owen dragged his palms down his face, trying to clear his vision. He'd been searching all night to no avail, and his sight was beginning to blur. He'd wandered clear up to the base of Mount Errigal and headed west from there, all the while calling out Saoirse's name. At one point, he thought he'd seen her silhouette curled up against the base of a stone wall, but it just turned out to be an ornery sheep who did not appreciate being jolted awake from its slumber.

Just as his fatigue threatened to overtake him completely, a shock of fabric on a tree caught his attention. He ran toward it, down the small knoll, feeling as though his boots had been filled with lead. Once he got closer, he could see that Saoirse was asleep in the low boughs of an oak tree. He gained his bearings. They were on the edge of the north side of Lough Lewey.

"Saoirse." Her name came out like a breath. She stirred and opened her eyes. "I've found you. At last, buíocihas le Dia."

Her eyes widened, and she rubbed them with her fists as though to make sure she could believe what she was seeing. "Owen? What are you doing here?"

"Funny, I was about to ask ye the same thing." He stepped forward, one hand raised. "Can I help ya down?"

Her expression tightened. "I'm not going back."

Owen huffed as if Lir had kicked him in the stomach. "Will you at least come down so we can talk?"

Saoirse stared down at Owen, his blue eyes blazing in the early morning light. With his hand outstretched to her like that, it took everything she had not to jump into his arms and never leave them again. But she couldn't. She had to be strong.

"Please?" he implored.

She let her gaze drift along the horizon, still warring with herself about whether or not to oblige. Could she trust herself? At length, she nodded, reached out, and let him help her down. Her bones ached and her neck was tight from the mostly sleepless night. It had been dreadfully cold, and the cacophony of strange noises had her checking over her shoulder all night long.

He held onto her hand and searched her face. Then he reached around and wrapped a thick blanket around her shoulders. "Are ya alright? What happened?"

She pulled the plaid tighter around her shoulders, grateful for its added warmth, and turned from his piercing gaze. There was no way she could say what needed to be said with him looking at her like that. "I'm fine. Nothing happened, I just . . . I need to leave."

"But why?" The confusion and hurt in his voice added fuel to the already blazing fire of her guilt.

She shook her head and turned farther away so her back faced him, her gaze sweeping the eastern horizon. "It doesn't matter."

He stepped up behind her, warmth spreading across her back from his nearness. She pulled in a slow, deep breath, trying to sustain her courage.

"Oh, but it does. It matters to me." He cleared his throat. "Very much."

Her hands balled into fists, and she dropped her head. "You wouldn't understand."

Slowly and tenderly, his fingers slid across her back to her shoulder and gripped it.

"Owen," she said, her voice barely audible.

His whisper was so near, his breath tickled her neck. "Help me understand. Please."

He tugged slightly so she faced him, then reached up and wiped the tears staining her cheeks. She nearly melted at his touch, and her eyes drifted closed. "I have to go."

"But why?" His voice was thick with emotion. "Don't you . . . I thought we . . . I think I lo— I need you, Saoirse."

"You'll find someone else who can help with the weaving, I'm sure." She sighed. "We're nearly finished, anyhow." She looked away, the force of his gaze too much to bear.

"Hang the weaving," he said, startling her with his intensity. He hooked a finger under her chin and lifted it. "Saoirse, I need *you*."

When she looked in his eyes again, her heart crumbled at the pain and confusion reflecting back at her. "Oh, Owen." Unable to stop herself, she reached up and cupped his cheek, his whiskers both soft and prickly beneath her skin. "I'm so sorry."

When he leaned in closer, she knew she should turn away. But if she was going to leave this place, never to see him again, she wanted the memory of the taste of his kiss once more. It wasn't fair—to either of them—but in that moment, she didn't care. She closed her eyes and brushed her lips against his. Then again. Suddenly, with the heat and intensity of a summer squall, they burst into the most passionate, toe-curling kiss that stole her breath and sent her head spinning. Her hands slid up and tangled in his hair. Owen's arms wrapped fully around her, pulling her close.

All at once, an alarm sounded in Saoirse's head. *What are you doing?*

She broke apart from him and spun away, taking a few steps to separate herself from this most intoxicating man. "I'm sorry. I'm so sorry," she said around puffed breaths.

He was quiet for a long moment, his own breathing sounding as though he'd just hiked Errigal in record time. At length he said, his voice rough, "What if I'm not?"

Saoirse gritted her teeth, tension snaking around her jaw and down her neck. "That's not what I mean."

"Then help me understand." He reached for her hand. "Come back with me and we can talk about it."

"I can't!" she yelled, yanking her hand free. "Don't you understand? It's all my fault!"

A look of confusion flashed across Owen's face, followed by a sly grin. "Well, that's just not true. I'm pretty sure it takes two to kiss like that."

"Och! That's not what I mean." She pressed both hands to her forehead and paced back and forth, trying to find the words that would let it all make sense to him. She huffed and held her arms out wide, letting the blanket fall to the ground. "You're in the position you're in because of me. Your hand, the sheep, the village, the landslide, all of it. It's my fault, and if I don't leave, I'm afraid I'll be the death of every last one of ye."

Owen's stance softened, as did his tone. "Hey, hey, that landslide was an act of nature. And if it wasn't for you, I'd probably be much worse off, if not dead. The same goes for Stout. None of that is your fault. You didn't send Haggerty and his men to steal my sheep."

He shrugged. "In fact, if it hadn't been for you and all you've done to help with the weavin' and the house and the flock, Aileen an' me would probably already be in the workhouse . . . You saved my life."

Saoirse's shoulders fell and her head dipped forward as it slowly wagged. "No, Owen," she said, her words measured, "I'm bad luck. I'm cursed. I brought this ill fate with me."

"No, no, no," he said, tracing a finger down her cheek. "You're not bad luck. You're the best thing that's ever happened to me."

He reached for her hand again, but she threw her arms in the air. "I killed my family!" she screamed.

Owen recoiled like he'd been slapped.

She coughed out a sob. "I didn't mean to. It was an accident, but I've paid for it ever since. And now I've made you and Aileen and the whole village pay for it too."

"What happened?"

Saoirse turned away again. She couldn't bear to look him in the face as she told him the story. She crossed over to a large rock and sat on it, her gaze trained over the valley in front of them. "I was a maid at Waterstown House and it was my job to get things all going in the morning. I'd start very early—or very late, depending on how you look at it.

"But for some reason I overslept that morning. I was rushing around getting ready to leave and trying not to wake my family. It was a frigid morn, and I'd set the fire extra hot. I tossed my apron on the peg near the hearth like I always did and rushed out the door without a second glance." Her chest shuddered with a ragged breath. "Apparently I missed the peg, and the apron knocked over a lantern from the mantel, because . . . the next thing I knew, the bells were clanging and a messenger came to the manor house and said there was a fire."

"Oh, Saoirse." She heard Owen's steps come up behind her. "I'm so sorry."

She scratched at a patch of moss on the rock. "I rushed back home, but it was too late. Everything was gone. Everyone was gone . . . even Finn, our dog." She squeezed her eyes shut, trying to block out the memory, but all that did was allow images of the charred rubble, still smoking, to shine brighter in her mind's eye.

"That's . . . that's awful. I'm so sorry."

Her head wagged slowly. "I've never been one for good fortune. My family always teased that if anything was going to go wrong for one of us, it would be me. I have a black thumb. Like when I tended the neighbors' stock while they were away and every last one of them fell ill. But ever since the fire, ill fate has befallen everyone I've come in contact with—starting with the man who was supposed to be my next employer, and it's just gotten progressively worse."

Owen's hand laid tenderly on Saoirse's shoulder. She resisted the urge to grasp it with her own and hang on for dear life. "Why didn't you tell me?"

A single laugh puffed from her chest. "You said it yourself—taking a life due to your own carelessness is unforgiveable. And I've taken five." Sobs shook her body once more.

"Saoirse, I—"

She shrugged his hand from her shoulder and slid from the rock. "I know. I'm a monster, and now I've allowed my carelessness to carry over and affect everyone else I love. I refuse to let anyone else pay the consequences for my mistakes anymore. I'm leaving so I can't hurt anyone else."

She turned, brushed past Owen, and continued up the hill to the road.

29

Owen watched as Saoirse walked away from him. Everything in him was screaming to run after her, to bring her home. But he couldn't move—the weight of all she'd just told him, and the shock of what he'd actually said to her, pinned him to the ground.

He mulled the remark he'd made about carelessness over and over, equal parts still believing what he said and also feeling like what happened to Saoirse's family was completely different. And yet . . . it wasn't that different at all from what had happened to his father. But he couldn't bear the thought of Saoirse having to shoulder the burden of losing her entire family in addition to the guilt she felt for their demise.

Show up.

The phrase drifted, unbidden, across his heart. "What am I to show up to?" he spoke to the brisk morning air, eyes searching the sky.

He was met with only silence and the distant mournful cry of a magpie. He looked back in the direction Saoirse had gone, but she was already over the far rise, nowhere to be seen. He stared at the horizon for several long, desperate minutes, hoping to summon her back with just his thoughts. When she didn't return, he decided he needed more help than just himself. If she kept heading on her current path, she'd hit Ballymann and then the Atlantic and would be forced to turn either to the north or south. He needed others to help him go after her and bring her home.

When John opened the door, Owen blanched at the dark circles that hung below his eyes and the crinkles of his skin that had seemingly deepened overnight. The poor man exuded exhaustion, and guilt washed over Owen like a rogue wave for potentially adding to the man's cares. Clearly the recent disaster was taking its toll on everyone.

"Owen, how are ya?" John said with a smile that didn't quite reach his eyes.

Owen shook his hand. "Well, I'm not grand, if I'm honest. But I can tell ya have a lot on yer shoulders already, so never mind." He started to go, but John's hand caught Owen's forearm.

John pinned a look on Owen that made him feel every bit the scolded schoolboy. "Ah, now, ya can't start a conversation like that and expect me ta just let ye go." He stepped aside and swung his hand into the house in a low arc. "C'mon in and we'll have a wee chat over a cuppa."

Owen blew out a long breath through his nose and pursed his lips. "I'd love to have some tea with ya, but I'm afraid there's no time." He met John's gaze and winced. "It's Saoirse. She's gone."

"Gone?" Confusion tightened John's features.

Owen quickly explained all that had happened since they left the village the night before.

"Och!" John snatched his coat and flatcap from the stand by the door. "That's the sorta information ya lead with, lad." He was already two steps out the door before Owen even had a chance to reply.

"Will we stop by and get Hugh?" John asked.

Owen shook his head. "He's up at the house with Aileen."

"Right." John's gaze swept the length of the village when he caught sight of another man. "Tommy! Goitse!"

Tommy O'Hanlon jogged over and greeted both men.

"Would yer new wife mind much if we stole ye away for a bit?" John asked. "Saoirse's gone and run off."

Tommy's eyes widened. "She won't mind 'tall. In fact, she'll want to help." The young man scurried off and was back in a flash with his wife and a couple of other folks, including Nora Boyle. The small group gathered in a half-moon shape around Owen and looked to him expectantly.

Owen scratched the back of his neck and tried to gather his thoughts. "There was a . . . a misunderstanding, and Saoirse's left. But she's truly nowhere to go, and I'm afraid she'll be in danger if she has to spend another night alone in the wilderness. I need yer help to find her and bring her home."

"Whadja do, lad?" Nora said, a knowing glint in her eye.

Heat flashed up Owen's cheeks. "I . . . I didn't do anything." *Liar.* "Like I said, there was a misunderstanding. And she's all alone—no money, nowhere to stay, no job. She needs our help."

"D'ya know where she's headed?" John asked.

Owen nodded. "She was heading west on the Moneybeg road when I saw her last. Once she reaches Ballymann, I don't know which way she'll go."

"Right." John turned to address the group. "Me an' Owen'll take the Moneybeg road on through to Ballymann. Tommy and Deirdre, ye head up where the road splits off toward Gortahork, in case she turns north before that."

"Grand so," Owen jumped in. "The rest of ye, split off south toward Annagary."

The group murmured their ascent and had already started to head to the main road when Deirdre asked a question. "But wait! What do we do iffen we find her?"

Everyone paused and waited for an answer, John's stubble scratching against his hand as he rubbed his chin the only sound. Suddenly, his eyes lit up, and he held up a pointer finger. "I've got it!" He scurried inside the house and a few moments later, he returned, arms laden with holly twigs.

"Is that leftover from Christmas?" Nora asked, disbelief coloring her voice.

John answered, matter-of-factly, "Aye." He shrugged and added, "We ended up not using all of it on Máirt na hInide. It smokes somethin' awful. If ya find her, light it, and we'll see the smoke and meet back here." He handed a few boughs to each pair, and they all set off again.

Once they reached the fork in the road, everyone split off. Owen and John walked—a bit too slowly for Owen's taste—in silence for a long moment. Owen's imagination ran rampant with all the horrific possibilities that could have befallen Saoirse in the half hour that had passed since they'd parted ways. Everything from being run over by a horse and buggy to being overtaken by Haggerty's band of misfits to—perhaps the scenario he dreaded most—meeting a dapper gentleman who swept her off her feet with riches and luxury.

"Yer army keeps dwindlin', eh?"

John's question jolted Owen from his thoughts. "Gabh mo leithscéal?"

Chuckling, John repeated his question, adding, "Just like auld Gideon."

Owen stopped walking, trying to figure out what on earth had made the man think of that. "Well," he said slowly, "aye, I suppose so."

"And ye've had to replace yer weapons too."

Owen's brows pulled together and he crossed his arms, annoyance beginning to bubble in his chest. "John, ya know I have great respect for you."

John nodded, a delighted glint in his eyes.

"So, I mean this with all due respect when I say, what on earth are ya on about?"

John's laugh echoed off the slate hills surrounding them. "Think back to what ya read." He hitched his thumb over his shoulder in the direction of the village and church. "Yer man Gideon had to reduce the size of his army, aye?"

Owen nodded, clarity slow in coming.

"And just like we said when we chatted in the church that day, God also reduced the size of yer own army."

Owen frowned and bobbled his head from side to side.

John's feet scuffed the ground slightly as they started along the path again. "And I don't know if ya noticed, but Gideon also had to replace his weapons. When the Good

Laird sent the tiny army to fight, what weapons did He send 'em with?"

"Um . . ." Owen's gaze drifted to the sky as he tried to recall. "Oh, they had torches, jugs, and trumpets."

"*Go díreach!*" John cackled. "He sent them into battle without a single sword among the lot. Instead, He sent them to fight with things no one in their right mind would consider takin' to war."

Owen looked at his friend from the corner of his eye. John must've sensed his continued confusion, because he went on to say, "What are the weapons—if ye will—that you use in yer daily life?"

Owen thought for a moment. "Well . . . I've used my shovel to fight off a fox before. Maybe a knife." He shrugged.

John tsked. "No, no, lad. Think about what yer true enemies are." He stopped walking again, his brows raised in question and his hands pressed onto his hips. When Owen was slow to answer, John listed off on his fingers, "Starvation, homelessness, sickness."

Oh, those enemies.

"How would you normally fight off those yokes?" John crossed his arms.

Owen lifted a single shoulder and let it fall. "I suppose by makin' sure I get the weavin' done, takin' good care o' the flock, and keepin' a good house so we stay warm and dry."

A sly smile slid up one side of John's face as he nodded. "And ye've lost a good portion of yer weapons lately, haven't ya?"

Sighing, Owen scratched his jaw. "By golly, ye're right."

They continued walking, each scanning the area around

them for any sight of Saoirse as they talked. "And the Laird saw fit to provide ya with Saoirse for a spell to help with that weaving. But if ye're not careful, you'll lose her too."

"I know." Owen's gut tightened along with his jaw. "That's one reason we're out here now lookin' for her."

John sent a playful wink in Owen's direction. "Aye. One reason." Then his expression became more serious. "Owen, ya need to take a sober look at yer life and what's happened in the last few weeks. Then ya need to look even closer to see what other weapons God's placed at hand fer ya—and they mightn't seem like weapons 'tall. All that's left to do, then, is show up and let the Laird fight for ya."

Owen opened his mouth to reply, but John's sudden shout and point stole his attention.

"Smoke!" John shouted. "They've found her. Let's head back to the village."

"Oh, thank you, Lord," Owen cried. John clapped a hand on his shoulder and nodded.

The trek back was mostly quiet, as John seemed to understand Owen needed some time and space to consider what he'd said.

Could John be right? Could God have placed other things in his lap to fight with that Owen hadn't even noticed? If his true enemies were hunger, homelessness, illness, and the like, he really saw no other way to combat them or hold them at bay than his work—both weaving and farming. But something niggled in his gut, and he suspected that what he was truly fighting against was a different beast entirely. As they rounded a bend, the tower of the church came into view. Suddenly it seemed very clear indeed. Owen's fight was not against man made of flesh and bone, or even situations that seemed bent on his demise. No, his enemy was far craftier and more treacherous than any circumstance or physical enemy could ever be. And if he wasn't careful, his lack of trust in God to sustain and provide would destroy all that he held dear.

30

Saoirse sat on the low stone wall lining the road that cut through the heart of the village—or what was left of the village. Then she stood, paced a few times, sat again, then hopped right back up. Tommy and Deidre had run to their house to fetch some tea and a blanket for her, but she insisted on staying here. On the inside, she tossed back and forth between deep relief that someone had come after her and bitter frustration that she was interrupted from doing what she truly felt to be the right thing.

A third emotion rose to the top—disappointment that it was the newlywed O'Hanlons who'd come after her instead of Owen. She swallowed that one down and tried to bury it beneath her sense of duty and a self-conjured relief. She'd told him he was better off without her. Safer. And she still believed that. But there was a part of her that desperately wanted him to find a way to convince her to see things his way. She blinked away the sting of fresh tears. Her cheeks were already raw from the nearly constant flow over the last two days.

"Ya best be careful cryin' beneath a hawthorn tree. The fairies'll come spirit ye away."

Saoirse startled at Bridie's voice, choking on the breath she sucked in quickly. As she coughed and sputtered, the older woman sidled up next to her on the wall. Soon Saoirse felt warm, gentle circles being rubbed slowly round and round her back.

"Aw, peata, I don't mean to poke fun. I was just tryna make ye smile." Bridie leaned forward to catch Saoirse's eye.

Saoirse offered a small, sad smile. "I dunno. It might be better if they do . . . spirit me away, I mean."

"Och!" Bridie flapped her free hand. "Why don't ya tell me what happened."

Saoirse's head hung low once more, and she gripped the edge of the wall so tightly the stones poked at her skin. While Bridie's kind eyes and tender soul invited—nae, beckoned—Saoirse to share her burdens, fear threatened to suffocate her. The more people who knew her shame, the fewer people she had left in her life. And while she desperately wanted to protect those she cared so deeply for, it felt nearly impossible to risk losing their companionship now that she was back in their fold.

But all it took was one look in her friend's eyes for the words to begin spilling out. She told Bridie the whole story, starting with the fire, to hiding in the McCreadys' barn and saving Stout, to Owen's kiss, and everything in-between. "And now," she said as she reached the present day in her story, "I just want to protect those I love. If I stay, who knows what else will happen."

Bridie was silent for a long minute, then her weathered hand slipped around Saoirse's. Her other hand reached over and patted it softly. "Oh, *a thaisce*," she crooned, "I can understand why ya feel that way."

Saoirse's heart sank, and she braced herself for whatever the woman might say next.

Bridie pulled in a deep breath and released it slowly. "If I were in yer shoes, I'd likely feel I was an ill omen as well." She tucked one corner of her mouth in and made a clicking sound as she shook her head. "But that's not how God works."

Saoirse opened her mouth to respond, but a squeeze of her hand stopped her.

Bridie chuckled lightly. "I know, it doesn't feel like that now. But we aren't instructed to live by our feelin's, are we?"

Saoirse's brow furrowed.

"Look," Bridie said as she pulled one knee up onto the wall so she could face Saoirse. "Can you tell me one person in the *na Scrioptúir* that God brands with bad luck because of a mistake?"

She considered Bridie's question and, for a second, the chaos and turmoil swirling in Saoirse's mind quieted. Despite her best efforts, she couldn't think of a single one.

Bridie went on, "The woman at the well, the adulterous woman people wanted to stone, Zacchaeus the tax collector"—she shrugged—"all of them made huge mistakes, and *Íosa* forgave and redeemed them all."

Saoirse turned a credulous look to Bridie. "Adultery and taking a wee bit too much money are hardly the same as what I did."

"Alright," Bridie replied without pause, "let's look at David, then. Not only did he commit adultery but he also plotted to have Bathsheba's husband killed so he could be with her. That was no accidental death on his hands. Yet he went on to be used by God in mighty ways, and He inspired him to write some of the most beloved Scriptures of all time. Never mind the fact that he planned the deaths he was involved in. Yers was an accident. A terrible, terrible accident."

Bridie stood, wincing as she stretched the leg she'd been sitting on. "And if that isn't enough for ya, how about yer man Gideon that Father Cunningham's been talkin' about. He doubted God, asked for sign after sign, and was scared to death at what God had called him to do. He eventually led his army to victory in the most unexpected way."

Saoirse wagged her head. "That's all well and good, Bridie. But how do you explain all that's happened? Why have I brought so much destruction with me?"

"Aw, pet." She laid a hand on Saoirse's shoulder. "I'd wager all o' that would have happened whether you were here or not. And I'd venture to add that if ye hadn't been here, Owen and Aileen would've been far worse off than they are now."

Saoirse stood and paced across the narrow road and back. She wanted to believe what Bridie was saying, but the heavy weight in her gut held her fast.

"Look at it this way," Bridie added, "our Lord said that the enemy has come to steal, kill, and destroy, aye?"

Saoirse nodded, the knot growing in her throat. She desperately wanted to believe what her friend was saying, but she couldn't get past all that she'd lost. All that she'd caused to be lost.

"But He"—she pointed to the sky—"said He has come

to give us life. And not just survival but a rich, full life. That has nothing to do with possessions or position and everything to do with fullness of spirit and joy. Are you living an exceedingly abundant life, Saoirse? Or is your life defined by what's been stolen from you?"

Owen rounded the corner and saw Saoirse in deep conversation with Bridie. As soon as his eyes caught sight of Saoirse's face, he took his first full breath in days. She was safe, and she was home. Well, nearly home. At the thought, the familiar pit resettled in his stomach.

What if she doesn't want this to be home?

As he drew nearer, he could see that whatever Bridie had said to Saoirse had hit her like a sucker punch. Her eyes were wide and she stared at the ground as if she could see seven miles beneath the surface and beyond. The curiosity of what they'd been talking about gave way to the utter relief to have her close again, and he had to resist the urge to scoop her up in his arms and carry her off into the sunset.

"Saoirse," he said, his voice breathy and rough. *Nice one, eejit.*

Her gaze flew up to meet his, and her jaw fell slack before she blinked hard and stiffened her posture. She nodded as though she were greeting a mere acquaintance. "Mister McCready."

Owen blanched, but quickly scrambled to regain his composure. "I'm glad ye're back, and that ye're alright."

The way she cocked her head to the side and sort of huffed out a breath seemed to say, "I'm not sure I'm alright."

If he was honest with himself, Owen felt exactly the same way.

Bridie touched Saoirse's arm. "Ye'll think about what I said?"

"Mm-hmm," Saoirse replied, her gaze drifting back to the ground as if the weight of their conversation had settled on her once again. Bridie laid a hand on Owen's shoulder and gave him a quick wink. "I'll let ye chat."

"Thanks, Bridie," he murmured, then shuffled over to join Saoirse on the wall, taking care to leave a comfortable space between them. *Well, comfortable for her.*

"Are ya?" he asked. "Alright, I mean?"

Her eyes darted in his direction, then back to the ground. "I will be." Under her breath, almost too quiet to hear, she added, "I hope."

He watched her for a moment, not sure what to say next. "Ya know ye're welcome back up at the house. I—er, we—would love to have you come home."

When she met his gaze at last, all the light was gone from her eyes, and a shadow of sadness clouded them. His heart clenched at the sight. "Thanks." Her gaze flitted toward Bridie's house and back. "I've been thinkin' about it, and I'll stay on and help ya finish the weaving like I agreed to."

Owen sighed and reached out to grasp her hand. "Oh, I'm so glad."

She stared at their hands for a beat before slowly slipping hers from his grip. "But I'll be staying with Bridie and John. I'll come up during the days to weave, but I'll come back here"—she jutted her chin toward the Sheridans' house—"in the evenings."

Owen stood and slipped his hands into his pockets, trying

to swallow the jagged disappointment that welled up in his chest. "Right. That's sensible."

"It's fer the best." She slid off the wall as well. "I'll be back up in the shed on Monday. Now, if you'll excuse me." She dipped her head and brushed past him and across to Bridie's house.

Owen turned to make for home when he spotted Aileen and Hugh strolling around the bend into town. When Aileen caught a glimpse of Owen, her pace quickened.

"Any word?" she asked, breathless.

Owen nodded, a sigh of relief and sadness puffing from his mouth. "Aye, she's back, and she's safe."

"Thanks be to God," Hugh murmured, and Aileen nodded emphatically.

It took a long moment for his sister to tear her gaze from the side of the schoolmaster's face, but when she finally did, her brows pulled together in concern. "What happened? Where was she?"

Owen pulled off his flatcap and ran his fingers through his hair. After a deep breath, he told them all that had transpired during the storm and what Saoirse had revealed to him about her family.

"Och, the poor *créatúr*," Aileen crooned.

"How awful," Hugh added.

Aileen shifted her weight between her feet. "What's she going to do now?"

Owen scratched his jaw and told them about the plan Saoirse had shared with him.

Doubt shadowed Aileen's features, and she stepped closer to Owen. "And ye're okay with that?"

No, I'm not okay with it! Owen shrugged. "What other choice do I have?"

Aileen looked to Hugh, her expression pleading. "Wouldja talk some sense into the man, please?"

Hugh just wagged his head and held up his hands in mock surrender. "I'm afraid I'm a wee bit too new to this whole situation to be of much use or to offer any sort of wise counsel."

"And you shouldna have to," Owen replied. Poor bloke, being dragged into this mess.

"Ya can't be serious," Aileen said, her voice hitching up an octave.

"What?" Owen tossed his hands and let them fall to his sides. A breeze kicked up around them, carrying the scent of turf fires with it.

Aileen pressed a hand to her forehead and mumbled something about the desperate state of men. "Ya do have a choice, Owen Sean McCready. Yer choice is to walk over there an' fight for that gairl."

Owen blanched, then shook his head. His sister was so naive. Owen had made it fairly clear how he felt about Saoirse that night in the shed. And from the way she kissed him back, he had guessed she felt the same way. But it wasn't until after that their real problems started. Maybe she'd had second thoughts, and after he'd kissed her, she decided he wasn't the man for her. As far as he was concerned, there was no question as to what her choice was. He wasn't going to force himself on her if she truly didn't want him.

"No."

Aileen scoffed. "Owen."

He gripped her shoulder. "I said no, Aileen."

She rolled her eyes. "I don't think you understand—"

"You don't understand. There's nothing to fight for." He dropped his head, his volume dropping with it. "I already tried."

31

Saoirse sat in the church service, trying desperately—and failing miserably—not to stare at the back of Owen's head from the Sheridans' pew two rows behind his. Father Cunningham called the congregation to prayer, and Saoirse bowed her head and closed her eyes, wincing at the burning as she did. She'd hardly slept a wink the last two nights. She couldn't stop thinking about the conversation she'd overheard between Owen and Aileen Friday afternoon.

One thing he'd said had echoed in her mind over and over again. *"There's nothing to fight for."*

"Amen."

The united declaration at the end of the prayer jolted Saoirse back to reality—more from the way it punctuated Owen's point than from the sound of the congregation all speaking together.

As the sermon began, Saoirse's gaze drifted back to Owen. He sat in his customary seat, with Aileen on his right. New to the row, however, was Hugh, who sat on Aileen's other side. A smile tickled the corner of Saoirse's mouth, but like a magnet, her eyes and mind pulled her attention back to

Owen. She could see the line in his hair from his flatcap, which she knew now rested on his knee. Brown waves with the occasional strand of silver curled at the nape of his neck, and his shoulders slowly rose and fell as he breathed. He shifted in his seat and cleared his throat. Saoirse's cheeks warmed as the guilt of eavesdropping the other day rose in her chest again. But she couldn't help it. Once she'd heard her name, she was desperate to know what Owen had had to say about her.

And Saoirse couldn't blame him for feeling as though there was nothing between them to fight for. But it still stung. As much as it pained her to admit, a part of her wanted him to throw caution to the wind, to tell her that it was utter nonsense and that the only devastation that would befall him would be if he couldn't have her by his side. Her mind drifted back to their conversation under the tree. Maybe in his own way, he had told her that. But she couldn't escape the nagging feeling that another disaster would be unleashed on him and his household should she stay.

This is how I'm fighting. This is what I deserve.

Perhaps this was her penance. Her sentence. To suffer the bitterness of a love unfulfilled in order to pay the price for her carelessness.

Movement caught her eye, and she managed to tear her gaze from Owen's head in order to follow the glint that had stolen her attention. The clouds were moving outside and, for a moment, the sun peeked out. Its light streamed through the windows, setting the marble walls aglow and landing on the cross at the front of the sanctuary. It almost appeared to glow, and Saoirse squinted at its brightness. Then, just as quickly as it had come out, the sun slipped once again under its blanket, dimming the interior. But Saoirse's eyes remained on the cross, and her ears became attuned to what the priest was saying.

"Let us read from His Word:

For Christ also hath once suffered for sins, the just for the unjust, that he might bring us to God, being put to death in the flesh, but quickened by the Spirit: By which also he went and preached unto the spirits in prison; Which sometime were disobedient, when once the longsuffering of God waited in the days of Noah, while the ark was a preparing, wherein few, that is, eight souls were saved by water. The like figure whereunto even baptism doth also now save us (not the putting away of the filth of the flesh, but the answer of a good conscience toward God,) by the resurrection of Jesus Christ: Who is gone into heaven, and is on the right hand of God; angels and authorities and powers being made subject unto him.

"My friends, don't you see?" Father Cunningham continued, "Our Lord paid the price for all of our wrongdoings. All our mistakes and shortcomings. He paid our debts on the cross—one time, for all time—so you and I might be free from the chains that come from those missteps and shortfalls. So, while we must often still experience the consequences of our sin, we no longer have to pay the debt for it."

Saoirse's pulse quickened and sweat prickled the palms of her hands.

"If you speak ill of your neighbor, you may have to work to repair that relationship, but our loving Father will not send you a new punishment to repay that sin, for that debt has already been paid." He paused and slowly scanned the congregation. When his eyes locked on Saoirse, they seemed to linger for a long while before moving on. When he spoke again, she felt like his gaze stayed trained on her, though in truth it hadn't. "I fear some of you are still living in bondage, trying desperately to make up for past mistakes. Or perhaps living in fear that God's judgment is just around the corner."

Father Cunningham smiled and held his arms out wide. "Breathe free, my dear friends. That burden is no longer yours to bear."

Saoirse's vision blurred behind fresh tears. Could it be that simple? Had Bridie been right—was all the devastation that had befallen Saoirse and those she'd grown to love merely happenstance and not reparation for her mistakes? It seemed too good to be true.

Once home, Owen set the kettle on and restoked the fire. Aileen had stayed in the village to visit with some of the ladies and make a plan with Hugh to help get the school cleaned out the next day. Owen settled into his chair by the fire with his cup of tea and tried to rest, but his mind was as agitated as the Atlantic on a stormy day.

He thought back to that morning's church service. Owen had resisted the urge to turn around and look at Saoirse to see if she was heeding the vicar's words and letting her heart be set free from the burden that had been weighing so heavily on it. In truth, Owen himself had struggled to focus on spiritual matters and the homily. He could feel Saoirse behind him. His neck tingled just knowing she was back there, so near, and yet she might as well have been ten miles away. But each time his mind had wandered, he uttered a silent prayer to help him attend to what was being said. And when he finally attended to the message, his chest burned at its timeliness—not just for Saoirse but for himself as well.

How many times of late had the word from Father Cunningham been the exact message Owen needed? His gaze drifted to the floor between his feet as he recounted how the intensity of his seeking the Lord had grown with each passing day, which then begged the question of why. Why was he seeking the Lord so much more intently the last several weeks? A list ticked off in his mind. Haggerty's first attack. Saoirse arriving. Haggerty nearly killing Owen and Stout. The increased tweed order. Many sheep stolen. The storm. The list rolled on and on. And as the calamity increased, so did Owen's pursuit of God and His guidance. Why did Owen not have such fervor in his faith and prayers before? Could he have grown too complacent? Could God have allowed these recent hardships in order to draw Owen back to Himself?

Owen's thoughts went round and round like a whirlpool, blurring together in a dizzying array. He pinched the bridge of his nose as the ache for simpler times filled his chest. It didn't seem like faith should be this much work. Surely if he was godlier, he'd have less pain. Wouldn't he?

Be strong and courageous.

Owen blinked hard at the thought. Where had that come from? And what did it have to do with all he'd been thinking before?

He thought back to the end of the service. When Father Cunningham invited everyone to join in the closing hymn, Owen had nearly heaved a sigh of relief, grateful for an escape from his dizzying thoughts. And when it had turned out to be the same song they'd sung last week, Owen could only laugh. Barely a sennight had passed since he'd made that fresh commitment to let God be the vision and focus of his life. And here he was, already honing back in on the doubts and worries rather than on the One who could guide him through them.

Owen chuckled and shook his head at the seeming co-incidence of it all. He shifted in his seat, struggling to get comfortable. Unbuttoning his waistcoat, he stood to let it slip from his shoulders. He then stepped over to the peg near his bed but paused before hanging it up. His thumb rubbed over the rough tweed, and he lifted it closer to inspect the pattern. To the untrained eye, it likely appeared to have no pattern at all, but nothing could be further from the truth. Hours of meticulous thought and planning had gone into every single stitch—knowing when to change the color on the shuttle or the pattern of the heddles was a painstak-ing decision-making process. And it dawned on him. Owen wanted his life, his faith, and the fruit thereof to be like his tweed. With weaving, he was able to control nearly every single element. When he tied on a spool of weft that was the color of the heather on the hills and wove it into the gray warp, he knew precisely what he was going to get before he even threw the shuttle for the first pass. But faith wasn't turning out to be like that at all.

He hung his vest in its place and made his way back to his seat, but before he could sit down, something else caught his eye. A weaving of another sort sat in pride of place on the mantel. A charming, rustic image of a thatched cottage—the very one in which Owen found himself now—was bordered by a stitched phrase about the comforts of home. The whole fabric was stretched across a backless, makeshift frame cobbled together with beechwood sticks. His mother had embroidered it when he was just a wee lad. He lifted the frame from its place and ran his fingers over the image, smiling at the memories that flooded his mind as he did so. When he set it back on the rough wooden mantelpiece, it fell forward, and Owen caught it just before it clattered to the ground. As he did, the back of the tapestry caught his eye, and he held it closer to the light of the fire. A tangled web of threads crisscrossed the fabric without rhyme or reason. Knots plagued many of the threads, and the whole thing looked more like an exercise in how not to embroider than the work of a master craftsman.

Owen's breath caught in his chest. He flipped the frame over to look at the front, then again turned to the back. Returning it to its place, he glanced at the waistcoat once more. No matter how much he wanted to control what happened in this world or in his circumstances, faith, it seemed, was nothing like tweed but much more like a tapestry. To look at the back of it—where the artist had begun each stitch—one might think it nothing more than a tangled mess. But the scrambled crisscrossing of threads and knots behind the scenes were the very things that allowed the beautiful design and image to shine through for others to see.

Owen had been trying to orchestrate his own life and manipulate it like he did his work on the loom, rather than let the Great Artist work through the mess and tangle to create beauty like only He could. It was why those battle plans Owen had read about seemed so crazy, if not a mite foolish. Those plans were the back of the tapestry. Had Gideon or Joshua or any of the others refused, the beauty of God's design would not have been shown. Owen now knew he had to be strong and courageous enough to release control. He needed to choose once and for all to trust the One with the pattern to take this mangled, jumbled mess in which he found himself and use it to create something that would declare His goodness, power, and beauty to all who would look upon it.

32

Saoirse had to remind herself to relax her shoulders and unclench her jaw as she made her way to the weaving shed the next morning. Not only was she anxious about getting the weaving done on time—the deadline loomed dangerously near—but she also felt anxious about working with Owen again. Would she be able to stay strong and keep her mind—and heart—on the task at hand and nothing more? Granted, they had made much more progress with the tweed than she had expected. They'd completed far more in their all-night weaving session than she thought possible before the storm blew out the window.

As the thatched roof of Owen and Aileen's home came into view, a relieved smile slid up her face, followed immediately by a pang of sadness. It felt so good, so familiar, to be back up here. But her heart broke anew realizing just how much it had come to feel like home but would never be so again.

Focus, Saoirse.

She pulled in a deep breath, drawing strength from the fresh scent of the grass anchored by the earthy aroma of the smoke from the turf fire that curled languidly overhead. The brisk morning was cool but calm—standing in stark contrast to Saoirse's mood. She paused and let her gaze sweep the horizon. A multitude of green patchwork squares spread before her, leading to jagged mountaintops in the distance. So much beauty and light even amid the pain and hardships she knew were scattered across this land. And in her own heart.

Sighing, she started for the weaving shed but stopped short and decided to head to the house and say hello to Aileen first. She knocked three times, then waited. No answer. She slid the door open and pressed her eye to the small crack of an opening.

"Hallo?"

When no response came, she peeked her head around the door. The aroma of their breakfast still hung in the air, but the fire in the grate was little more than a low smolder. Swallowing the familiar pang of guilt that always accompanied thoughts of fire, she pulled the door shut and headed to the shed.

The ground was still fairly soaked and soft, so she opted to follow the road up and around the barn rather than climb the small but steep hill behind the house. As she rounded the north end of the barn, Stout came bolting toward her, his happy yips and yaps echoing in the breeze as he ran.

"Oh, there's a good dog!" Saoirse crouched down to greet the pup. He skidded right in front of her and raised up to put his paws on her shoulders as if he was giving her a hug. The force nearly knocked Saoirse onto her rump.

"Oof! How are ya, Stout, huh? How've ya been?" Saoirse crooned over the dog as she scratched his head, ears, and back. Stout responded with several licks to her cheek and tail wags that wobbled his whole body. Laughing, Saoirse rose and brushed the dirt from his paws off her shoulders and skirts. Stout trotted a few steps toward the weaving shed, then stopped and turned back to her. His mouth hung open, making it look like he was smiling as he panted. Then he continued to trot happily toward the shed, peeking over his shoulder every few steps to make sure Saoirse was following. She smiled as she trailed behind him. As they neared the building, the loom was silent allowing Owen's voice to drift out through the open door. His deep baritone singing warmed Saoirse to the core. It was the same song he'd taught her, and it instantly filled her with equal parts delight and heartache.

As she approached, she noticed the piles of small logs flanking either side of the door, stacking nearly halfway up the wall. She stood in the doorway for a moment before entering. Owen had his back to the entrance and was winding light yellow thread around a shuttle.

"I see ya got the tree moved," she said, stepping just inside.

Owen stilled, then finished wrapping the last couple of inches onto the shuttle before setting it in the basket at his feet. Then he turned. "Mornin'." He smiled but it didn't reach his eyes, which fairly glowed in the morning light. "Hugh did that fer me." He swallowed hard. "While I was out searchin' for ye."

An awkward silence enveloped them as her gaze drifted to the floor. At length, Saoirse cleared her throat and hitched her thumb in the direction of the house. "I stopped by to say hello to Aileen, but she wasn't there."

Owen nodded. "She and Hugh went down to work on the schoolhouse. They're gettin' it cleaned up."

She fidgeted with her hands. "Ah."

After another awkward pause, Owen said, "Eh, thanks for comin'."

Saoirse nodded and licked her lips, which had suddenly gone very dry. She'd seen him just yesterday, but somehow, standing with him now, it felt like ages since they'd been face-to-face. She tugged her cloak from her shoulders, more for a distraction than anything else, as it almost felt colder inside the shed than outside. After hanging it on the peg, she crossed over to the loom. "Same place we left off?"

Owen nodded, his intense blue gaze boring into hers, shining with an emotion she couldn't read. She forced her attention to the stack of finished rolls of tweed in the corner and stepped over to them. Running her fingers along the edges, she marveled at what they'd been able to accomplish in such a short amount of time. "I didn't realize we'd finished so much."

"I can scarcely believe it myself," he said. "But I have you to thank for it."

Her head spun back to look at him, heat flashing in her cheeks. "I have no doubt you'd have found a way."

His mouth twisted up to the side, and he made a clicking sound as he wagged his head. "I don't think so." He busied himself moving the basket of weft spools to the end of the loom. "When you first offered to learn the trade and Aileen was pesterin' me to let ya, I thought ye'd both lost yer minds. That plan made absolutely no sense, and I couldn't see any way it would work."

Saoirse's brows lifted and she nodded. "I'd had the same fear."

He slid his hands into his pockets, his shoulders rising then falling with a deep breath. "But it's been made very clear to me—and to you too, I think, based on our conversations—that God's plans very often seem foolish to those He asks to carry them out." He closed the distance between them until only a foot or so was left. "But I've come to see that it's in those times that He is able to show himself more faithful and powerful. And that experience would be lost if things were to be done any other way."

Saoirse wrapped her arms around her middle, trying to stay the fluttering that his nearness set loose there. "That's . . . that's very . . . insightful." Her eyes flitted up to his face, then fell to her hands as she pretended to pick at a jagged nail. His gaze was too intense. Too inviting.

A soft chuckle slipped through his lips, and he moved half a step closer. "You still don't see it, do ya?"

She turned away, not wanting him to see the fresh tears that stung her eyes. She didn't even know why she'd been moved to tears. There was just something about the tenderness in his voice, the faith drenching his words. It was too much.

"You think that you brought a curse when you showed up on my doorstep, but it's not true. It was never true."

Saoirse squeezed her eyes shut and pulled her arms tighter around her waist. How could he still not see?

Gentle hands warmed her shoulders. "You were never a curse, Saoirse." His voice hitched, and he cleared his throat. When he spoke again, it was a hoarse whisper. "You were the answer to my prayers."

A sob choked out and she clapped a hand over her mouth, shaking her head. It couldn't be. His hands tightened on her shoulders protectively, and warmth spread across her back as he moved so a mere handbreadth separated them.

"After all that's happened, I'm absolutely convinced . . ." He paused again as his breath shuddered. Tears laced his voice as he finished, "I'm utterly convinced you were God's plan for me all along."

Saoirse's eyes slid open as she let his words wash over her and sink in like rain on a parched desert land. She turned her head to finally look back at him. His sapphire eyes were brimming with unshed tears and alight with something Saoirse couldn't bring herself to name. "Really?" she whispered.

He lifted one hand and brushed a stray ringlet from her face, then tenderly grazed the backs of his fingers down her cheek. He nodded slightly. "None of it made a lick o' sense. And then suddenly it did." His arm slipped around her waist, and he pulled her closer still.

Saoirse's eyes drifted closed, and she leaned her head back against his chest. "Owen?"

"Mm?" He was pressed so close, she felt his hum rumble in his chest.

"I'm scared." The statement came out in a small, timid whisper.

"Oh, Saoirse." He released his embrace and turned her to face him. Cupping one of her cheeks, he held her gaze and said, "I can't begin to imagine what ye've been through. My heart aches for the loss you carry. But I've come to believe that no tear is ever wasted in God's economy, and I know without a shadow of a doubt that He meant for you to come here."

He reached up and held her face with both hands, one thumb tracing gentle arcs on her cheek. Saoirse's skin came alive at his touch, and her heart thudded in her chest. She searched his face for any hint of jest or doubt but found only confidence and—dare she believe it?—love.

He lowered his voice to a whisper. "I'd be lost without you." He trailed his fingertips along her jaw, sending chills skittering down her arms and spine. "In absolutely every way."

His face blurred as fresh tears filled her eyes. She blinked them away, not wanting to miss one second of gazing at his face. She slid her hands onto his waist. "So would I," she replied, her voice barely audible.

A small smile lifted the corners of his lips, and Saoirse found her gaze tracing the outline of them. Finally, she forced her eyes to meet his again, and the intensity she found in them electrified her. The air between them stilled, and her fingers curled to grip his shirt. Slowly, he lowered his head, his own gaze now dipping to her lips and back up. Just as he was so close she could feel the warmth of his lips on hers but not yet their touch, her eyes fluttered closed. She held her breath, eagerly anticipating the feel of his kiss. Suddenly, Stout's head burst up between them as he pawed at her apron, then Owen's stomach.

Disappointment flooded Saoirse's soul even as she burst into laughter.

Owen's face reddened beneath the stubble of his beard, and he ran his fingers through his hair. "He never was one for sharing," he said, his head wagging.

Saoirse's cheeks burned. She reached down to scratch the dog's head.

"I, uh," Owen said, rubbing his jaw, his whiskers scratching against his skin, a sheepish glint replacing the intensity in his eyes. "I s'pose we should get to work."

"Right," she said, dipping her head, hoping to hide the disappointment that he didn't suggest they pick up where Stout had interrupted them. And yet, she had to let him know she'd heard him. His words had soothed her raw and weary spirit like a cup of tea after a trying day. Already, she felt lighter. Freer. As she brushed past him to get to the foot of the loom, she reached out and took his hand. Slowly raising her eyes to meet his, she said, "And thank you."

He smiled softly and his stance relaxed. Lifting her hand, he pressed his lips to the backs of her fingers and held for a long moment. "Ye're welcome."

33

Owen sang along with Saoirse's weaving tune as he wrapped the last two shuttles with thread—one with lavender, one with his favorite rusty red color. The singing was a good distraction. He glanced over his shoulder at Saoirse. She was intently focused on the job, brows pulled together in concentration as her hands and feet moved in the coordinated dance that is weaving. She looked like a seasoned master of the craft. Well, mostly. Her tongue poked out of the corner of her mouth, and Owen couldn't help the chuckle that rumbled in his chest. But then he had to look away from those lips, lest he be pulled back into the daydream of what could have been had Stout not come between them.

He finished wrapping the last spool and shuffled behind Saoirse to drop it in the basket at her side. More than the longing for her kiss, he was overwhelmed with a deep sense of gratitude. It seemed that, perhaps, his words had sunk in and she was beginning to see that God wasn't punishing her for what happened to her family—she'd been doing that to herself. And while he wouldn't wish that sort of tragedy on even the likes of Haggerty and his ilk, he was so grateful that God used those terrible circumstances to bring Saoirse here.

He turned and studied the loom. Only a few inches remained until they were finished with their last bolt of tweed. His gaze drifted to the stack in the corner. Even in the waning light, he could make out the unique blend and twill he'd designed and was slowly becoming known for. He counted the rolls again just to make sure his mind hadn't played a trick on him the last seventeen times he'd tallied them.

All at once, the loom fell silent.

"I . . . I don't believe it," Saoirse said. "'Tis done."

Owen's hand drifted up to cover his mouth. Then he ran it down his chin, a strange sensation filling his belly. "Dáiríre?" he said, his voice thick.

She nodded. "Really."

A slow smile lifted his face, and he walked the length of the loom, his hand running along the finished tweed. When he got to the foot of it, he bent close to the fabric to ensure it was all done and ready to be tied off. He straightened and met her gaze, then held out a small pair of shears. "Would ya like to do the honors?"

Saoirse's jaw fell slack, and a small grin lifted the corners of her mouth. "Are ya sure?"

Owen grinned and waggled the scissors in his hand. "I'd say ye earned it."

She took the cutters from him, bent, and double-checked the weaver's knot she'd tied the weft off with, then she reverently snipped the shuttle thread close to the weave. They made quick work of cutting down the heddles and pulling the finished tweed from the loom. Once they had it rolled and stacked with the others, they both stood and stared at the fruits of their labor for a long, quiet moment.

Finally, Saoirse sighed and looked at Owen. The brightness and joy in her eyes threatened to undo him. He'd do anything to make sure he saw it there every day. "We did it," she said, sighing once more.

"Aye." He smiled. "We did."

They both burst into laughter and then he swept Saoirse up in his arms and spun her around. When he set her down, they held the embrace for a moment. "Thank you," he murmured into her ear. "For everything."

She shook her head against his shoulder. "No, thank *you*."

Saoirse relaxed into Owen's arms, both exhausted and elated that their task was finally complete. They stood that way, each holding the other, for a long while. When they finally parted, Saoirse took one more look at the tall stack of fabric bolts and shook her head in wonder. "I won't know what to do with m'self now." She chuckled and looked back to Owen.

"I can think of a few things," he said, a sly grin tipping his mouth.

Heat flashed up her cheeks, and her pulse quickened as they drew closer to one another again. She shrugged slightly. "I suppose I could think of something to keep me busy." Good gracious, she was getting bold.

He took her hand and laced his fingers through hers. Saoirse reached up with her other hand and ran her fingertips down his cheek.

"Owen! Saoirse! Come eat!"

Owen huffed a breath out his nose, and his head drooped as he chuckled. He leaned down and pressed a slow, tender kiss to Saoirse's cheek, then her forehead. He then tugged her hand to lead her outside. "We'd best not keep Aileen waiting."

Saoirse giggled and followed him out into the chilly evening. As they strolled over to the road, she took in the view. The stars overhead twinkled in the unseasonably clear sky, the windows of the house glowing with the soft golden light of a turf fire. In the distance sheep bleated contentedly, and the air was filled with the most comforting and familiar potpourri. Overwhelmed with gratitude and overcome with love for this place, these people, this man, she stopped walking. When Owen's hand tugged against hers, he looked back, his face questioning. Saoirse closed the distance until barely a breeze fit between them. She reached up and stroked his cheek, then lifted on her toes and pressed her lips to his. Owen stiffened in surprise for a split second before engulfing her in his arms and melting into her kiss.

When they pulled away, Saoirse pulled in a deep breath and let it out in a huff. "Now we can go eat."

Owen laughed, shaking his head. Then he took her hand, laced his fingers through hers again, and led her down the road to the house.

When they went in, Hugh was setting plates and flatware around the table as Aileen stirred something in a pot on the stove. Next to Saoirse, Owen's stomach rumbled.

He pressed a hand to his belly. "Pardon me," he said, his cheeks reddening. "I reckon I'm a mite hungrier than I realized."

Once coats and hats were hung up and hands and faces had been washed, the four sat down to a delectable supper of stew and brown bread.

"Well, it seems ye two have kissed and made up," Aileen said as she dipped her bread into the broth.

Saoirse choked on the bite she'd just put in her mouth, nearly spewing it all over the table. As she tried to right herself and take a sip of tea, Owen asked, "What d'ya mean by that?"

Aileen rolled her eyes. "I just mean ye lot came in here all smiles and hellos when ya couldn't even look at each other yesterday."

Saoirse, finally recovered, cleared her throat. "Oh, right. Yes, I believe we've worked things out." She glanced at Owen from the corner of her eye. He flashed a subtle wink in her direction, and she warmed at the gesture.

"It doesn't hurt that we've finished the order," Owen added.

"Have you now?" Aileen's eyes rounded, and she grinned wide. "That's wonderful!"

"Well done," Hugh said. "*Comhghairdeas*!"

Owen nodded. "Thank you." He looked to Saoirse, eyes shining. "I think we both thought we weren't going to make it there for a wee while."

Saoirse agreed but couldn't help feeling his statement addressed more than the weaving. "Indeed." She dabbed the corner of her mouth with her napkin and turned her attention to Aileen and Hugh. "How go things down at the school?"

Hugh sighed and shifted in his seat. "Well," he said, "in some ways better than expected. We've been able to salvage a great deal more than we'd originally thought we might."

"Oh, that's good," Saoirse said.

Aileen nodded and looked at Hugh. "Unfortunately, the building itself is far more damaged than we originally expected as well."

"Exactly," Hugh added. "In fact, several of the buildings in town have shown signs of slipping. Even ones not directly affected by the landslide."

Saoirse's hands dropped to her lap. "Oh, that's awful."

"Which buildings?" Owen asked.

Hugh shook his head. "A great many, actually. Now I think of it, there's only one or two that still seem stable." His gaze flitted to Aileen and back. "There's talk of leaving."

"Leaving?" Saoirse and Owen asked in unison.

Aileen set her spoon on the table and settled her gaze on them. "There's going to be a meeting in the village in two days' time to talk about abandoning it and everyone goin' their separate ways."

Saoirse's heart sank. So many lives would be affected by that. Not just those who lived in Glentornan itself but everyone in the surrounding area and glen as well. The school, the church, the doctor's office—all were utilized by the greater community in the Poisoned Glen. Sadness filled Aileen's eyes, and Saoirse looked from her to Hugh. Clearly the two were very fond of one another. What would it mean for them if Hugh was assigned to a different school farther afield?

"I'm so sorry," she said. "Where would everyone go?"

One of Hugh's shoulders lifted and fell. "That remains to be seen. Some folks have family in the area. Others are talking about leaving Donegal altogether. And one or two have mentioned using this as a chance to finally make the voyage over to America."

Saoirse looked to Aileen, whose eyes swam in fresh tears. Saoirse reached across the table and squeezed her friend's hand. Was this one of those plans that didn't make sense? Or was this more hardship simply for the sake of hardship?

Under the table, Owen slipped a hand around Saoirse's free one. She drew strength from its immediate warmth and lifted a prayer for courage and wisdom. It would seem they were going to need it.

34

The next morning, Owen was up early to ready the tweed order for when the courier from Murphy's arrived. After every twig snap and gust of breeze, he checked the horizon for signs of Saoirse coming up the road. He'd offered for her to stay last night, back in Aileen's room like before. She'd blushed and thanked him for the offer but said Bridie would be expecting her and she didn't want to worry her hostess.

That was something Owen greatly admired about her. She was one of the most thoughtful and considerate people he'd ever known. Which made knowing how the fire that took her family started all that much more difficult to swallow—and his remarks about carelessness as well, for that matter. He still felt that those who caused the death of another human through their own negligence should be held accountable. However, there was a difference between true negligence and sheer accident. What happened to Saoirse's family was the latter, as far as he was concerned. But had Saoirse truly come to believe that for herself?

When the wind picked up, Owen tugged his flatcap down over his ears and glanced toward the sky. A few wispy clouds skittered across the vast expanse of blue, but dark, ominous ones were building out over the sea. If the weather followed its typical pattern, they'd be in the middle of another squall by nightfall. Once again, his gaze drifted toward the road leading up from the village as he wished, not for the first time, that he had insisted on going to John and Bridie's to collect Saoirse in the wagon this morning. He'd offered last night, but she'd refused, saying the walk would do her good. However, at this moment, he wanted nothing more than to have her by his side.

Finally, he saw a shock of strawberry-blond ringlets bobbing its way toward the house. A wide grin split his face, and he scampered down the hill from the shed like a schoolboy who had just been called in for pudding. He arrived at the front door, breathless, just about the same time Saoirse rounded the final bend before the house.

"'Mornin'," he said, still grinning like an eejit.

"And good mornin' to yerself, sir," she replied, an equally big smile lighting her face. He met her halfway to the door and pressed a kiss to her cheek, which turned the loveliest shade of pink. "Are ya all set for yer man from Murphy's?" she asked.

Owen glanced back toward the weaving shed and nodded. "Aye. I've got it all by the door. Just waitin' for the man himself."

"I still can't believe we did it," she said looking up at him, eyes aglow.

"You did it, really." He held up his right hand. "And I mean that quite literally."

She took his hand and kissed the back of it. "It was a team effort. I had the best apprenticeship master."

Owen scoffed playfully. "Well, when ye're right, ye're

right." He laughed, and she bumped his side with her elbow. "Cuppa while we wait?"

Saoirse nodded and they headed inside.

Just as they were finishing their tea, the Murphy's wagon rumbled up outside. Owen and Saoirse exchanged a glance, both clearly eager to see if their work would pass muster. They met the man outside. Owen greeted him and shook his hand. "Conn, how are ya?"

"Can't complain now, so I can't," Conn replied. "Rain's a'comin' though. Can feel it in my bones."

Owen looked to the sky. "Aye," he said. "I believe it is. Let's get ye loaded up and back on the road, then."

Owen and Saoirse led Conn and the wagon around to the weaving shed door. As they loaded the bolts of fabric into the wagon bed, Conn inspected a few of them. He bent closer, brows furrowed, and rubbed the cloth between his fingers. "Hmm" was all he said.

Owen's stomach sank, and the familiar weight of worry settled on his shoulders once more. Next to him, Saoirse slid her hand through the crook of his arm. "Be strong and courageous," she whispered.

Thunder rolled overhead, and the wind began to pick up.

"Help with this, will ya, lad?" the man said, holding up a large leather cover.

"Cinnte," Owen said, rushing to help him spread it over the bed of the wagon and secure it down.

"Can't risk the damp settlin' in to it, y'know?"

Owen knew all too well.

"Right. I think that'll do nicely. Well done, and thanks very much," Conn called over his shoulder as he scrambled onto the seat at the front of the wagon. "Till next time."

Owen and Saoirse walked behind him down the hill. When he faded out of sight around the bend, Saoirse slipped her hand into Owen's. His fingers curled around hers and he squeezed.

Saoirse gasped and looked up at Owen, mouth agape.

"What?" Owen asked, his heart kicking up in pace.

She smiled and lifted his hand up. Only then did he realize that it was his right hand holding hers. He laughed once and opened his hand, letting hers slip free. Slowly, he flexed his fingers. They felt stiff, almost foreign, but at least they were obeying his commands. He worked until they curled all the way into a fist, then carefully opened them again.

"Buíocihas le Dia," she said on a sigh, eyes closed.

"Aye." He nodded. "Thanks be to God, indeed."

Thursday morning, Owen stood at the hob waiting for the kettle to boil. He yawned and scrubbed his hand down his face. He'd barely slept the last two nights. Just after Conn had left, the skies opened and didn't stop until late last night. Even the town meeting had been postponed until this afternoon. Aileen and Hugh had gotten stuck in the village yesterday evening. They'd gone down to continue working at the school Tuesday morning, and when the storm hit, there was no safe way for them to return. Owen presumed Aileen had stayed with the Sheridans since then.

But that had left Owen and Saoirse here alone. While being alone with Saoirse was top of his list of things he wanted in life, this was not the way in which he wanted to do it. Given their newly rediscovered affection for one another, both were so concerned about propriety that they'd hardly spoken for two days.

Between the racket from the storm and the magnetic pull of knowing Saoirse was just through the next door, sleep had eluded Owen both nights.

It wasn't that he felt they were both incapable of controlling themselves but more that he wanted to do whatever he could to let her know that her honor mattered to him and that he wanted to preserve her reputation. If spending a night trapped in a weaving shed together could've set village tongues wagging, how much more so could spending two full nights alone in his own home?

The door to Aileen's room scraped open, and Saoirse shuffled into the living room. Purple shadows ringed her eyes, and her hair—which had been pulled up into a tidy bun the night before—now half-dangled down the side of her head. She scratched her arm and yawned. "Mornin'."

Owen smiled. She'd never looked more beautiful, and he counted himself lucky that he got to be the first one to greet her that morning. "Get any sleep?"

She lifted weary eyes to meet his. "Not much."

"Me neither." The kettle whistled, and he poured the boiling liquid into the teapot, stirred, and put the lid on. He gestured to the table. "Come sit. I've got just the thing."

She shuffled over and flopped into the chair. He poured a steaming cuppa and placed it in front of her, along with a slice of brown bread and a rasher of bacon.

"I'm afraid I burned the bacon a bit." He shrugged. "Aileen usually does the cookin'."

Saoirse drew in a long sip of tea, eyes closed, and sighed. "Thank you." She sounded like she'd been crawling in the desert and that had been her first drink of water in days. The power that a mere cup of tea had to improve just about any situation had always struck Owen funny.

"I wonder how she's doing?" Saoirse asked, sounding a bit more awake.

Owen tried to infuse a lightness in his voice. "I'm sure she's grand. Bridie's probably fed her so much, she's about to burst." Saoirse laughed. Owen only hoped he was right and that nothing sinister or disastrous had befallen his sister.

"What's on the docket today?"

Owen stretched as he thought. "I need to get out to the fields and see to the sheep. Check their water, make sure Haggerty's not been back."

Saoirse nodded. "Need any help?"

Owen smiled. "If you'd like, I'd love the company."

Her head bobbed again, and she took another sip of tea. Owen stood and went down the hallway to a small press to grab some things he wanted with him in the fields. When he returned, Saoirse's head lay on the table. Her eyes were closed, and she was snoring softly.

He watched her for a moment, wanting to soak in the peace that finally rested on her face. Quietly, he tiptoed over and brushed the hair from her face, then carefully scooped her up in his arms. He carried her to one of the chairs by the fire and set her down. Then he grabbed a plaid from his bed and draped it across her. Bending at the waist, he pressed a kiss to her forehead. "Sleep well, my love," he whispered.

35

Saoirse awoke with a start. Her back was cramped, so she stretched her legs out in front of her and reached her arms high overhead. Where was she? She blinked a few times and finally recognized her surroundings. She was in a chair in front of Owen's fireplace. She had a blanket over her lap and a crick in her neck.

"Well, hello there."

Saoirse yelped and jumped to her feet. Owen sat at the table in the kitchen, a funny little smile on his face.

"You snore." The playful glint in his eyes sparkled as he chuckled.

"Och! I do not." She pretended to be offended and made herself busy folding up the plaid Owen had apparently covered her with.

He stood and set an empty teacup in the basin. "Well, of the two of us, I was the one awake for the event in question, so we'll be taking my word for it."

Saoirse tried to hold back the laugh building in her chest, but she couldn't. Suddenly, she felt very self-conscious. "Were you . . . did you just . . . sit there? While I slept?"

"No," he said nonchalantly. "Some of us actually work around here."

Saoirse scoffed and threw the blanket at him. He managed to dodge it before rolling laughter bubbled up and out his mouth. Saoirse adored the sound of it.

"I'm only jokin'," he said as he closed the distance between them. "If anyone deserves to rest, it's you. Besides," he said as he took her hand and kissed the back of it, "I've only been in here for a few minutes. If you hadn't have woken yourself up, I would've done. We need to get to the meeting."

Saoirse clapped a hand to her forehead. "I completely forgot about the meetin'! Are we late?"

"No, no." He laid his hand on her shoulder. "We don't need to leave for another hour."

"Right," she said, relieved. She reached up and squeezed his hand on her shoulder, then turned toward the hall. "I'll get myself ready."

"There's some bread and fish on the table if yer hungry." He gestured to the kitchen.

As if on cue, Saoirse's stomach rumbled, sending heat creeping up her neck to her cheeks. "Thanks," she said, then she disappeared into Aileen's room.

She quickly changed out her apron for a clean one and put on a fresh pair of stockings. Then she approached the looking glass and gasped. Even in the smoky reflection, she could see she looked an absolute fright. Her hair was completely disheveled, and somehow dirt had gotten smudged across her cheek. How long had that been there?

Without a washstand in the room, she had few options. So she licked her finger and cleared the dirt from her face, then she pulled all the pins from her hair and twisted the locks up in a fresh style, allowing a few ringlets to fall down around her face and neck. That was about as good as it was going to get. She pinched her cheeks and bit her lips, hoping to add a little color, and left the room.

In no time, they had the wagon hitched up to Lir and were rumbling down the road toward the village. Both were quiet, though the silence that stretched between them was comfortable. It was a nice change from the strained silence they'd been living in the past two days. The fresh air, it seemed, did them good. That and having an escape from the growing romantic tension building between them. Saoirse had hoped kissing him Tuesday morning would relieve some of that and help them keep their minds on other matters. Instead, for her at least, it had only served to ramp up the intensity of her attraction to and affection for him. Adding how he'd been a complete and utter gentleman during their time alone only served to endear her even further to the man.

We just need to get married and be done with it. Saoirse's cheeks burned at the errant notion. If that idea were to escape her lips on accident, someone might presume her intentions were untoward or carnal. But nothing could be further from the truth. Owen McCready had proved himself to be a trustworthy man, an able guardian, a man of faith, and a wonderful companion. And while being in his arms was entirely delightful, it was all those other things she was most eager to experience for the rest of her life.

"Penny for your thoughts."

Saoirse felt Owen studying her, but she kept her gaze trained forward as she willed her pulse to slow. "Oh, nothing much." She shrugged. "I'm just wondering about the meeting and what might happen in the future for everyone." Well, it was mostly true.

Sighing, Owen nodded. "I've been thinking the same thing." He glanced her way, then back at the road. "I have a hunch of what the village might decide, but it could go one of several ways." He paused for a moment, then added, "Well, I s'pose it's really only one of two ways. Either they decide to stay, or they decide to scatter."

As they neared the church, Saoirse's mind returned to Aileen and what this might mean for her if Hugh had to take a headmaster position somewhere else.

Owen parked the wagon and helped Saoirse alight, then they joined the stream of people making their way into the church. When they entered, Aileen caught Owen's eye.

"God be praised," she cried and ran to her brother before wrapping him up in an embrace. "Thank God yas are alright."

Owen held his sister tight and cradled the back of her head with his hand. "I was just about to say the same thing about ye." He gripped her shoulders and held them at a distance as he looked her over. "Are ya truly alright?"

"Aye," Aileen said, nodding. She looked absolutely knackered. Dark shadows hung below her eyes, and her hair clung to her shoulders. Her dress was covered in dried, caked-up mud.

Saoirse hugged her friend as Owen and Hugh shook hands.

"Might I have a quick word?" Hugh asked. Owen glanced to his sister, then back to Hugh, and nodded. They walked to the back of the church.

"How was it down here?" Saoirse asked. But before Aileen could answer, John Sheridan called the meeting to order.

His face was ashen with the same fatigue as everyone else's as he stood and patted the air with his hands to quiet the crowd. "A chairde," he began. "What I'm going to say will be no surprise to those who live here in the village. But we've kept this meeting because we know that ye who live in the hills need to hear what's going on."

Worried murmurs rippled through the crowd, which Saoirse noticed was a mite larger than any service she'd been to. Owen and Hugh shuffled down the aisle and joined Aileen and Saoirse in their row. Saoirse almost missed Hugh give Aileen a small nod. Aileen blushed and tried to hide a smile before turning her attention to the front of the sanctuary.

John scanned the group, a deep sadness shadowing the light that could usually be found in his eyes. The bright afternoon sunlight streaming in through the tall windows and pooling in a golden puddle at his feet contrasted the dim mood of the crowd. "The village of Glentornan . . . is no more."

Gasps and cries went up from the people.

"Níl!"

"Say it's not so!"

"What's happened?"

"What about the church?"

John patted the air again. When the mumbling quieted, he continued. "'Tis true we first called this meeting in order to discuss if it was necessary to abandon the village, or if there might be a way to make it so we could stay." He paused and scratched the back of his head. "However, during this most recent storm, another slide occurred"—more gasps— "Thankfully no one was hurt or trapped. But it has made it so the foundations of our buildings are no longer safe."

Saoirse grasped Owen's hand and squeezed. He wrapped his fingers around hers and held tight. What would this mean for them?

John went on, talking about what he knew most of the residents of Glentornan itself were planning to do, but Saoirse couldn't follow his words. Her mind was swirling with questions of her own. While Owen and Aileen didn't live in the village, they certainly relied on it for many things, including worship and fellowship. Not to mention medical care and schooling, should that need ever arise. But if that was all gone, could they sustain themselves just on the farm with the sheep? And what of Saoirse? If they were limited to the resources they could source from their land, having a third mouth to feed would tax that supply even further.

Next to her, Owen shifted in his seat and looked behind him, then around at the rest of the crowd. He leaned close to her and whispered in her ear, "Brace yerself. There could be a big fuss from the community."

Saoirse peered up at him, worried and wondering. What sort of fuss?

A few rows ahead of them, a large, muscular man rose to his feet. "Uh-oh," Owen muttered. He leaned in again, his breath tickling her ear as he spoke. "That's Big Ed. Used to be a prized boxer in his younger days."

Saoirse tightened her grip on his hand.

"First t'ing," Big Ed said, holding up a meaty finger, his booming voice echoing in the large room. "I want to say I'm terrible sorry to hear yas hafta flee yer homes."

The crowd erupted in agreement.

"Hear, hear."

"Go díreach!"

"Good man!"

John Sheridan's chin quivered as he nodded his thanks.

"And second," Big Ed continued, "whatever yas need—be it a helpin' hand or a bracin' cuppa, we're here." Applause erupted and Saoirse's grip loosened as she looked at Owen. Astonishment was painted on his face.

John was quiet for a long moment. It appeared he was trying to compose himself. At length, he said, "Thank ye, truly. Very much. I know all of us in Glentornan appreciate it."

Father Cunningham joined John at the front of the room. "Let's pray for all those who will be displaced by this unfortunate turn of events." A rustling filled the room as people shifted in their seats, some to kneel and bow their heads.

As the vicar prayed, Saoirse lifted up her own prayers in agreement with his, though she added an extra prayer for Father Cunningham, as this likely meant he would be transferred to another parish.

After the prayer, the crowd slowly filed out, but a few stayed back. Conversation was almost absent, and the only sounds to be heard were the shuffling of feet and the occasional sniffle or quiet sob. John and Bridie approached their row and stopped, both offering sad smiles.

"What say ye to one last cuppa at our place? For auld time's sake?" Bridie said, her voice cracking.

"That would be lovely." Aileen's eyes were red and puffy. Hugh laid his hand on the small of her back and gently guided her into the afternoon sun. Owen and Saoirse filed out behind them.

As they headed down the hill to the Sheridans', a messenger rode up on a horse. "Beggin' yer pardon, folks, but I'm lookin' for an Owen McCready? I went up to his place, but no one was there. Someone on the road said to look here for 'im."

Owen stepped forward. "I'm McCready."

The messenger extended his arm, an official-looking envelope in his hand. "This is from Murphy's of Donegal."

Saoirse's heart felt like it thudded to a stop in her chest. She instinctively drew closer to Owen, who was staring at the envelope. She could almost see the wheels turning in his mind as he tried to figure out what it could be.

"Would it be payment for the order?" Saoirse asked.

"No," Aileen said behind her. "Yer man would've paid the balance when he collected the tweed."

Saoirse looked up at Owen, who nodded slightly. She'd missed that part altogether.

Slowly, as if in a trance, Owen broke the seal and pulled the letter out. His eyes scanned the page, and his hands began to shake.

"What is it?" Saoirse placed a hand on his arm. "Are ya alright?"

Aileen was suddenly on the other side of him, as if she thought he might need holding up.

Owen stepped away from them, his head rocking side to side. "I canna believe it."

Saoirse and the others held their breath, waiting for Owen to tell them if it was good news or ill.

He turned to face them all, still staring at the page, disbelief painted across his face. "They . . ." He swallowed and dropped his hands to his sides. "They want me to work for them. Full-time."

"What?" Aileen exclaimed. "That's incredible! Doin' what?"

He looked at the paper again. "They're wanting to centralize their production. They want me to oversee all the weavers and teach 'em my new twill and dying techniques and then manage all the production." He looked at the group again. "Says Conn will be out here again tomorrow to discuss the particulars."

Saoirse felt a little breathless. "That's . . . that's wonderful!" And she truly meant it. But it was not lost on her that Murphy's was based in Donegal Town. If he accepted that job, he'd be leaving his farm. And while she wanted only the very best for him, it did leave her feeling a mite worried about where she would go if he left. Could she and Aileen manage the farm on their own?

Aileen sidled up to Owen and began peppering him with questions he surely didn't know the answers to as the group wound their way toward Bridie and John's house. Saoirse kept to her own thoughts but couldn't help the sadness that had begun to settle in her chest.

Once at the Sheridans', Saoirse helped Bridie gather the cups and saucers and serve the tea. As Bridie settled into her chair after everyone had been served, she turned to Aileen. "So, any thoughts for what you might do if Owen accepts this new opportunity?"

Aileen blushed and dipped her head as she smiled. Her gaze flitted to Owen, then Hugh. "Well," she said, "it's funny ye'd ask. It just so happens I do have some plans of m' own."

"Oh? Do tell," John said, a small glint returning to his eyes. Saoirse couldn't tell if he knew what was about to be said or if he just had an idea.

Aileen reached over and took Hugh's hand. "Hugh's been offered a position at a boardinghouse that's openin' up just east of Letterkenny."

Hugh smiled and kissed her hand. "And I've asked Aileen to go with me." He scanned the group, beaming. "As my wife."

Chaos erupted as hugs and congratulations were given out. It was only then that Saoirse noticed the thin silver band on Aileen's left hand. She hugged her friends. "That's wonderful. I'm so happy for you," she said.

"Father Cunnigham said he'd marry us next weekend." Aileen grinned from ear to ear. "He said 'tis usually forbidden to wed during Lent, but given the circumstances, he felt it appropriate to bend the rules a bit."

"This calls for something a mite stronger than tea!" John exclaimed and scurried to a cabinet in the corner. "Uisce Beatha all around!"

When everyone had a dram of the fine whiskey in hand, John led them in a toast. He raised his glass, and the rest followed suit. "To the lovebirds!"

"To the lovebirds!" everyone repeated. Glasses clinked together and wishes of "*sláinte*" were given. The whiskey was happily drunk by all, and joyous chatter filled the room for a long while before Saoirse, Owen, and Aileen took their leave.

Saoirse was truly happy for her friend. Aileen had waited so long for love to find her and had nearly given up hope. She deserved every happiness she and Hugh would find. But selfishly, Saoirse couldn't help feeling like she was losing her family all over again. As the wagon rumbled over the road in the dim light of the setting sun, she hoped no one noticed the single tear sliding down her cheek.

36

The next morning, Owen awoke early in order to tend to the sheep before Conn's visit around lunchtime. He made his tea and toast as quietly as he could, then tugged on his jacket and flatcap and slipped out into the morning mist. As he crested the first hill past the barn, he stopped short. Saoirse sat on the low stone wall overlooking the valley, lazily scratching Stout's head as he sat next to her.

"Ye're up early," he said as he stepped over the wall and sat beside her. Stout wagged his tail a few times but didn't move from his place on the other side of Saoirse.

She glanced at Owen and smiled softly before turning her gaze back to the valley. "Couldn't sleep."

Owen studied her profile as he tried to get a read on her mood. What was going on in her mind? Her hair cascaded over her shoulders in a pile of ringlets, and the light he usually found in her eyes was muted and dim.

He reached over and took her hand. "Everythin' alright?"

She squeezed his hand softly but then slid hers from his grip. "It's fine. Just needed some fresh air."

He let his gaze drift along the horizon. Experience with

Aileen had taught him that when a woman said she was fine, she very rarely actually meant it. But he also wanted to give Saoirse any space she needed. He wasn't so arrogant to think he could be the solution to all of her problems. And yet the idea of her struggling under the weight of any hardship sat ill with him, and he wanted to do anything he could to ease her burden. "Ye're sure?"

She looked at him fully for the first time that morning and smiled, though it failed to reach her eyes. "Yes, I'm alright. I promise." She reached over and patted his knee. "Thank you though." Then she stood and made her way back to the house.

Owen watched after her, still feeling like something was off. "I'll see to the flock, then I'll be back," he said. Saoirse nodded, then disappeared inside the house.

Once out in the fields, the tension in Owen's shoulders began to melt. Between the weather, the weaving, and the women in his life, he felt like it had been ages since he'd been able to roam the hills with his flock. He inhaled deeply, reveling at the unique aromas of the damp grass, wet wool, and turf fires, then set to work checking the lambs and moving the herd to the next field.

Before he knew it, it was time to head back to meet with Conn. As he approached the house, doubts began to creep into his mind. How did Murphy's envision this happening? What did they truly want him to do? What if the letter was sent by mistake and Conn was going to have to take back the offer?

Be strong and courageous. Show up and shout the Lord's victory.

Owen's steps stilled. He closed his eyes, drew in another

deep breath, and reminded himself the circumstances around him didn't matter. Whether he worked for Murphy's or stayed here and eked out a living from the land, he knew he could trust God in any and all of it.

Rounding the barn, he saw that Conn had already arrived and was likely inside having tea with Aileen and Saoirse. Owen quickened his pace and joined them inside.

Conn stood as he entered. "Owen, good ta see ya," he said, extending his hand.

Owen took his hand and shook it. "Same to ye." He gestured to the table. "Come, sit. I presume Aileen's given ya some tea?"

Conn nodded as he returned to the chair he'd been in. "Oh, aye. And she's been tryin' to get me to explain why I'm here, but I wanted to wait until ye were home."

Owen took the seat next to Saoirse and pinned a look on his sister, who just shrugged innocently.

"Can't blame a gairl fer tryin'," she said.

"Now"—Conn leaned forward and rested his elbows on the table—"the letter told ye that Murphy's wants ya to oversee their new centralized weaving operation."

Owen nodded.

"And they're just over the moon about yer new twill design, especially the colors." He settled back against his chair. "The customers love it. Especially the wealthier yokes from abroad. They love how it looks like a piece of Donegal plucked right off the map and onto their shoulders.

"And this new batch, there was just somethin' about it." Conn shook his head. "It's special."

The warmth that had spread across Owen's chest at Conn's praise dissipated. He agreed—there was something special about Saoirse's work. But he couldn't have Conn believing Owen was the one responsible for it. He cleared his throat. "I hafta be honest with ya about something."

Conn crossed his arms across his chest. "G'on."

Owen looked to Saoirse, then back to the man. "I didn't weave most of that. It was Saoirse here. I'd been badly wounded not long after accepting yer order"—he lifted his right hand and pointed to the scars. "But we couldn't afford to back out of the contract, so I taught Saoirse how to do the weavin' so we could fulfill the order."

The laughter that erupted from Conn startled everyone else in the room. "Oh, we know that," he said between guffaws. "I could tell when I first laid eyes on it that is wasna yers." He wiped his eyes. "I thought ye were gonna tell me ya didn't want to weave fer us or somethin' like that."

Owen's jaw slackened. "You knew?"

"Oh, aye." Conn nodded emphatically. "To the average customer, it all looks the same fer the most part. But to the trained eye, each master weaver has his own unique tell in his work. Or should I say, hers. Most of us at the shop can tell who wove what just by lookin'."

"That's incredible," Saoirse said. Then her head slowly lowered. "I'm sorry if the tweed was subpar. I was just tryin' to help my friends."

Owen reached over and squeezed her arm.

Conn flapped his hand. "*Seafóid.* Yer work was as fine as any I've seen." He turned back to Owen. "We want ye to teach the weavers yer twill, or design, if you will, and then oversee the lot of 'em to ensure our orders get filled. The royals have just discovered us, and many are startin' to choose Murphy's over Harris and we need help managin' the workload."

He grabbed the teapot and helped himself to a fresh cup of tea. "An' then ye're free to join in the weavin' whenever ye like," he said after he'd gulped down a slurp.

Owen grimaced. Would they still want him if they knew he couldn't weave anymore? He'd regained quite a bit of mobility in his right hand, but the dexterity needed for weaving and tying knots simply wasn't there.

Owen stared at his hands. "I'm afraid I'm goin' to hafta decline."

"Owen Sean McCready, have ye gone mad?" Aileen rounded the table and smacked his shoulder. "What's the matter wit' ye?"

Saoirse laid her hand on his forearm. "'Tis a very generous offer."

Shaking his head, Owen said, "I'm sorry. It is a very generous offer and an amazing opportunity." He turned his hands over and back. "I'm just afraid I can no longer weave. I've lost most of the use of my right hand." He lifted sorrowful eyes to Conn. "Please extend my deepest gratitude to everyone, especially Mister Murphy."

Conn set his cup down with a loud clank, confusion pulling his brows together. "I don't think ya understand—"

"I'm sorry, Conn. If I canna use my hand, I canna weave."

Sighing, Conn flopped his hand flat on the table. "I only added the weavin' part because I figured ye'd want to continue yer trade. The real bulk o' the job is trainin' and managin'. And if ya truly taught her"—he nodded at Saoirse—"to weave with that level of expertise in a manner of weeks, that just goes to show we've found the right man fer the job."

Owen shook his head. How would they have known he could teach people how to weave the way he did? Why did they want him? It simply made no sense. He slowly turned to Saoirse. She looked back up at him expectantly. Could this really be what everything had been leading up to?

"How did you know?" he asked, his gaze still trained on her.

"Know what?" she replied.

Owen turned to Conn. "How did ye know I could teach weavin'?"

Conn shrugged. "We didn't. What we're really after is that pattern of yorn. Ye're the only one weavin' that design with those colors, but we simply need more of it. We figured we'd give it a shot to have you show others how to do it. But hearin' ya taught Saoirse here confirms ye're the man for the job."

Owen looked at Saoirse once again.

"If it's the lass ye're worried about, there's no need," Conn said. "They want her too."

"What?" Owen and Saoirse asked at the same time.

"Aye." Conn nodded. "I meant it when I said that there's something special in yer work. We want ya to be one of our full-time weavers."

Saoirse's hand fluttered up and covered her mouth. "I can't believe it." She turned wide eyes to Owen, fresh tears threatening to spill over. She searched his face, a million questions being asked without a single word.

Owen lifted his brows slightly, and she did the same. He nodded and she smiled.

He turned in his chair and took both her hands in his. "What do you say? Will you be strong and courageous with me and be my wife?"

A wide smile spread across her face, and she pressed her

forehead against his. "I thought you'd never ask," she whispered. "Yes."

Across the table, Aileen squealed and clapped her hands together. Owen took Saoirse's face in his hands. "I love you, Saoirse." When he pressed his lips to hers, she responded immediately, wrapping her arms around his neck and stealing his breath with the intensity of her kiss.

Conn cleared his throat. "Does that mean yes for me too?"

Owen and Saoirse laughed. Her cheeks flushed. They both turned to Conn and said together, "Aye."

Author's Note

Thank you, dear reader, for joining me on this journey through the *Heart of the Glen*. If you read the author's note in my most recent novel, *The Irish Matchmaker*, you may remember me saying how difficult that book was to write. That was due to writer's block, for lack of a better term. This book, however, has been an entirely different beast altogether. I knew the bulk of this story almost right away. But I was hit with more spiritual warfare during the writing of this story than I have with any of my other books. I pray that as you've read, your spirit has been encouraged and that you have been challenged in your own faith walk. And if you've not come to the place where you trust God with all the knowns and unknowns of your life (and beyond), my prayer is that you would understand now how deeply loved you are and how trusting Him with your soul is the best thing you could ever do. He loved you before you were even born and sent His Son, Jesus, to pay that debt for your mistakes that Father Cunningham spoke about in his final homily. God's forgiveness is a free gift we only need to reach out and take. The Bible promises that if you confess with your mouth that Jesus is Lord and believe in your heart that God raised Him from the dead, you will be saved (Rom. 10:9–10). If you've never done that but you would like to, take a moment now to tell God that. And then drop me an email at jennifer@jenniferdeibel.com—I'd love to pray with and celebrate with you!

Glentornan was a real village that was abandoned suddenly around 1912 or 1913. No one knows why the residents left, and I wanted to explore what that reason(s) might be. As far as I know, there wasn't a landslide in that exact area at that time, but there have been several over the years. It truly was the heart of the glen for a while, as it's striking church attests. Known mostly now as The Roofless Church or The Old Church, it stands in the middle of the Poisoned Glen as a stark reminder of both God's faithfulness and life's unexpected changes. The church itself carries a sad history—which Bridie shared about in the story.

Owen and Aileen are entirely fictitious, but the cottage-weaving industry was a cornerstone of Donegal's economy for quite some time. I was inspired to write the McCreadys' story after watching a fascinating documentary about two brothers who weave for Magee's of Donegal—which Murphy's Tweed is fashioned after. There is a link to that video on the Pinterest board for this book, which I share at the end of this note. Tweed weaving is still a massive part of Irish (and Scottish) culture and trade, with Magee's of Donegal often rivaling Harris Tweed in popularity.

Beyond the construction paper placemats I made in VBS as a kid, the actual art and craft of weaving was something unfamiliar to me. So intense research was certainly required. I learned a lot of the history and terminology from books, particularly *This is Donegal Tweed* by Judith Hoad and *Irish Folk Ways* by E. Estyn Evans. But I really found the heart of understanding through an entirely delightful chat with master weaver, Colm Sweeney—no relation to the beloved Colm Sweeney found in *A Dance in Donegal.* ☺ Colm was gracious enough to spend an hour or so chatting with me on Zoom about the craft, as well as to respond to countless emails with detailed answers to my crazy questions. You can learn more about Colm, see his work, and even find out how to take one of his weaving courses at his website, https://colmsweeneyartist.com/.

One of my favorite parts of writing this story was Stout. A sweeter dog was never known. I enjoyed researching sheep dog training, commands, and more, especially those specific to farmers in the northern part of the Republic of Ireland. One of my favorite places to find firsthand accounts is Away to Me Sheepdog Trial Demonstrations.

If you'd like to see photos of the area where this story takes place, pictures of how I envision the characters, videos of the songs mentioned in the story, and more, be sure to check out my *Heart of the Glen* Pinterest page at https://pin.it/HKKRuq5cN.

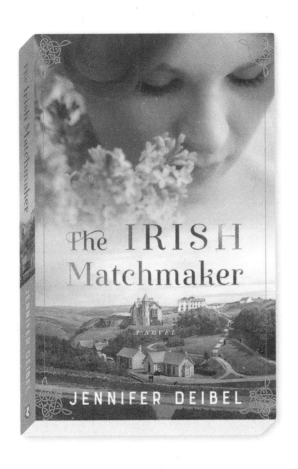

Ready for more from Jennifer Deibel?

Turn the page for a sneak peek of another charming Irish romance!

1

Lisdoonvarna, County Clare, Ireland
August 25, 1905

The warning came far too late, and before Donal Bunratty could register what his daughter was saying, he was slammed into with the force of a locomotive. Arms akimbo, he craned his neck to anchor himself in space while his feet flew up and over his head. The rustic odor of wet hide assaulted his senses, and Donal groaned and rolled onto his back. Wiping the muck from his eyes, he looked up to find *Bó* standing over him, huffing.

Donal grunted. "Hallo, auld man."

Bó sniffed Donal's hair and forehead and then, as if deciding his master was alright, he snorted heavily and trotted off away from the barn, the deep timbre of his hearty *moo* trailing after him.

Donal rested on his elbow and turned to see where the bull was headed. A chorus of lowing filled the bog. The whole herd of cattle now roamed as free as jaybirds. Flopping back down, Donal studied the heavy slate clouds mixing ominously overhead as he seemed to sink deeper into the spongy turf. The rain had passed—for the moment. But it wouldn't be long in returning.

"*Daidí*!" Sara splish-splashed toward him in her wellies. "Sorry 'bout that, Da. I couldn't latch the gate. It's rusted again."

Suppressing a sigh, Donal sat and squinted up at his daughter. Her sleek brown hair clung in wet strands to her cheeks, which held the rosy glow of childhood. She looked off in the distance—toward the herd, no doubt—and in the waning evening light, and from that angle, she looked just like her mother. He swallowed hard and lowered his gaze. Nearly six years later and he still missed his wife, though the grief was more of a distant foggy ache than the harsh knife to his heart it had once been.

He stretched his hand out to his daughter. "Help an auld man up, will ya?"

She giggled and clasped his forearm with both her hands, then tugged with all her might, her feet slipping on the puddled grass. But at last, she managed to help him up. "C'mon, Da, they're gettin' away!" Off she took like a flash toward the errant cattle.

Donal followed suit, though with much slower, heavier steps than his daughter. The next hour played out like a comedy of errors. The pair managed to wrangle the cows into a group fairly easily, but getting them back to the barn was another thing entirely. If father and daughter both walked behind the animals, some at the front would wander off to investigate an inviting shrub or thistle. But if they both walked in front, the group would break up, and the rounding up would start all over again. The fleeting thought that perhaps he should've gotten a dog after all skittered through

Donal's mind, but he shook it free. They could barely feed themselves and keep up with the livestock, as it was. At last, Donal and Sara fell into a sort of rotating dance, circling around the mob of stock—that kept the animals in their places. Confused, but in their places.

As they approached the barn, the skies broke open, and rain lashed down even heavier than before. Tugging his flat-cap lower over his eyes, Donal squinted through the deluge.

"Go open the door!" he called.

Sara, her hands shielding her forehead like a shelf, hurried to do as she'd been told.

The wind picked up and whipped Donal's coattails and yanked Sara's hair in every direction. He shouted to the girl again, gesturing wildly in case the storm distorted his words. "Now, stand there! No, no, in the open space. Yes, that's it!"

It took another feat of engineering, and a large dram of luck, to get the excited cattle back where they belonged. Once they wrangled the door closed, Donal and Sara efforted to get the latch to catch.

"We need a new one," Sara shouted over the maelstrom.

Donal nodded, water sluicing down the brim of his hat like Ennistymon Cascades. "This'll have to do for tonight." The hasp was secured, but Sara looked at him, her eyes questioning, doubting. "'Twill hold for the night, at least."

It has to. The uninvited thought invaded Donal's mind despite his efforts to stave it off. He refused to entertain any idea of what would happen should they lose the livelihood of their stock.

Back in the cottage, Sara changed quickly and saw to stoking the fire. Donal lumbered into his bedroom, closed the door, and crossed to the window. Pressing his palms to the sill, he rested his forehead against the cold glass as the storm raged on outside. Still breathless from their pursuits, he watched as the panes fogged and cleared, fogged and cleared. He'd always presumed the farming tasks would get easier as Sara grew and her abilities to help grew with her. Yet, for some reason, it seemed the difficulty was only increasing—compounding exponentially alongside Sara's growth . . . and the Irish pound's ever-shrinking reach.

The thud of iron against iron drew his attention back to the kitchen. By the sounds of it, Sara was starting on their tea. Not yet nine years old and already the woman of the house. It shouldn't be this way. And yet it was all they'd known—it certainly felt that way, at least. The three short years they'd shared as a family of three seemed nothing more than a daydream these days. This farm, this land, this life was all Donal had ever wanted as a lad. And now, if something didn't change, he would have to give it all up. The thought churned his stomach.

Catríona Daly leaned closer to the looking glass. Touching her fingertip to the corners of her eyes, she traced the fine lines making their home there. The frown that slid onto her face only deepened the creases, and she scoffed. Flapping her hand at her reflection, she straightened and then smoothed her hair. Neither blond nor brown, it reminded her of the color of water rushing from the bog after a heavy rain.

The haunting whine of a single fiddle note seeped up through the floorboards of the flat she shared with her father on the second floor of the Imperial Hotel. It was followed by the hollow groan of the *uilleann pipes* and the shrill call of a tin whistle. The *seisún* would be starting soon and Father would be looking for her.

Tightening her apron around her slightly-too-thick waist, she gave herself one more look in the mirror. Too old to be young, too young to be old, and having inherited her mother's "big bones," 'twas no wonder she remained single. She grimaced. Lisdoonvarna's unmatched matchmaker. That ought to draw confidence from her customers this year.

Her eyes slid closed, and she steadied herself with a breath before bounding down the steps.

She burst around the corner into the Imperial Pub, which was nestled on the ground floor of the hotel, then tossed her arms with a flourish and let out a laugh that failed to reach her heart. "What's the *craic* now, lads?"

"Caty!" the musicians called over the din of their warm-up.

Catríona made her way to the bar where Peadar polished the wood to a high shine. "The usual, Caty?"

"Aye." She nodded, her eyes scanning the dark, wood-paneled interior. Reflections from hurricane lanterns hung around the room danced on the tabletops, while the soft glow from the turf fire in the hearth pooled in a golden puddle on the floor. Every table was clean and equipped with no fewer than four chairs. "Expectin' a mob, are ya'?" she asked. "The festival doesn't start for another week."

Peadar shrugged as he set a steaming pot of tea in front of her, alongside a pint of water. "Seems some folk are startin' early."

Catríona poured the molten liquid into her cup, then added a splash of milk as she watched the door. She rolled around the idea of another matchmaking season in which their sleepy little village overflowed with interesting new people from all over. Hope fluttered in her weary soul at the thought. Maybe this would be the year. When someone would miraculously swoop in, ignore all the other perfectly coiffed merrymakers, and whisk her away to a life she could only ever dream of. One of excitement and city life that would take her far away from cattle and bogs and the never-ending loneliness that permeated every nook and cranny of her life in Lisdoonvarna. She lived in the famed home of romance, where people found love waiting around every corner—often orchestrated by Catríona herself. For everyone else, this village represented all their hopes and dreams of finding their one true love. For Catríona Daly, it was a reminder of all she failed to be.

Scooping up her tea service and water, she shuffled to the side room—not much bigger than a wee closet—that served as office for her and her father. Catríona scooted to the center of the bench that filled the rounded bay window. As she settled in for the long evening ahead and arranged her things on the table just so, a ruckus erupted at the main door. She didn't even need to raise her head. Jimmy Daly's chaos surrounded him like a thundering cloud, and Catríona would recognize its unique cadence anywhere.

"Ah, there she is." Her father's broad smile appeared around the corner. His graying hair stood out in all directions from the strengthening near-autumn wind. Though, in truth, it mattered not if the wind blew. The man's hair had a mind of its own. "The finest matchmaker woman in the whole of *Éireann*."

Catríona scoffed. "Oh, Da."

He scurried around and plopped onto the bench next to her, his well-worn woolen jumper scratching at her elbow. 'Twas true, her father carried an air of utter disarray about him. To look at the man, you'd think he'd lost his marbles long ago, along with any information or documents of any import. But the truth was, Jimmy Daly had a mind like a steel trap and could recall every detail of every deal he'd ever made—whether land, livestock, or love. Indeed, some deals involved all three! Catríona had no idea how he did it. She had to settle for keeping detailed notes when working with a brand-new client. Though she could hold more in her memory banks if it was someone with whom she was already well acquainted.

"Ya all set for *anocht*?" he asked, his bushy brows lifted.

Catríona nodded. "Aye, though I must duck out around ten."

"Ten?" His voice cracked. "Ye do realize 'tis a Friday night in Lisdoonvarna? There'll be plenty o' matchmaking work to be done well into the wee hours."

"Yes, Da, I know." For the locals, matchmaking took place all year long. She pulled out the small notebook she carried in her skirt pocket and flipped through it. "But I've the plucking of the gander with the O'Malleys and the Duncans."

He inhaled sharply. "That's right, that's right." He tapped his pointer finger to his temple. "The auld trap's startin' to slip a mite."

"It is not." Catríona slapped his arm playfully, shaking her head. "Ya just only have enough room in there for yer own deals, that's all."

Jimmy's features softened, and he leaned over and pressed a kiss to her forehead. "Ye're a good daughter, Caty. The best." Movement in the main room caught his eye, and he shimmied off the bench. "There's Black-eyed Jack. He's after me to make him a match."

Catríona followed her father's gaze to Jack. At over six feet tall and nearly sixty years old, Black-eyed Jack had been looking for a wife for ages. None of their matches ever seemed to work for him though. This one was too tall, that one too fat, this one not fat enough. Catríona suspected the real fault lay with Jack and his brusque, heavy-handed ways. But that didn't stop her father. He was bound and determined that there was a love out there for everyone.

She flapped her hand in Jack's direction. "Go, go." As she watched her father approach the giant of a man, her smile faded. Feigning interest in her tea, she couldn't help thinking that Jack wasn't the only one who was beginning to doubt her father's credo of true love waiting for all.

Acknowledgments

First and foremost, all thanks and praise must be given to God, who so graciously allows me to live this dream of writing books. I'm so grateful, Father, that Your ways are so much better than my own and that I can trust Your plans, even when they don't make sense.

I also would be remiss if I didn't offer special and specific thanks to my dad, Jerry Martin. You see, readers, I've been going to church since nine months before I was born. My dad was my pastor for the first eighteen years of my life. His sermon on Gideon—affectionately then called "God's Stupid Battle Plans," now renamed simply "Gideon"—was my most favorite ever. The three main points of that sermon are as follows: (1) replace weapons with what God places at hand, (2) worship, praise, and believe God, and (3) show up and shout His glory.

Dad—thank you for your faithfulness to not only pour into the spirits and lives of your family but also into countless others. I know it wasn't always easy—in fact, I often wonder if it was ever easy—but your faithfulness to God's call on your life set the foundation for mine. I love you.

Seth—my partner in crime, my coffee date, my taskmaster (when I really just want to watch one more episode of *Suits*)—there is no way on this earth that I could live this dream without you. Thank you for your understanding as I try to manage all the spinning plates of our lives—especially when I drop a few. Thank you for encouraging me not to give up and for cheering me on every step of the way.

Mom—thank you for joining Dad in leading our family to follow hard after God and for being faithful to your calling as a pastor's wife. Your example showed me what true servant leadership looks like.

The Panera ladies—Liz Johnson, Lindsay Harrel, Sara Carrington, Erin McFarland, Kim Wilkes, Ruth Douthitt, Sarah Popovich, Breanna Johnson, and Tari Faris—where do I even begin? You guys were my lifeline during this book. Thank you for brainstorming, encouraging, praying with me, and sharing your chocolate. Not a week goes by that I don't thank God for bringing us all together.

Rachel McRae—I don't think you'll ever fully know the significance of that email you sent a week before my deadline. Those prayers carried me across the finish line. Thank you for being an editor who prays. Thank you for your encouragement and for trusting me to tell these stories.

Cynthia Ruchti, my incredible agent-friend—thank you for your leadership, your messages, your phone calls, and for going to bat for me when I don't have the confidence in myself or my gifts.

The Revell team—Brianne Dekker, Robin Turici, Karen Steele, the design team, marketing team, proofreaders, and beyond—thank you all for all you do to champion these stories. Thank you for letting me be a welcome member of the Revell family and for caring about these crazy casts of characters as much as I do.

And last but not least, YOU, dear reader—thank you for trusting me with your precious time. I know you have about a million choices for where to place your attention. I'm honored that you've chosen to put it on these pages with me. It's a delight, joy, and honor to share these stories with you. If we haven't connected yet, I do hope you'll reach out to me on social media and sign up for my newsletter. You can find all of that on my website, JenniferDeibel.com. And, finally, if you loved this story, please drop me a line and let me know what touched you most at jennifer@jenniferdeibel.com. Blessings, dear one.

Jennifer Deibel is the award-winning author of *A Dance in Donegal*, *The Lady of Galway Manor*, *The Maid of Ballymacool*, and *The Irish Matchmaker*. With firsthand immersive experience abroad, Jennifer writes stories that help redefine home through the lens of culture, history, and family. After nearly a decade of living in Ireland and Austria, she now lives in Arizona with her husband and their three children. You can find her online at JenniferDeibel.com.

Journey to the 1930s *Emerald Isle* in this fresh take on the Cinderella story

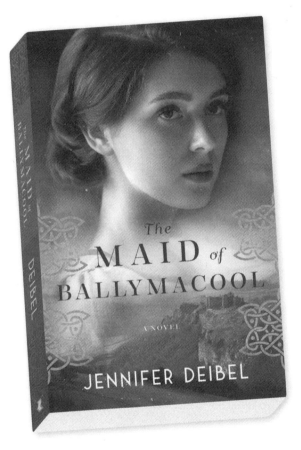

The only home Brianna Kelly has ever known is Ballymacool Boarding School, but when the son of local gentry arrives at the school to deal with his unruly cousin, an unexpected discovery uncovers the truth about her past—and the key to her future.

MORE
HISTORICAL ROMANCE
from Jennifer Deibel

"Deibel's descriptions of Ireland's landscape, enticing cuisine, sonorous language, and vibrant culture converge to form a spectacular background for the story."

—**BOOKPAGE**, starred review of *A Dance in Donegal*

Meet *Jennifer*

Find Jennifer online at
JENNIFERDEIBEL.COM

and sign up for her newsletter to get the latest news
and special updates delivered directly to your inbox.

Follow Jennifer on social media!

 JenniferDeibelAuthor   ThisGalsJourney   JenniferDeibel_Author